THE BOOK OF
CANDLELIGHT

THE BOOK OF CANDLELIGHT

ELLERY ADAMS

WHEELER PUBLISHING
A part of Gale, a Cengage Company

GALE
A Cengage Company

ALL RIGHTS RESERVED
Wheeler Publishing Large Print Cozy Mystery.
The text of this Large Print edition is unabridged.
Other aspects of the book may vary from the original edition.
Set in 16 pt. Plantin.

LIBRARY OF CONGRESS CIP DATA ON FILE.
CATALOGUING IN PUBLICATION FOR THIS BOOK
IS AVAILABLE FROM THE LIBRARY OF CONGRESS

ISBN-13: 978-1-4328-8190-0 (softcover alk. paper)

Published in 2020 by arrangement with Kensington Books, an imprint of Kensington Publishing Corp.

Printed in the United States of America
2 3 4 5 6   24 23 22 21 20

For my Loves,
Tim, Harrison, Sophie

She had only a candle's light to see by, but candlelight never did badly by any woman.

John Fowles,
The French Lieutenant's Woman

The Secret, Book, and Scone Society Members

Nora Pennington, owner of Miracle Books

Hester Winthrop, owner of the Gingerbread House

Estella Sadler, owner of Magnolia Salon and Spa

June Dixon, thermal pools manager, Miracle Springs Lodge

The Inn of Mist and Roses

Lou Simmons and Patty Meacham, proprietors

Sheldon Vega, guest

Micah Foster, guest

Bo and Georgia Gentry, guests

CHAPTER 1

And in this moment, like a swift intake of breath, the rain came.

— Truman Capote

Nora Pennington had no idea how much the rain would change her life.

According to the saying, spring was supposed to come in like a lion. And so it did.

It plodded into the little western North Carolina town like a wet cat looking for a comfortable place to nap. Having settled in, it was in no rush to leave.

The rain began on a Monday in early April. It was tentative at first. Gentle. The kind of rain that coaxed people into slowing their pace and speaking in softer voices. It was chilly. Thick cardigans, already packed away in anticipation of balmier weather, were unpacked. Extra cups of coffee were brewed. People craved soup and homemade bread for supper.

11

It rained all day. The roads glistened. The soil turned dark. The vegetation was weighed down by fat water droplets. When the storm tapered off late in the evening, the townsfolk assumed that Tuesday would bring a change. A little sunshine. A rise in temperatures.

The next morning revealed another gray sky. By lunchtime, it was raining again.

The rain fell every day that week. As the consecutive days of wet weather drove the locals and the tourists indoors, Nora's bookstore became a sanctuary for book lovers and for those searching for a cozy place to wait out the rain.

Miracle Books had never seen such a steady stream of paying customers. They bought books and hot drinks — one after the other — until Nora feared she'd run out of coffee beans or tea bags. She'd never had to stock so much milk before. By Friday, she was down to her last twenty sugar packets.

Her coffee bar supplies weren't the only things being depleted. Her stock of shelf enhancers was also thin. Shelf enhancers were what Nora called the antique and vintage items decorating her bookshelves. As beautiful as books were on their own, Nora felt they shined even brighter when surrounded by interesting objets d'art like an etched cranberry glass vase, a Steiff fox terrier, a hand-painted wooden rooster, chintzware candleholders, cut-glass powder boxes with silver lids, a singing bird toy in a brass cage, and, because Easter was around the corner, a selection of vintage plush bunnies, wind-up chicks, alabaster eggs, and handwoven baskets in every color of the rainbow.

Nora couldn't complain about the rapid disappearance of her inventory. She was selling stacks of books and a dozen shelf enhancers a day. In addition to these sales, she was taking in a tidy profit from the coffee bar, which included the sale of the book pastries made by Hester Winthrop of the Gingerbread House bakery. In short, Miracle Books was having a banner week.

By Friday, the bookshop was a mess. Not an eclectic jumble. Not charming dishevelment. A flat-out mess.

Due to gaps on the shelves, books leaned against one another like tired children. The Holistic Medicine section needed a good dusting, as did the shelves in Romance. Nora noticed that the display of vintage teacups she'd lined up in front of Victoria Holt's novels were no longer quaint but pathetic looking. A few days ago, the ten

13

floral teacups had been filled with sprigs of dried lavender and rosebuds. Since then, eight of the cups had been sold and someone had removed the posies from the remaining two cups.

I can't blame them, Nora thought, listening to the steady drumbeat of the rain outside her window. *Everyone is desperate for a little color. A bit of cheer.*

After hanging the CLOSED sign that evening, Nora did some tidying up and then rode to the grocery store on her bicycle. By the time she returned to her tiny house located behind the bookstore, she was drenched. Leaving her bike on the deck, she entered what had once been a working train car. The locals called Nora's house Caboose Cottage, and as she peeled off her wet clothes, she wished she could push it onto the tracks and ride to a place awash in sunshine.

Too tired to return the phone calls or texts she'd received from Jedediah Craig, the handsome, charismatic paramedic she was dating, or any of her Secret, Book, and Scone Society friends, Nora dropped on her bed and fell into a deep sleep. Neither the rumbles of thunder nor cracks of lightning could wake her.

The next morning, there was finally a

break in the rain.

Buoyed by the sight of a pale sun fighting its way through the haze, Nora rode to the old tobacco barn where the flea market was held every weekend.

Hoping to find a treasure trove of new shelf enhancers inside, she shopped the booths of her favorite sellers first. These were the people who treated her like a human instead of a burn victim. They were the people who'd look into her hazel eyes before letting their gazes stray to the octopi-shaped burn scars on her neck or the jellyfish bubbles swimming up her right arm. Eventually, they'd find the space above her pinkie knuckle. A space created by hungry flames.

Nora had been an attractive woman before the fire had marked her. She didn't regret her scars. She regretted the event that had caused them. Her recklessness had almost cost a mother and her young son their lives, which was why Nora refused to allow the plastic surgeon who'd operated on her face a few months back to repair the skin on her neck, arm, or hand.

"You already worked a miracle on my face," she'd told him during one of her follow-up visits. "If I wear the right makeup, you can hardly tell that I was burned."

She chose not to use the makeup, preferring to let her skin breathe, to let the thin scars show along her hairline where Dr. Patel had worked his magic. Nora didn't want to erase the evidence of her car accident, the fire, or the months in a burn unit. The married, suburbanite librarian she used to be had died that night, and the woman who'd left the hospital to start a new life in Miracle Springs was a better person. She was uglier, poorer, stronger, and more compassionate than the woman who'd sped along that dark highway, fueled by rage and alcohol.

"You want me to take off three bucks because of that tiny wrinkle?" a vendor named Beatrice asked Nora. "You want my six kids to starve?"

Beatrice loved to haggle. Her eyes were already glimmering at the prospect of a good back-and-forth session with Nora.

"Six? Last week, it was five," Nora said, holding back a smile. "And you know how fussy my customers are. They won't focus on the blue butterfly inside this paperweight. They'll focus on the crack."

"That's no crack. It's a dimple," Beatrice objected.

Nora put the paperweight aside and held up a vintage Bakelite alarm clock. Its yellow

16

hue reminded her of a ripe lemon.

"What about this? If I buy both of these, will you knock five bucks off the total?"

"Five?" Beatrice acted affronted. "There's not a damn thing wrong with that clock."

The haggling continued for several minutes. When it was over, Nora left the booth with the paperweight and clock as well as a hammered copper inkwell and blotter.

She moved around the flea market, asking for discounts from every vendor. Though it had been a record-breaking week for Miracle Books, there was no telling what would happen next week. Life in retail was filled with uncertainty.

An hour later, Nora's backpack was stuffed with treasures wrapped in newspaper. Deciding to return for more on Sunday, she headed for the exit and ran into her friend June.

June Dixon managed the thermal pools for the Miracle Springs Lodge, the biggest hotel in town. June was in her fifties but looked a decade younger. Her café au lait skin glowed with health and her close-cropped, black curls accentuated her high cheekbones and drew attention to her best feature: her golden-brown eyes.

"Are you coming or going?" June asked Nora.

17

"Going. You?"

June frowned. "I stopped by to find out about booth rental. I want to sell my socks here, but it's too pricey. I'd have to knit around the clock to pay for the privilege of sitting on my ass all weekend. No, thanks."

"I told you I'd sell your socks in my shop."

"And you wouldn't burn me like the folks who run the gift shop at the lodge, but that experience made me realize that I don't want to owe anybody anything. I want to sell my stuff my way."

The two friends ambled over to the last booth in the row. Situated close to the door, the booth belonged to an artisan known to the locals as Cherokee Danny. Every weekend, he and his wife arranged their wares on tables covered with handwoven blankets. Danny was a potter and his wife was a basket maker. The couple had been at the same spot since Nora had moved to Miracle Springs, but she'd never purchased anything from them.

Living in a tiny house meant that Nora only had space for items she used on a daily basis. Other than her favorite books and a few antiques, she bought collectibles for resale only. No matter how wonderful the item, it was priced and put on a bookstore shelf.

Nora looked at the wares in Danny's booth and remembered telling Jed that he could jazz up his spartan kitchen by buying a few pieces of pottery. She now knew that most of his salary went toward his mother's medical expenses, so he couldn't afford pottery. He didn't even own a couch. He lived like a monk so that his mom could receive the very best care. Jed was a good man.

As Nora admired a bowl glazed a rich, walnut brown and stamped with swirls, she realized that she and Jed weren't the kind of couple that exchanged gifts. She wasn't sure what kind of couple they were, but she felt like buying him a gift anyway.

"Are you looking for yourself or for someone special?" asked Danny's wife. Nora didn't know her name.

Nora wasn't sure what to call Jed. She was in her forties, and it seemed silly to say that she had a boyfriend. The term sounded juvenile. *Significant other* was no good and Nora wasn't the type to use idioms like *partner in crime* or *my better half.*

"A friend," she said. "He could use a bowl like this for pasta. Or salad. If he ate salad."

The other woman laughed. "The only way I can get Danny to eat veggies is by drowning them in butter."

"Hello, I'm sitting right here," said Danny.

"I know," his wife retorted playfully. "I wasn't trying to be quiet."

There was a smile in Danny's voice as he said, "Like you've ever been quiet a day in your life." To Nora, he said, "If you've got any questions about my work, let me know."

"Can your pieces withstand everyday use? Like microwaving or dishwashing?" she asked.

"Not all," he said. "That bowl you and my girl were talking about can handle high heat, though."

Nora picked up the pot and saw the price sticker affixed to the bottom. "I'll take it."

While Danny's wife wrapped the bowl in newspaper and chatted with June about her baskets, Nora and Danny griped about the rain.

"We live thirty minutes away," said Danny. "Our house is right on the mountain, and I don't know how much longer it'll stand if the rain doesn't let up. If we get another week of this, our place will slide down the mountain like a sled."

He made a downward motion with his hand.

Wanting to offer him a little hope, Nora said that the upcoming forecast called for two days of partly cloudy weather.

Danny shook his head. "That's wrong.

More rain is coming. I've seen the signs. It's coming today, and it won't budge until it's made us even more miserable."

After thanking Nora for her purchase, Danny moved off to help another customer. His wife handed Nora the bowl, now cocooned in white paper. "May this humble pot bring many blessings to the home it enters."

Nora didn't know how to respond to the woman's words or to her warm fingers lingering on the back of Nora's scarred hand. The touch itself felt like a blessing. She managed a quick "thanks," before she and June made for the exit.

Just outside the doors, the two friends parted. June headed for her car and Nora walked to the bike racks. As she put the paper-wrapped bowl in her bike basket, it began to rain.

Cursing under her breath, Nora pulled the hood of her raincoat over her head and donned her helmet. A few hours of weak sunlight weren't enough to dry the muddy parking lot, which meant Nora had to maneuver around dozens of deep puddles. The shoulder of the main road was just as bad. In a matter of minutes, Nora's sneakers, socks, and pant legs were completely saturated with muddy water.

She rode across the bridge and entered the downtown shopping district, surprised by the number of cars on the road. Seeing a line of red taillights ahead, Nora decided to cut through the park.

This seemed like a brilliant idea until she came upon a tree branch in the middle of the sidewalk. She tried to swerve around it, but her tires slipped out from under her and she went down hard.

She'd fallen before, but not directly onto her hip and elbow. Pain tore through her entire left side as water splashed over her pinched face. It took her a few seconds to sit upright.

Her jeans were torn at the knee. Blood soaked the frayed denim around the hole, turning the blue fabric purple.

Nora heard the sound of boots in the water. Someone put a hand on her shoulder.

"Are you okay?"

It was Hester, looking adorable in a red-and-white polkadot raincoat.

"Yeah." Nora got to her feet. "But I don't think I can say the same for my flea market finds."

Shoving a tendril of frizzy blond hair out of her face, Hester said, "Come into the bakery. I'll make you some tea."

Hester carried Nora's backpack and the

bag with the pottery bowl into her warm kitchen.

"Have you ever thought about buying a car?" she asked once they'd shucked off their raincoats. The aromas of melted butter, baking bread, and cinnamon wafted through the space, settling around Nora's shoulders like a cashmere shawl. Spilled flour, halos of powdered sugar, and bits of dried dough covered every surface.

"I don't need a car. I don't go anywhere," said Nora. She gestured around the kitchen. "What happened? It looks like a spice rack exploded."

After pulling a tray of dinner rolls out of the oven, Hester slid one onto a plate. She cut the roll in half, buttered it, and pressed the halves together. Putting the plate in front of Nora, she said, "I can't keep up with the work. I thought the rain would slow things down. Nope. People want my food more than ever. My cash box is stuffed, but I'm running on empty."

Nora took a bite of the roll and moaned. "No wonder they line up for your stuff. This tastes like the feeling of putting on PJs at the end of a long day."

Hester smiled. "Thanks, but the bakery's popularity might also have something to do with my over-the-top April Flowers theme."

Seeing Nora's quizzical look, Hester beckoned her to the front of the store.

Nora gazed at the display cases in astonishment. They held baked apple roses, tulip cake pops, daisy lemon tarts, sunflower cupcakes, pansy sandwich cookies, and more. Every muffin, roll, and loaf of bread was shaped like a flower or embellished with a floral design.

"This is right out of *The Secret Garden.* Except the flowers are edible. Amazing," Nora said. Then she sighed. "I need to change my window display, but who has the time? I'm running back and forth between the checkout counter and the ticket agent's office like a madwoman. Last night, I was too tired to eat dinner. On Thursday night, I fell asleep in my clothes."

Hester plucked at her shirt. "This is my last clean T-shirt. And it wasn't like I was on top of things before the rain came. I can't remember when I last changed my sheets or washed my towels. My house smells like a high school locker room."

Nora understood. At home, she'd been using the same plate, fork, and glass for days. She'd wash them and leave them on the counter to dry. She didn't bother putting things in cabinets or drawers. That required too much energy.

"Are you thinking about running another ad?" she asked, returning to her roll.

Hester frowned. "Ever since the Meadows was bought, a bunch of the people who lost their jobs after the community bank scandal have gone back to work. Now, no one is interested in my part-time gig. Especially since I'm not offering any benefits. Unless you count free food."

The Meadows was a planned housing development on the outskirts of town. No houses had been built because the investment firm heading the project was run by scumbags. These scumbags colluded with more scumbags from the Madison County Community Bank to commit major mortgage fraud. The crooks had been caught, partially due to the efforts of the Secret, Book, and Scone Society, and the bank had gone belly-up. The recent purchase of the development by a legitimate firm meant homes and jobs for many of the fraud victims.

Nora put on her raincoat. "My applicants were a high school kid who wouldn't work weekends, an empty nester who wanted a higher wage than I make, and a chain-smoker who couldn't name the last book she'd read."

"Ouch."

"Whoever works with me has to be a book lover. That's nonnegotiable." Nora reached for the door handle and paused. "Speaking of books, should I grab my book pockets while I'm here?"

Hester slapped the counter with her oven mitt. "I totally forgot! I'll bake them right now and ask Jasper to drive them over. Otherwise, they'll be water-logged."

Nora grinned at the image of Hester's boyfriend, Deputy Andrews, transporting pastries in his sheriff's department cruiser.

"Good idea. Besides, I want to ask him if he finished *Ready Player One* yet."

Hester filled a measuring cup with flour and said, "Not everyone devours books like we do. Some people savor every page."

"I need books like I need oxygen." Nora glanced out at the rain. "A little sunlight would be nice too."

Inside the dry and cozy haven that was Miracle Books, Nora set the coffeemaker to brew and inspected the contents of her backpack.

The results were depressing.

The inkwell of the hammered copper desk set was dented, the butterfly paperweight was chipped, and the Bakelite clock was cracked. A vintage leather canteen had also been flattened. The only survivors of her fall were a Russian nesting doll and a silver plate bowl.

"Damn it," she muttered, stuffing a screwdriver into the canteen to push out a few dents.

The coffeemaker beeped, and Nora checked her watch. It was almost ten and both she and the shop were completely disheveled.

Nora looked at the hole in her pants. She didn't have time to change. Instead, she turned on lights, straightened throw pillows, and ran a rag over the dustiest shelves. With one minute to go, she switched on some music and ran a brush through her hair. As she fought with a knot at the nape of her neck, she thought, *I need to clean this cut on my leg. I need to change the window display. I need to open boxes. I need to restock the shelves.*

Her mental list scrolled on as she put the old brass skeleton key in the front door and unlocked it.

The door immediately swung open, and the sleigh bells dangling from its hinges clamored.

"Don't you get tired of that noise?" asked a doppelganger for Colonel Sanders. He removed a gray fedora and shook it out, his gaze moving from Nora's face to her torn pants. "Honey, you're a hot mess. What can Sheldon do to help you?"

Normally, Nora would have delivered a terse reply and gone about her business, but genuine kindness radiated from the man's dark eyes. She liked his fedora and his pink bowtie. She liked how his sweater vest seemed to hold his belly in check.

Before she could say a word, the man looped his arm through hers. "I smell coffee. Let's go to where the coffeepot lives, and you can tell me everything. I'm an *excellent* listener."

Minutes later, to Nora's surprise, the short, round, bearded stranger was in the ticket agent's office, making coffee for them both.

"So many mugs! I love them," Sheldon declared. "Especially the snarky ones."

Nora watched him. She was so tired that it was a relief to sit back and let him take over.

Sheldon handed her a mug emblazoned with the text TALK DARCY TO ME, and said, "There's no problem that a Cuban coffee and a heart-to-heart can't fix. Go on. Take a load off."

Nora sat. "Cuban?"

"No talkie before coffee." Sheldon mo-

28

tioned for her to take a sip.

Nora was immediately smitten with the strong, sweet brew. "Magical."

"Not magical. Cuban. I'm only half-magic because I'm half-Cuban," he said. "Sheldon Silverstein Vega, at your service."

"As in, Shel Silverstein the poet?"

Sheldon spread his hands. "Mom was a school librarian who wanted her son to love words. And I do. My Cuban papa wanted me to love food." He rubbed his belly. "And I do."

Studying her guest, Nora realized that Sheldon was too handsome to be compared with Colonel Sanders. Sheldon's skin held a hint of bronze and his white hair was mixed with a generous dose of silver.

The sleigh bells clanged. Nora called out a hello before turning to Sheldon. "Thanks for the coffee. I'd better get to work." She held out her hand. "Nora Pennington, by the way."

He took her hand as if she were a queen and he, her courtier. "Lady Nora, I've been in town for three days, and I'm terrifically bored. The inn where I'm staying is being renovated, and I didn't emerge from the thermal pools to find my chronic pain miraculously gone. I don't do yoga, I have a therapist back home, and I can't stand kale.

So when I saw your shop — this glorious den of books and trinkets — I thought, here's the place for me. I can arrange the bric-a-brac, I can shelve books, I can make Cuban coffee. Whatever you need. Give my day some purpose. *Please.*"

A middle-aged couple appeared from around the corner of the fiction shelves and Nora asked if she could help them with anything. The man wanted a coffee and the woman wanted a vegan cookbook. Nora promised to make the man's coffee after showing his wife the cookbook section, but she never got the chance. By the time she returned to the ticket agent's office, the man was settled in the purple velvet chair, contentedly sipping coffee out of a Dilbert mug.

"Do you want a job?" Nora asked Sheldon. She was only half teasing.

"I might," he said. "But I'm a complicated man. I come with baggage."

Nora smiled at him. "Don't we all?"

With Sheldon handling beverages, Nora was able to load a shelving cart with inventory from the stockroom. She even managed to put out some of the new books in between making recommendations and ringing up sales.

When Deputy Andrews arrived carrying

two boxes of book-shaped pastries, Nora asked if he had time to look for a new book.

"I've gotta go." He jerked his thumb out the window. "Multiple fender benders."

The mention of car accidents reminded Nora that she'd forgotten to examine the pottery bowl she'd bought for Jed.

Later, after bagging *Goodnight Moon, Harold and the Purple Crayon,* and *Maisy's Bedtime* for a woman who'd be babysitting her rambunctious grandson at the end of the month, Nora decided to check on both the bowl and Sheldon.

Sheldon had tidied the ticket agent's office from top to bottom. The coffee machine sparkled. The counters gleamed. He'd also lit one of the scented candles from the display in the Home & Garden section.

"You'll sell more candles if people can sample their smell," Sheldon said. "I mean, I had no clue what to expect from a candle called Beach Reads. It could smell like cocoa butter and sweat for all I know."

Nora grinned. "Thanks for cleaning up back here. I've been meaning to do it, but the rain has kept me super busy."

Sheldon pointed at a cardboard box. "I put your broken stuff in there. I'm guessing that the hole in your jeans and your busted antiques happened at the same time."

"I fell off my bike," Nora said as she reached for the plastic bag in the sink. She peeled off the layers of newspapers and released a heavy sigh. The rim of the bowl was chipped. Red clay peeked out from a dime-sized area where a chunk of brown glaze was missing.

Seeing her stricken look, Sheldon came up behind her and asked, "Have you ever heard the story of the cracked pot?"

Nora shook her head. She was in no mood for a story.

"It's about a water bearer who has to walk a long way to fetch water for his master. He carries a pot in each hand. One pot is flawless. The other is cracked. Every day, when the water bearer returns to his master's house, the perfect pot is full of water. The cracked one is half-full."

As Sheldon spoke, Nora searched through the newspaper for the glaze chip. She hoped to ask Danny to repair the bowl. She'd see him at the flea market tomorrow.

Sheldon continued his story. "The cracked water pot was ashamed that he couldn't carry as much water as the flawless pot. One day, he apologized to the water bearer."

"The pot speaks?" Nora asked wryly.

"Yes. Now, listen. This is the important part. The water bearer told the pot to pay careful attention to the flowers they passed on the way home. The pot did, and he saw that they were beautiful. There were flowers of every shape and color. They filled the air with a lovely perfume and brought joy to all the people on the road. The flowers existed because one day, the water bearer dropped seeds on the dirt along the side of the road. He then watered the seeds with the water leaking out of the cracked pot. The water bearer told the pot that he had no reason to feel shame. After all, it was his flaw that had created so much beauty."

Nora looked at Sheldon. He was a curious man. A quirky and capable man. She didn't know him, but she liked him.

Sheldon tapped his temple. "I know what you're thinking. Who is this marvelous Mr. Miyagi? This glam Gandalf? This winsome Obi-Wan? This dreamy Dumbledore?"

The moment had come for Nora to learn more about Sheldon Vega. Gesturing at the circle of chairs on the other side of the ticket agent's office, she said, "I'm thinking that I lucked out when you showed up today. You're like a fairy godmother." She gestured at the circle of chairs. "I always thought fairy godmothers were too good to be true. They never had any visible flaws, which made me distrust them. Why don't you tell

33

me about some of yours?"

"Some of my flaws?" Sheldon rolled his eyes and released a theatrical sigh. "Honey, we do *not* have that kind of time.

CHAPTER 2

The air moves like a river and carries the clouds with it; just as running water carries all the things that float upon it.
— Leonardo da Vinci

"You let him take care of your customers?" Hester asked Nora in astonishment. "Just like that?"

June pointed at the ticket agent's office. "A total stranger? Back there, making drinks?"

"I'd like to meet this man. He sounds like a force to be reckoned with," Estella said, coquettishly twirling a strand of crimson hair around her index finger.

Nora smiled at her. "I don't think he leans in your direction."

"I don't want to seduce him. I just want to meet him." Estella crossed her shapely legs and leaned back in her chair. "It's so out of character for you to trust a stranger."

"The rain is making Nora a little crazy," June said in a stage whisper. "Shit, it's making everyone a little crazy. You gals know that I don't sleep well. You know that when I wake up at two in the morning and can't get back to sleep, I throw on a cap and go for a walk."

Hester grinned. "With your army of cats."

"They're not *my* cats."

Though June refused to accept kinship with the cats, half the town had seen her in the dead of night, walking through the quiet shopping district. They'd seen her in her hooded sweatshirt and baseball cap. With her dark skin and dark clothes, June practically melted into the night, but there was no mistaking the herd of cats trailing after her. No matter what the weather, the cats accompanied June. Sometimes, they mewled or growled as they moved around her, orbiting her like planets around the sun. June wasn't even fond of cats, but they were uncannily fond of her.

"Anyway," June said, casting a glare at Hester. "My nocturnal strolls have been especially miserable these days. My shoes are soaked through before I reach my own mailbox. Last night, when I walked by that little inn on Chestnut Street — the one that's being renovated — I saw a light on in

a second-floor window. It was half past two."

"Another night owl," said Nora.

"It was your barista." June took a cookie from the platter on the coffee table. "As soon as you described his looks, I knew he was the same the guy."

Estella leaned forward, eager for a tidbit of harmless gossip to dole out to her customers as she colored their hair or painted their nails.

"He was sitting on the window seat, reading," June said. "He must have sensed me out there because he waved. Actually, he stared at the cats for a few seconds. Then, he waved."

Hester exhaled in relief. "For a second there, I thought you were going to go all Stephen King on us and say that he had red, glowing eyes or that he didn't cast a shadow."

June bit into her flower-shaped cookie. Hester had made cherry blossom sugar cookies decorated with pink, cherry-flavored buttercream. The soft, fruity, sweet cookies made Nora forget about the rain.

"Speaking of Mr. King, are we ready to discuss his hair-raising novel?" Nora asked. "Or do you all want to keep talking about Sheldon Vega?"

"Don't get prickly," June scolded. "Sheldon is an outsider. The book we read is called *The Outsider.* I don't think we could find a better segue. What makes someone an outsider?"

Estella tapped a manicured fingernail against her plate. "Let's not deal with boogeymen and blood without our King of Horror cocktails. I made a pitcher of Red Rum punch. Prime yourselves for a killer blend of rum, lime juice, simple syrup, and muddled blackberries."

June rubbed her palms together with glee. "Oh, that sounds good! I wish I could give you some of the Dom Pérignon from *Misery,* but I couldn't find any coupons for champagne in the paper. So I made *Green Mile* appletinis instead." She hurried into the ticket agent's office and returned with a glass decanter. "Check out this shade of green."

"Whoa. Freaky. It makes me think of *Pet Sematary.* Or, wait a minute, what's that book? Yeah, *Cat's Eye,*" Hester said, winking at June.

Estella and Nora laughed while June hurled a throw pillow embroidered with the words CARPE LIBRUM at Hester. "Respect your elders, girlie."

"Elders? You have, like, ten years on me," Hester said, which wasn't strictly true. At thirty-five, Hester was the youngest member. Estella had just turned forty and Nora was in her mid-forties. June was almost twenty years older than Hester, but it didn't matter. The two women were thick as thieves.

"All right, ladies. I am ready to get my drink on." Estella got to her feet. "It has been a *very* long week. Hester? What did you whip up in that magical kitchen of yours?"

"Cookies," said Hester. "I tried making a cocktail, but I'm a crappy mixologist. Really crappy. What about you, Nora?"

Nora pointed at the ticket agent's office. "In honor of the first Stephen King novel I ever read, I made *Firestarter* mocktails with OJ and grenadine. I was a freshman in high school when I randomly picked up the paperback, and I finished it in two days. I went on a Stephen King binge after that. Next up was *Carrie.* Then *Salem's Lot.* That one messed with my sleep. I kept hearing vampires scratching at my bedroom window with their long nails."

"Mocktails?" Estella gave Nora a puzzled look. "It's Saturday night. No one's working tomorrow."

Nora didn't want to confess that she was trying to avoid alcohol. She liked its numb-

39

ing power far too much, and she was tired of being numb. She was ready to feel again.

When she'd first moved to Miracle Springs, she'd made it clear that she didn't want to join clubs, churches, charitable organizations, or political parties. Even though she was a small business owner in a small town, she hadn't sponsored the Little League team or invited Girl Scouts to sell cookies under the Miracle Books awning.

However, Nora had reluctantly opened herself up to the women in this room. Over the past nine months, the four of them had told one another their deepest, darkest secrets. In the telling, they'd learned to trust again.

Despite this, Nora wasn't ready to tell them that she might be an alcoholic. She had yet to look in the mirror and admit that fact to herself.

"I have tequila if you want to turn it into the real deal," Nora said as she walked into the ticket agent's office. She felt Estella's gaze on her. "I just thought I'd give everyone a choice."

Hester raised a hand. "I'll take a mocktail. I'm not in the mood for booze. The rain makes me drowsy as it is."

Nora took drink orders from Estella and June and delivered glasses filled with red or

40

green-hued liquids The four women clinked rims, sipped their drinks, and waited for someone to start the book discussion.

Never one to shy away from attention, Estella picked up her copy of *The Outsider* and said, "I can really relate to Ralph, the doubting detective. Like him, I don't believe in the supernatural. The monsters I've known have all been flesh-and-blood men."

"I stayed up late last night finishing this," said Hester. "When I was done, I was pretty unsettled. I couldn't sleep, so I got out of bed and walked around my house, making sure everything was locked up tight. When I looked out the front window, I thought I saw someone on the sidewalk. He was wearing a white T-shirt. No raincoat."

"That shirt must have been stuck to his skin," said Estella, her eyes shining with interest.

"I guess." Hester shrugged. "Anyway, seeing him reminded me of a ghost story I used to hear at sleepover parties. On a rainy night, a man pulls over to pick up a hitchhiker. The hitchhiker is a teenage boy. He tells the man his name and address, and the man drops the boy off at home. Days later, he drives by the house and sees the boy's mom in the yard. He pulls over and tells her that he gave her son a ride home the

41

other night. She nearly faints. When she can talk again, she says that her son died on a rainy night ten years ago. The man stopped for the boy at the exact spot he was killed in a hit-and-run."

June shuddered. "One of the guests at the pools this week was an old Japanese woman. She told me a story about a female rain spirit who snatches babies. She looks like an old hag. She puts the stolen babies in a black bag and celebrates when their distraught mothers go mad." June took a swallow from her glass. "This woman couldn't have known about me and Tyson, of course, but I wanted to tell her that there are many ways a mother can lose her child. There doesn't have to be a rain demon with a black bag. I got real close to going crazy after Tyson stopped talking to me for good."

Hester gave June's hand a quick squeeze. Hester was also a mother. Unlike June, who was estranged from her child, Hester had been forced to give up her baby. She'd had only a glimpse of her daughter's face before the baby was whisked from the delivery room and handed over to her adoptive parents.

Glancing at her two friends, Nora wished she could do something to make them feel better. She decided to distract them with another story. "Back when I was a librarian, I used to read a scary story to the kids around Halloween. It was about a little girl who was scared of the rain. She believed the drops came together to form a monster. This monster would stand at the edge of her property where the woods gave way to grass. The little girl was so petrified by this watery shape that she refused to go outside. She told her family about it, but they didn't believe her. One rainy day, the girl's family went to town, leaving her alone in the house. When they came home, the girl was gone. They never saw her again."

Estella raised her tumbler. "I think Mr. King would be proud of our storytelling session. But I still don't believe in the supernatural. When we die, we die. Ashes to ashes, and all that. There are no ghosts, vampires, or boogeymen. Don't you think the bad things non-supernatural beings do to each other is frightening enough? I do."

Nora had to agree. The four of them had grown close because they each had a shameful secret. Though they'd shared the secrets with one another, they kept them hidden from everyone else.

Our secrets are our monsters, Nora thought. *Dark and shadowy. Watery and cold.*

"It's not about ghosts and werewolves,"

43

said June, pulling Nora out of her reverie. "I'm a God-fearing woman, but I'll be the first to say that there's more to this world than we can explain. Take your scones, Hester. No one can convince me that there isn't something beyond human comprehension that allows you to reach into people's souls and *know* what flavors will transport them back in time — straight into the heart of a memory."

"And your cats," said Nora. "You don't want to be a feline Pied Piper, but you lead a merry band of fur balls every night. I don't really believe that they do it because the woman who used to live in your house fed them chicken and planted lots of catnip. There's something more to it. I just don't know what it is."

"It's the same with your bibliotherapy," said Hester. "There are hundreds of thousands of books out there, but you can find the five or six titles that a customer *needs* at that moment in their life. You just *know.* Where does that knowledge come from?"

Estella held out her copy of *The Outsider.* "Just because seemingly unrelated incidents came together to spawn a boogeyman doesn't mean we should read too much into an intuitive baker or a nighttime meanderer who smells like catnip. This is fiction, remember?"

"Look at all the things that had to happen to bring the four of us together," Hester argued. "We were like baby Moses, floating in a river. Yeah, we were surviving, but we were never going to start living until someone took us out of the water."

"I got myself out, thank you very much." Estella was irritated. "But this sort of mumbo-jumbo belief system is what you'd expect in a place called Miracle Springs. I mean, what kind of name is that for a town? The thermal pools aren't miraculous. The superfood shakes and sunrise yoga can't cure cancer or reconcile couples on the brink of divorce. We're just another stop on the False Hope Railroad, and when people have spent their seven days here and we've made our money off them, they get back on the train and return to their same sorry lives."

Nora stared at her friend. Estella often displayed flashes of temper, but this bitter tone wasn't like her.

"Hey," Nora said as gently as she could. "What's going on with you?"

Instead of replying, Estella gulped down her cocktail. She then held out her glass as if a waiter stood at her elbow. Hester took the cue and refilled the glass from the pitcher on the coffee table and they all watched Estella take a dainty sip of her second cocktail.

"Magnolia Salon and Day Spa is in trouble. Financial trouble," she finally said. "Nora, you and Hester are tired, but you're also making money hand over first." She turned to June. "Your job comes with a guaranteed salary, health insurance, and other benefits. The salon is all I have. I built it up from nothing, and I've put everything I have into it."

"I don't get it." Hester's voice was quiet. Hesitant. "You were so busy by the end of summer that you had to hire part-time help."

"But that was right after the Meadows scandal. Once the media and the rubberneckers left, I was back to my regular clients. They're not enough." Estella put a hand to her heart. "Don't get me wrong. I love my wash and sets and my standing mani-pedi appointments. Those ladies are my bread and butter. But the women closer to my age only come to me if it's an emergency. They don't like my tight skirts or low-cut dresses. They don't like how their men look at me." She paused for breath. "I don't care what they say about me behind my back, but I do care about all the blank spaces in my appointment book. With the cancellations I had because of the rain, it's going to be hard to pay the bills this month."

Nora was stunned. The Secret, Book, and Scone Society met once a week to discuss books over drinks and dessert, and Estella hadn't said a word about her financial woes. How had none of them known she'd been so stressed? Nora knew that if Estella lost her salon, she'd lose her purpose in life.

"Making women see themselves in a new light is a gift," Estella had once told them. "A woman who believes that she's beautiful also believes that she's worthy of love and success. A woman who believes she deserves love and success is a confident woman. If she can hold on to these feelings after she leaves my salon, she's capable of anything. That's why a new haircut or a makeup session is a kind of therapy. Women talk about what's eating at them while I listen. After I'm done listening, I encourage. Still, plenty of local ladies dislike me. They refuse to see that I'm a champion of women."

Estella spoke the truth. Many women drove up to an hour to visit other salons, despite Estella's skill. And she was skilled. Nora could attest to that. She'd become one of Estella's clients out of necessity. After her hair had been singed in a fire last summer,

Estella had insisted on giving her the works: a scalp massage, a deep conditioning treatment, and a cut and style. The session had been pure bliss.

In her former life, Nora had treated herself to monthly salon visits. But after the fire, after the right side of her body was covered in shell-smooth scars, she gave up on beautification rituals. She cut and colored her own hair a mouse-brown shade and rarely wore makeup. She was the polar opposite of Estella, who was perfectly coiffed and styled at all times.

Estella had worked wonders on Nora. She'd painted golden brown highlights in her hair before cutting it in flirty, face-framing layers. Her touch had been deft and gentle, and Nora had felt compelled to talk throughout the process. Estella was an excellent listener. She definitely possessed a gift when it came to making women feel beautiful, inside and out. Nora had walked out of the salon with a confidence she hadn't felt in years.

"I could lend you some money," Nora said now. She didn't have much, but she would give all that she could spare.

"I'm not looking for handouts, but thank you," Estella said. "But I'd welcome some ideas. How do I get more local women as clients? How do I make my salon trendy?"

The four of them brainstormed for a while, their discussion of *The Outsiders* temporarily forgotten. Twenty minutes passed without Estella falling in love with any of her friends' suggestions. As they talked, Hester's yawns increased in frequency. Her eyelids were heavy. Her shoulders were drooping. It was time to call it a night.

"Ask your new barista if he has any thoughts," said Estella as she made to leave. "Maybe he got stuck here during the worst weather week in history for a reason. Maybe those forces we can't see are conspiring for our benefit."

June touched Estella's cheek. "You'll get through this, honey. It's just a bump in the road."

"More like a sinkhole," Estella grumbled.

Talk of bumps and roads reminded Nora that she wanted to be at the flea market when it opened tomorrow. She hoped to catch Danny before church let out and the old barn filled with Sunday shoppers.

Stifling a yawn of her own, Nora said good night to her friends and locked the bookshop.

As was her habit, she did a walk-through of the empty store before leaving. This final stroll through the stacks infused her with peace. Tonight, however, when she reached the front, she glanced through the display window and saw a blur of movement from across the street.

Startled, Nora moved closer, peering through the streaks of the water running down the glass. There was nothing now, but she could have sworn that she'd just seen exactly what Hester had seen last night.

There had been a man standing out in the rain. A man in a white T-shirt.

When thunder woke her the next morning, Nora shouted, "Are you kidding me?" at the bedroom ceiling.

Her annoyance grew as she prepared to ride to the flea market. She donned her raincoat and baseball hat for what felt like the hundredth time that week and glared at the sky.

"If I hear one more joke about building an ark, I will kill someone."

After loading the chipped pot into her bike basket, she pedaled through the parking lot behind her shop.

She'd made it to the end of the block before a car drove by, splashing muddy water over her whole lower body.

Nora yelled and was about to wave her

middle finger at the driver when she realized that he hadn't done anything wrong. He was driving in the center of his lane at a reasonable speed. It wasn't his fault that the puddles had multiplied overnight. He couldn't avoid the standing water covering the road.

It's over an inch deep, Nora thought, studying the wavelets moving over the double yellow line. She then glanced at the closest gutter. The water flowing toward its grilled mouth roiled like a crocodile drowning its prey. A tangle of branches, leaves, and trash vied for access to the storm drain, but nothing was getting through the metal grates. All the drains were clogged with debris.

Despite her recent accident, Nora decided to cut through the park. It seemed safer to look out for branches than to share a flooded road with anxious drivers.

It was slow-going. Water shot out from under Nora's tires as the bike moved over the sidewalk. A tree had fallen into the playground, flattening the swing set, and Nora wondered how many more would topple before the rain stopped. The soil was completely saturated. The grass was an unreal green, like a black-and-white movie suddenly colorized. The bushes were drooping, their leaves spotted with brown. Fungus had begun to creep over the mulch beds.

This morning's rain, relentless and steady, felt like an attack. This wasn't the gentle rain from the beginning of the week. This was a blinding curtain of water. The longer Nora was out in it, the more she thought of what Danny had said yesterday.

"More rain is coming," he'd said. "I've seen the signs."

What had he seen? She was hoping that he'd tell her that it would all be over by tomorrow and that he could fix the damaged bowl. She wanted some good news to dispel the dampness that had seeped into her skin and permeated her bones.

As she exited the park, Nora saw an ambulance heading in her direction. At the next corner, it pulled to the curb and Jed rolled down the passenger-side window.

"Nice day for a ride." He jerked his thumb toward the back of the rig, his eyes dancing with mischief. "Are you trying to get on my gurney?"

"It wasn't one of my goals." Nora tried to smile at Jed from beneath her baseball cap while keeping the rain from hitting her face. "I'm on my way to the flea market."

"You should think about gettin' a car," said the paramedic behind the wheel. Nora couldn't remember his name. "Even if it's a piece of crap, it would put a roof over your head."

Jed looked concerned. "We could give you a lift. We're public servants, after all, and you're a member of the public. You —"

His speech was interrupted by a stream of animated squawks from the dashboard radio. Nora heard something about a bridge and saw the two paramedics exchange surprised glances.

"What happened?" she asked.

"The footbridge collapsed and fell into the river," Jed said.

The driver leaned over the center console. "People have taken that shortcut into town for a long as I can remember. Good news is that no one was on it when it dropped. Bad news is that the wreckage is gonna float downriver and get stuck around the base of the main bridge. It'll be a helluva mess."

The voice on the radio barked out a code. After months of dating Jed, Nora knew what a few of them meant. In this case, there'd been a car accident near the Meadows.

"We have to roll," Jed said. He put his arm out and squeezed Nora's shoulder. "Be careful, okay? Things have gone from inconvenient to dangerous. The sooner you get off the road, the better."

Nora nodded. "Stop by the shop later if you get the chance. If my new friend is there, he'll brew you a cup of Cuban coffee. You'll love it."

"A new friend?" Jed asked. "Should I be jealous?"

"Maybe." Nora flashed him a grin and pedaled away.

The flea market was nearly deserted. Nora was disappointed to see that Danny hadn't opened his booth. Then, she remembered that Danny and his wife lived over thirty minutes away and that their house was perched on a mountainside.

It's probably not worth it for them to leave home, she thought.

Fighting an increasing feeling of gloom, Nora started shopping for more shelf enhancers.

Though she didn't find as many treasures as yesterday, none of them were fragile. After filling her backpack with a tin toy cash register, a bronze statue of a greyhound, a copper mold in the shape of a fish, a pewter box, and vintage fireplace bellows, she asked Beatrice if she'd keep the chipped bowl in case Danny came in later.

"I don't think he's comin', honey. The roads are real bad and the river's already over the banks. Did you see how high it was when you crossed the bridge?"

"Higher than I've ever seen it," Nora said. "Trees are falling in too," she added, thinking of the big willow she'd seen half in and half out of the water. A tire swing was tied to one of its branches.

"Did you see pieces of the footbridge?" Beatrice asked.

Nora had been so focused on reaching the dry, well-lit barn that she hadn't stopped to look for debris from the footbridge. Shouldering her backpack, she told Beatrice that she'd check on her way home and trudged out into the ceaseless rain.

An hour had passed since she'd left home. Since then, the world had become a darker shade of gray. There was so much water — in the sky, on the ground, dripping from Nora's face — that everything was blurred.

I need more coffee, she thought.

Nora mounted her bike and pedaled toward the bridge, wondering if Sheldon would make an appearance at the bookshop tomorrow. She hoped so. She liked his blend of sarcasm, humor, and sincerity. She wanted to get to know him better, which was unusual for her. Nora was friendly, but she avoided getting close to people. The only time she connected deeply with her customers occurred during a bibliotherapy session. A person would tell Nora why they'd come to Miracle Springs. They'd share their story of pain and she'd recommend book titles to address their feelings and put them on a path toward healing.

It didn't always work. No book would cure a terminal disease, but there were many books on how to navigate end-of-life situations with grace and courage. Though Nora had a list of titles for the most common sources of distress — sickness, death, divorce, child estrangement, depression, career unfulfillment, and conflicts with their friends, family, or significant others — she never gave two people the same list. She customized the titles based on the person's situation. Every person was unique. As was their pain.

What pain brought Sheldon here?

He'd mentioned chronic pain, but Nora suspected that there was more to his suffering than that. She sensed his loneliness. It was probably why she was drawn to him.

She began crossing the bridge, sticking close to the side to avoid being splashed by passing cars. When she reached the middle, she stopped to peer over the railing.

Broken planks of wood from the foot-bridge smacked against the base of the

56

bridge Nora stood on. Chunks of trash churned in the angry water. There was plastic sheeting, fast food bags, soda cans and bottles, rectangles of cardboard, and thin pieces of wire.

There was another object in the flotsam. Something that didn't belong there.

The shape was familiar, as was the red-and-black flannel fabric. Nora stared at it, trying to remember where she'd seen it before.

And then, it came to her.

Danny had been wearing a red-and-black shirt yesterday.

Nora stared down at the buoy of swollen flesh until she understood exactly what was floating among the wreckage.

It was a body.

CHAPTER 3

Oh, my soul, be prepared for the coming
of the Stranger.

— T. S. Eliot

Nora wiped water from her eyes and prayed
that she wasn't staring at a dead man.

But nothing else in the water looked human. The building materials had hard edges.
The man did not. The garbage was soft and
somewhat colorful, but it didn't have limbs.
Or skin. Or black hair that fanned out in
the rippling water.

Nora covered her mouth with her hand,
fighting a wave of nausea.

She closed her eyes and breathed in
through her nose. In. Out. In. Out.

She remembered Danny's pretty wife. She
remembered the way she'd teased him
yesterday. How he'd teased her back. The
smiles they'd exchanged. The ease between
them. They'd made a good team.

The rain kept coming.

It didn't care about the man in the river. It struck against him, hitting him while he was already down.

Nora's shock gave way to anger. She was angry at the rain. Angry at the broken bridge. Angry at the chipped pot. Most of all, she was angry that a man — a kind, young man — was bobbing in the river like a dead fish. She was angry at all the water. The water pushing Danny's body around. The water filling his lungs. The water covering his eyes.

Nora screamed into the rain.

Hearing her own voice was somehow calming. She had control of that, at least.

Taking out her cell phone, she held it under the brim of her baseball cap and called Sheriff Grant McCabe.

"I hope you're in the mood for chicken and waffles," the sheriff said when he picked up. "I could really use a change of scenery."

Nora and the sheriff were friends. Not close friends. Theirs was a friendship where Nora recommended books, the sheriff recommended recipes, and they shared the occasional meal. McCabe was fairly new to Miracle Springs and enjoyed trying a different restaurant every week. He'd taken over for the previous sheriff, a corrupted misogynist now serving what Nora hoped would be a very long jail sentence. McCabe had been in their little town for only three weeks when a local woman was found dead. He'd handled the case with a dogged professionalism, impressing everyone in Miracle Springs.

McCabe and Nora had crossed paths during the investigation of the local woman's death and found that they enjoyed each other's company. They especially liked driving to Pearl's, a soul food restaurant three stops down the railroad line. When the sheriff crossed the county line, he could leave his badge at home and just be Grant. He could split a basket of the best hush puppies in North Carolina with a beautiful woman whose hazel eyes lit up whenever she talked about books.

"Sorry," Nora now told the sheriff. She wasn't sorry for letting McCabe down. She was sorry because Danny would never have a restaurant meal with his wife again. They'd never try each other's food or figure out the server's tip. They'd never clink glasses or hold hands until their meals came. They'd never talk about their day or smile at each other across the table.

"I'm standing on the bridge over the river," Nora said, her voice flat with sorrow.

"I'm looking down at a body. I think it's Cherokee Danny."

"Is he dead?" the sheriff asked.

Nora looked down at her feet. Water pooled around her boots. "Yes."

"Sit tight. I'll be there in five minutes," the sheriff said.

Nora slid her phone back into the zippered pocket of her raincoat and wheeled her bike under the awning of the hardware store. She stood there, shivering and waiting.

She saw the sheriff's department cars approaching but didn't leave her shelter. The closer the cars got, the more she wondered if she'd really seen a body in the river. What if she just thought she saw a body? What if her mind had leapt to a conclusion because it seemed logical?

Danny's down there. Floating.

Sheriff McCabe put his car in park and jumped out into the rain. Within seconds, water was streaming off the brim of his hat and landing on the shoulders of his electric yellow raincoat. He glanced to the right and, not finding Nora, looked to his left. When he spotted her, he signaled for her to wait and walked to the railing, Deputies Andrews and Fuentes followed close behind.

The three men leaned over the metal rail

and looked down. Nora couldn't see their faces clearly — the rain continued to blur details — but she saw them shake their heads in a universal sign of regret.

The sheriff spoke to his deputies. They listened, nodded in understanding, and returned to their cars. Fuentes slid into the passenger seat of the first car and raised a walkie to his lips. Nora guessed that he was calling for backup. The fire department's water rescue team would have to fish Danny out of the river — a dangerous job with the rain, the flooding, and the shifting debris in the water.

When he was done talking, McCabe walked to Nora, his head lowered against the battering rain. Safely under the awning, he removed his hat and gave it several violent shakes.

"Goddamn rain," he muttered. Nora appreciated his anger. She felt the same anger over the flooding, the fallen bridge, the car accidents, and now, the death of a young man. It was an anger born of powerlessness. There was nothing they could do against nature's willfulness.

"Are you okay?" he asked, giving his hat a final shake.

"Yes." Nora touched the bulge in her backpack and said, "I'd been to the flea market to see him. Danny. I wanted to ask him to fix a chip in a bowl I bought from him. He's a potter. His booth was empty, and I was so disappointed because I wanted to get that chip fixed. A goddamn chip. And all the time, he was down there."

The sheriff turned to follow her gaze. On any other day, it would be difficult to see the river from where they stood, but it was so swollen that its bubbling, muddy water was easily visible.

"Fire and Rescue are on their way," McCabe said, turning back to Nora. His eyes, dark and intelligent, studied her in concern. "You should go home. Dry off. We can get your statement later." He was about to walk away when he added, "I really wish you'd called about chicken and waffles. It would have been the only good call from today."

Nora thought of Jed and his partner rushing off to respond to a car accident. She thought of how tired both men had looked. They'd already been to the scenes of multiple accidents that morning, which meant the sheriff's department had too.

And I went out to fix a broken pot, she thought, marveling over the disparity between her life and that of the first responders.

"Whenever you want to stop by for a coffee, it's on the house," Nora told the sheriff.

"Thanks," he said. He gave her a weary smile and donned his hat.

Nora mounted her bike and paused. This was her day off. Her day to replenish her shelf enhancers, to hike on the Appalachian Trail, or to spend a luxurious afternoon reading. She pictured her bare refrigerator, the hamper stuffed with dirty laundry, and the mess that was her bookshop. She should go grocery shopping, clean her house, and straighten her store, but she'd just discovered a dead man in the river. She needed a distraction. She needed light and noise. And people. Not to talk to. She didn't want to talk. She wanted to sit among warm and vibrant bodies, anonymously sharing their company.

The best place in town to find comfort food was the Pink Lady Grill. It would probably be mobbed with churchgoers, but Nora didn't care. She'd be glad to see neighbors in their Sunday finest, sleepy tourists venturing out for brunch, and waitresses in their bubblegum-pink uniforms. She wanted sound and color. Anything to lighten the endless grayness of the sky. Anything to replace the image of Danny's floating corpse.

Stepping into the diner, Nora was hit by a wave of warm, grease-scented air. And noise. Talking, laughing, the clink of silverware. Every booth was occupied. Even the counter was full.

Nora looked around for the owner, Jack Nakamura. Jack was a Japanese-American transplant from Alabama who cooked traditional Southern comfort food as if his family had been making biscuits, fried chicken, grits, and ham steak for generations. The Pink Lady's name and color scheme were a tribute to his late mother. After breast cancer claimed her life, Jack became a passionate advocate of breast cancer prevention. Letters and photographs from women who'd battled the disease were displayed on the diner's pink walls, and Jack paid for early detection screenings for area women who were either uninsured or needed a little financial help.

Jack was working the grill. He had blueberry pancakes cooking on one side and an order of fried eggs on the other. Nora watched him line up three strips of bacon next to the eggs before expertly flipping the pancakes.

"Looks like there's no room at the inn," said a voice from behind Nora. She turned to find Sheldon Vega smiling at her. "You look like a character from *Les Mis.* Come with me. You need something hot to drink and a plateful of carbs."

So much for sitting among people without interacting, Nora thought.

But she was happy to see Sheldon. He was exactly the sort of distraction she needed. Unfortunately, he wasn't dining alone.

"You make friends fast," she said.

"What can I say? People fly to me. Like little moths." His smile wavered. "It's not easy to be my friend. When I hurt, I'm not a nice man. After working at the bookshop, I was sure I'd wake up on the wrong side of the coffin, but I was okay. It was a nice surprise."

Nora studied him in concern. "I hope you didn't overdo it helping me."

Sheldon dismissed this with a flick of his wrist. "Honey, I'm a big boy. And before you ask, I'm here with the lovely ladies who've given me shelter. At a reduced rate, no less."

Nora decided that it would be interesting to meet the proprietors of the Inn of Mist and Roses. Ever since she'd seen the sign, she'd wanted to know the origin of the inn's name. It sounded like something out of a gothic novel.

"I hope they don't mind your picking up

a stray," she said.

"These ladies are angels. And they seem to like strays."

Sheldon led the way to a booth at the far end of the diner where a pair of sixty-something women sat together. Both had reading glasses perched on their heads. The first woman had glasses with bright red frames, which stood out against her silvery hair. The second woman had purple glasses. These were nearly lost in a sea of blue and purple curls.

"Nora Pennington, these are my hostesses with the mostesses." Sheldon gestured at the woman with the red glasses first. "This is Louisa Simmons. She might let you call her Lou if you ask her nicely."

The woman laughed, causing fine lines to spring out from the corner of her eyes. "Don't listen to him. Everyone calls me Lou."

Next, Sheldon indicated the woman with the colorful hair. "This mermaid is Patricia Meacham."

"Call me Patty," she said, shaking hands with Nora.

"We ordered more coffee," said Lou. "We're on our second pot, but it's that kind of day."

Sheldon tapped the rim of his mug. "All I

can say for this stuff is that it's hot. Some-times, it's best to just shut up and count your blessings."

"Sheldon is a walking cross-stitch pillow," Patty said, her mouth curving into a smile.

When their waitress arrived with a fresh pot of coffee, Nora ordered Jack's famous breakfast sandwich. She'd already eaten a bowl of grits that morning and wasn't particularly hungry, but the idea of fried egg and melted cheese sandwiched between two pieces of buttery toast might warm her up from the inside. And she needed warm-ing.

"How many people have you taken in because of the rain?" Nora asked the women.

Lou replied while pouring Nora the last of the coffee in the carafe. "We have four guests right now. Sheldon, a young hiker named Micah Foster, and the Gentrys, a couple from Toledo."

"The Gentrys are keeping busy by going on short car trips," Patty added. "Their car is a muddy mess. Good thing it's a rental. Micah came on foot because he just started hiking the Trail. He doesn't have money to spare, so he's lending a hand with some of our DIY projects. As for Sheldon, it feels like he's a family member, not a guest. He told us about your shop. I'm sorry that we haven't been in yet, but we're up to our eyeballs in work."

"How are the renovations going?" Nora asked.

Lou added a splash of milk to her coffee. "The major stuff was done while we were still in Pennsylvania. The roof, the gutters, a whole new kitchen. That left us with the rest of the public spaces, the guest rooms, and the carriage house where Patty and I will eventually live."

"A brand-new kitchen, eh? And where are we having breakfast?" Sheldon arched a brow.

"Everyone needs a break, you tyrant." Patty tossed a wadded straw wrapper at him.

The waitress returned carrying Nora's food in one hand and a coffeepot in the other. She topped off everyone's cups before moving on to the next table.

"It's been a challenging process," Lou continued to answer Nora's question. "We just found out that the library chimney needs to be rebuilt. Of course, the crew can't start with this rain."

"And we're stuck inside, stripping wall-paper," Patty said. "I think the previous owners put the stuff on with Krazy Glue."

Lou shook her head in dismay. "Actually,

I think it might be contact paper."

"That makes it vintage," said Sheldon. "Give it to Nora. She can sell it at Miracle Books."

Patty asked where Nora searched for her treasures. Apparently, she and Lou wanted to decorate the inn with vintage pieces.

Nora hesitated. She'd prefer to sell the items to Lou and Patty instead of sharing her trade secrets. However, she didn't know how to avoid answering without sounding like a shrew.

They invited you to join them, she reminded herself, and told the B&B owners how she visited area garage sales, the flea market, and occasionally bought items online. At the mention of the flea market, an image of Danny's body rose up in her mind. She tried to push it away. She'd come to the diner to forget about what she'd seen. If only for a little while.

"I guess all the garage sales were canceled yesterday," Patty said. She'd been looking out the window and hadn't noticed Nora's stricken expression.

Lou had, though. She paid the bill and then asked Nora if she'd ever been inside their inn.

"No," Nora replied. "I never met the previous owners. They kept to themselves."

"Well, we plan to be very neighborly. We like people. We'd better since we're going to be sharing our home with a bunch of strangers." Patty suddenly brightened. "I have an idea. Let's have an impromptu potluck supper tonight. What do you guys think?"

Lou and Sheldon immediately agreed. Patty turned to Nora with an expectant smile.

Nora hesitated. She wasn't good at small talk unless it revolved around books. In the shop, the books spoke for themselves. Their cover art, back cover blurbs, catchy titles, and colorful spines made them irresistible to readers.

Nora was always friendly to her customers. She did her best to match them with the perfect books or to give them space to browse. Until she'd become close to the women of the Secret, Book, and Scone Society, she'd avoided lengthy conversations because polite chitchat was exhausting. Now that she had June, Estella, and Hester, she didn't feel like she needed anyone else.

She didn't want to widen her circle. She liked her small, intimate circle just the way it was.

"I think she's hesitating because she gets around on a bike. How would she get a dish to the inn in the rain?" Sheldon gave Nora's arm a pat. "Don't worry. I have a car, and I know where you live. I'll pick you up at six."

Since it was too late to object, Nora thanked Patty for the invitation. She wasn't ready to leave yet, so she said that she was going to stay for another coffee.

She didn't really want coffee. Her belly was full, and she felt warm and drowsy. She wasn't in a rush to step back into the wet and dismal world outside the diner.

Everyone seemed to be lingering. People ate slowly, sipped from their coffee cups, and chatted. They visited other tables to catch up with acquaintances, filling the room with noise and movement. Nora watched them until she was distracted by a streak of red passing outside the window.

A fire truck drove by, followed by an ambulance. Close behind these vehicles was the fire department's pickup. The truck pulled a trailer bearing the water rescue raft.

Danny, Nora thought.

All the warmth inside the diner vanished. The pleasant din faded too far into the background. Nora felt cold and alone.

She gazed at the road long after the emergency vehicles were out of sight, which is why she saw another flash of movement on the deserted sidewalk. At the mouth of the alleyway separating the insurance agency and the florist, she saw a man. A man in a white T-shirt.

Nora got to her feet, pulling on her raincoat as she headed for the exit.

"Have a nice day! Thanks for comin' in," the hostess called after her.

Nora didn't hear the hostess. She was too focused on the man. But when she glanced outside again, there was no one at the mouth of the alley.

Instinct propelled her to go after the man, to prove that he existed.

That he wasn't a ghost.

This was the second time Nora had seen him. And it wasn't just her. Hester had seen him too. On the street in front of her house. He'd stood there for a moment. And then, quick as a blink, he was gone.

Nora didn't like the way this man melted into the rain. She didn't like how he seemed to be made of mist.

She jumped on her bike and pedaled toward the alley. As she rode, several thoughts crossed her mind. Why was the man out in the rain in nothing but jeans and a T-shirt? The white made him stand out. It stuck to his dark skin like a wetsuit. Nora realized that she hadn't noticed the color of his skin the first time she'd seen him. It had been a rainy night and he'd been bathed in shadow.

She glanced around the street, searching for the man.

Who are you? she wanted to ask him. *Why are you watching me?*

His behavior wasn't normal. At best, it was furtive. At worst, he was stalking her. He'd been staring directly into the diner, as if he knew Nora would meet his gaze. And she had. She couldn't even see his eyes, but his bold stare had felt predatory.

Nora slowed her pace. Did she really want to confront a man like that in a deserted alley?

No, she didn't. All she wanted was proof of his existence. And when she reached the mouth of the alley, she found it.

In a patch of ground kept dry by the eaves of the florist building was a smoldering cigarette butt.

Nora took a long look down the stretch of empty alley before glancing back at the glowing stub. As she watched, the light went out and a whisper of smoke started to drift skyward.

The second it cleared the shelter of the eaves, it was pummeled into oblivion by the rain.

CHAPTER 4

Out of suffering have emerged the stron-
gest souls; the most massive characters
are sealed with scars.

— Khalil Gibran

Because they enjoyed eating together, Nora
had become a better cook since she and her
friends had formed the Secret, Book, and
Scone Society.

After their book club meetings, a potluck
supper was usually the meal of choice.
Hester always organized the food, doling
out assignments like an army general. She
took care of the entrée and left the side
dishes to the rest of them.

Nora was tired of lettuce in all its forms,
so she decided to make a watermelon and
berry salad for tonight's supper at the Inn
of Mist and Roses. She was in the middle of
chopping the watermelon when the phone
rang. It was Lou.

"I'm sorry, but we have to reschedule our potluck," she said, sounding glum. "Sheldon isn't feeling well, and it's all our fault. Our attic is full of junk — old trunks and boxes filled with who-knows-what — and Sheldon heard us moaning about having to go through it. He volunteered to take a preliminary look. He wasn't up there long before he said that he was going to his room to rest. Patty went to check on him, and she said his face was as gray as the sky."

"Is he in pain?"

"From what Patty said, it's really bad. She heated two rice bags and brought them up to him. He said that he has absolutely no appetite and wants to be left alone."

Nora understood Sheldon's need for solitude. She remembered her days in the burn unit. All she'd known was pain. It was her only company. Pain and guilt.

Unlike her, Sheldon hadn't driven another car off the road. He hadn't been the cause of his own suffering. Still, he had to live with it, and Nora had enough experience with physical pain to know that medicine had its limits. At best, it took the edge off the hurting. At worst, it did nothing. Which is why people came to the thermal pools. The heat was a blessed respite. But the pain always returned. Always.

Nora stocked lots of books on pain relief. Her inventory was a blend of traditional Western medical advice, holistic treatments, and the tenets of Chinese medicine. She'd spoken with hundreds of customers desperate to find a cure for their suffering, and by this time in her career, she had a deep understanding of chronic pain and its debilitating effect on people's lives.

"I have lots of books on chronic pain," Nora said. "Maybe I can find a holistic treatment he hasn't tried yet. What does he have?"

"Rheumatoid arthritis and fibromyalgia. He wanted me to tell you that this is why he'd be an unreliable employee." Lou paused. "Are you thinking about hiring him?"

It was Nora's turn to hesitate. "I don't know yet. We need more time together."

"We can reschedule our potluck when Sheldon's feeling better. I'd call it a rain check, but . . ."

"The word rain is now taboo?" Nora asked.

Lou let out a dry laugh. "Seriously taboo. The local news channel says that the you-know-what will be over by tomorrow, but their credibility was shot to hell when they claimed that the whole system would move through in a day or two. Idiots. What are they doing with their fancy computers? Playing Candy Crush? They should try a Magic Eight-Ball for this week's forecast."

Someone knocked on Nora's door and she frowned. She did not encourage visitors. Jed and her friends came over by invitation only. No one dropped by unannounced. They knew better.

Nora told Lou that she needed to go. "Tell Sheldon that I hope he feels better," she added before hanging up.

There was another round of knocking. It sounded impatient. Still holding the knife she'd been using to cut the watermelon, Nora approached the door.

"Who is it?" she called out.

"Grant McCabe."

Nora opened the door. The sheriff looked like a dog left out in the rain. She stepped aside to let him in.

"I don't want to track water all over your house," he said, hesitating in the threshold.

"Leave your boots on the mat. I'll get you a towel."

Nora dropped the knife on the cutting board and got a clean towel from her bathroom. When she returned to her living area, McCabe was glancing around for a place to put his wet hat. Nora set it on top of her tiny wood-burning stove.

McCabe dried his face with the towel before spreading it over a section of Nora's sofa. "May I?" he asked.

Nora gestured for him to sit and asked if he wanted anything to drink.

"I'd like a shot of whiskey, but I'm on duty." His attempt at levity was half-hearted. "I'd ask for a glass of water, but I've had it with water. If I complain about the heat in July, remind me about this week."

Nora waited for him to continue. She expected him to talk about Danny. Instead, he pointed at her right hand. "Do you always answer the door armed?"

"I was cutting fruit. I hope you don't mind if I finish while we talk." Nora returned to the kitchen and continued chopping the watermelon. It was so juicy that the grooves in the cutting board had overflowed, pink rivulets flowing onto the counter.

The sheriff let his body sink a little deeper into the sofa cushions. He radiated fatigue. "The person you saw in the river was the man known as Cherokee Danny. I've already mispronounced his last name too many times today, so I'm going to call him Danny."

"What is his last name?" Nora asked.

McCabe carried his phone into the

kitchen and showed Nora the name on the screen.

Amo-adawehi.

Nora wiped her hands on a paper towel. "There's a website with a list of Cherokee pronunciations. I can't promise this name will be on it, but I can look."

"Please."

Nora found the site and an audio recording of the second part of Danny's surname. She pressed a play button and a man with a deep baritone said, "ah-DAH-way-hee."

"I'll bookmark this for you." Nora indicated another word on the list. "It says here that Ama sounds like AH-ma, so maybe Amo sounds like AH-mo."

"Would you like to work for the Miracle Springs Sheriff's Department? You could be our official researcher."

Nora smiled at him. "No, thanks. Your uniforms don't look very comfortable."

McCabe took a seat on a kitchen stool and grew serious again. "Marie is Danny Amo-adawehi's wife," he began, pronouncing the name correctly. "Last night, Danny told Marie that they wouldn't be driving to the flea market today. He thought they should stay put because the roads in their area were going from bad to worse and he didn't expect many customers at the flea market."

"He was right about that," said Nora quietly.

"Despite what he'd said, Danny got up and got dressed very early. He wrote a note telling Marie that he loved her and to be careful. She said that even though he wrote her little notes all the time, this one made her worry. She couldn't understand why he'd gone out when they'd agreed not to."

Nora remembered watching the couple interact. She remembered them exchanging smiles and playful digs. Danny and Marie were good together. Anyone with a pair of eyes could see that. She told McCabe as much.

"If she hadn't mentioned that Danny left her notes on a regular basis, I might have viewed it as a good-bye."

Nora said, "No. He wouldn't."

McCabe gave her a quizzical look.

"I didn't know Danny or Marie, but you can't fake the kind of quiet contentment they had. They were man and wife. They were also friends. It was plain to see. I don't think a man who had a true friend in his wife would jump off a bridge."

"I guess Danny was in the wrong place at the wrong time." There was sadness in the sheriff's voice.

"But why?" Nora asked. "Why was he on

the bridge in the first place? He told his wife that they should stay home. He knew the roads were bad, but he drove to town anyway. And if he had a car, why was he on the footbridge?"

McCabe's expression was solemn. "I wish I knew. I also wish I could figure out why Deputy Andrews found Danny's truck parked near Cherokee Rock. It's pretty far from town."

Nora hadn't been to Cherokee Rock, but she'd heard of it. Hikers often left the Appalachian Trail to take a brief detour to the famous site. The rock itself was an unremarkable outcropping, but it featured a pictograph created by a Cherokee artist thousands of years ago. A group of hikers visiting the bookshop told her that the paint used to create the mysterious pattern was still bright after all this time.

"It'll be there long after we're all dead," one of them had said.

It's already outlived Danny Amo-adawehi, Nora thought sadly.

"Cherokee Rock is three miles away," she said while mopping up the watermelon juice with a sponge. "Why would he park there and walk through the rain?"

"I have no idea. Neither does Marie. She also doesn't know why he had three boxes of pottery in the back seat. According to Andrews, Danny would have to take a trail through the woods to get to town. It would have been a long and miserable walk."

Nora asked if he'd been wearing hiking boots.

"Tennis shoes. Though he owns rain boots. I asked his wife. They would have kept him dry, but they wouldn't have been comfortable for a long walk."

The story was getting stranger and stranger.

"Was he meeting someone?" Nora wondered aloud. "Why else would he park in a place he wouldn't be seen?"

McCabe didn't reply. He seemed on the verge of a decision, and Nora knew it was best to stay silent.

"There's more," he said. "This doesn't leave this house, but Marie told us that Danny has been acting jumpy lately. Full of nervous energy."

Nora immediately thought of the man in the white T-shirt.

"When did this start?"

"A few weeks ago. Marie said that nothing has changed at home. They live pretty simply. It's just the two of them in a two-bedroom house. They have a small network of friends but spend most of their time working." The sheriff spread his hands. "Something must have been going on with Danny, but Marie had no ideas and I didn't want to press the point. She'd already had to identify her husband's body and suffer through an interview. Speaking of which."

McCabe asked Nora to recount every detail from her interaction with Danny and Marie at the flea market to how she'd come to spot his body in the river.

She finished up with a question of her own. "What about the cause of death?"

The sheriff frowned. "Why do you ask?"

"Because maybe he never meant to walk to Miracle Springs. Maybe he was never on the footbridge. Maybe . . . something else happened to him."

McCabe sat very still. "Such as?"

"What if he ended up in the river because someone put him in the river?"

"At this point, there's no evidence of foul play," McCabe said. "We'll wait for the ME's ruling, but for now, we're treating it as an accidental death." He stood up and walked to the living room to collect his hat. Holding it in his hands, he looked at Nora. "As much as I'd like to dry off some more, I'd better be on my way."

Nora was torn. Should she mention the man in the white T-shirt? What could she say about him?

He doesn't seek shelter from the rain. He stood there, looking right at me, and then vanished. He's like the monster from the story I used to read to the kids at the library. He becomes whole in the rain, and only certain people see him.

The sheriff would listen to her with an open mind. But even if she told him, what could he do with the information? The stranger hadn't committed a crime. He was just . . . there. For a few seconds at a time. Staring. And then, he was gone.

Nora readied to open the door. "What about through-hikers? Maybe some of them checked into a hotel to wait out the rain? It's a long shot, but one of them might have seen Danny this morning."

"Through-hikers," McCabe repeated the term that referred to the men and women hiking the Appalachian Trail in its entirety. "I'll check on that."

Nora handed him the bowl of fruit, which was now covered in plastic wrap. "Take this with you. I'm sure everyone at the station could use a little taste of summer."

McCabe thanked her and left.

Nora listened to his footfalls on the deck's metal stairs. When she turned back to her kitchen, she realized that she had nothing for dinner. Other than a box of Raisin Bran, she'd just given away the only food she had.

"Cereal it is," she murmured.

It wasn't a total loss. The great thing about cereal was that it only required one hand to eat, which left her other hand free to turn the pages of a book.

Nora read while she ate. Afterward, she moved to the sofa and read some more. Two hours passed. She made a cup of chamomile tea and carried the book and the tea to her bedroom. She sipped and read until her eyelids felt heavy.

Just one more chapter, she told herself.

The softness of her pillow and the steady rhythm of the falling rain lulled her off to sleep. She slept with her lamp still burning, her book pressed against her chest. The feel of it brought her comfort. The words between its covers were a bridge to dreams, and Nora crossed it without looking back.

The next morning, the sun came out. After a week of rain — of endless, drenching, hammering rain — there was finally sunshine.

It was a joy to hear a sound other than rainfall. Birds sang. Insects buzzed. The streets thrummed with traffic noise. There was activity everywhere.

In town, the sidewalks were jammed with people. The merchants swept their stoops and cleaned their windows. Visitors left their hotel rooms in droves, eager to shop, to eat out, to feel the sun on their skin.

Customers congregated on the sidewalk outside Miracle Books well before opening, and though Nora would have loved to get a jump on sales for the week, she wasn't prepared for a crowd. Coffee had to be brewed, the floors needed vacuuming, and the shelves were crying out to be restocked and rearranged.

After deciding that the floor was only going to get dirty again, Nora focused on the coffee. She had two pots brewing when she remembered the book pastries. She'd have to hurry if she wanted to get them from the Gingerbread House and still open the shop at ten.

The bakery was packed. Nora gently pushed her way through the eager customers and waved at Hester.

Hester waved back and called out, "I haven't boxed them. Can you do it?"

Nora gave her a thumbs-up and continued into the kitchen. She packed the chocolate- and raspberry-filled book pockets into a large cupcake box, slapped on a few pieces of tape, and returned to the front of the store.

Hester was cutting a slice of brown sugar coffee cake embellished with pecan flowers and a coffee drizzle when Nora came up and whispered, "I saw the man in the white T-shirt."

"When?" Hester asked in a hushed tone.

"Saturday night, outside the bookshop. After the rest of you left. I saw him again yesterday. It was the middle of the day. I was at the Pink Lady."

"Do you recognize him?" Hester handed the piece of cake to a woman who smiled with childlike delight. Hester smiled back and turned to the next customer in line. "What can I get you?" she asked.

Nora didn't have time to wait for Hester to fill another order, so she asked her friend to tell Deputy Andrews about the man and left.

Hester and Deputy Jasper Andrews had been dating for six months. Andrews was a good guy, and Nora knew that he'd listen to Hester. If Andrews thought the strange man's presence had any bearing on Danny's death, he'd raise the subject with the sheriff.

Nora hurried back to Miracle Books and arranged the pastries on a platter. The rest of the morning passed by in a blur as she made coffee and sold books. Around one, a middle-aged man entered the shop holding a piece of paper in his right hand.

"Do you have a notice board?" he asked. "We're selling our daughter's moped."

Nora was taking her first breather of the day. She really wanted to drink her cup of coffee while it was still warm and spend a few minutes perusing the newspaper, and her inclination was to tell the man that she couldn't help him. However, as she studied his haggard face, she had a feeling that he needed to talk to someone. He was practically brimming with unspoken words. If Nora's hunch was correct, he would need books too.

"May I?" she asked, pointing at the paper.

He passed it to her. The moped was canary yellow with pink daisy decals, was less than a year old, and was priced to sell. Nora had no idea what a new moped cost, but this one seemed like a bargain, despite the garish color scheme.

"How old is your daughter?"

"Sixteen. And at the rate she's going, she'll be grounded until she graduates," the man said gruffly. He tapped his index finger on the paper. "When we got this for her, we told her that it came with certain conditions. Since then, she's ignored every one of them."

The man exuded exasperation. It was in his voice, in the furrows he plowed through his hair with his fingertips. He was frustrated and tired.

Nora smiled at him. "I might be in the market for a moped. Would you like a cup of coffee? I just poured myself one."

The man said that he'd love a coffee and followed Nora to the ticket agent's office. As they walked, he said this his name was Richard Kerr and that he and his family were new to town. "I'm the foreman at the Meadows. My wife, Jess, does interior design. Our daughter's name is Lily."

Nora showed Richard the menu board and he took his time reading the selections.

Ernest Hemingway — Dark Roast
Louisa May Alcott — Light Roast
Dante Alighieri — Decaf
Wilkie Collins — Cappuccino
Jack London — Latte
Agatha ChrisTEA — Earl Grey
Harry Potter — Hot Chocolate with
  Magic Marshmallows
Assorted Book Pocket Pastries

He ordered a Jack London. Nora served

him his coffee and then dropped into a chair across from him.

"The moped is pretty new. Has your daughter taken good care of it?" she asked.

"*She* hasn't, but *I* have." Richard pursed his lips in annoyance. "I don't know where we went wrong. Lily doesn't take care of anything. Her room is a pigsty, her grades are terrible, and she does whatever she can to avoid helping around the house. She used to be a sweet, hard-working girl. All she cares about now are her friends and her phone. She spends hours posting selfies and videos and God knows what else. Last weekend, we found vodka in her bookbag."

His words had poured out in a flood, and as soon as he finished Richard seemed abashed by his openness.

"Sorry," he said. "This situation is making me crazy. Jess too. We're . . . afraid."

Nora saw the fear in his eyes. "Of?"

"Of losing our daughter," Richard said. "The more we try to hold on, the faster she slips away. We don't know how to control our own kid. She doesn't listen to anything we say. I'm worried she'll get hurt. Drinking is just the start."

Nora let this hang in the air for a moment. "Will she miss the moped if you sell it?"

"I don't think so. She'll catch rides with

older kids who have cars. She did that this weekend. She didn't even tell us she was going out. Probably because she's grounded for failing three classes. That didn't stop her, though. She ran out into the rain and got in someone's car. We didn't see her again until after midnight. My wife and I were sick with worry."

Book titles were already scrolling through Nora's head. Richard and Jess had every reason to be concerned, but they also needed to consider Lily's point of view. Being a teenager was hard, but being a teenager in the digital world was particularly challenging. Social media provided an endless stream of feedback, and some teens were exhausting themselves trying to appear perfect. The high schoolers Nora saw around town were far more sophisticated than she'd been at their age. Then again, she was the type of girl who wanted a new book more than a new eye shadow palette.

But I wasn't judged by my number of online followers, she thought.

"It sounds like the lines of communication between you and your daughter aren't working," Nora told Richard. "Lily probably doesn't talk to you and your wife because she doesn't think you'd understand what she's going through. She's giving you the silent treatment and saving her words for her friends. Is that right?"

Richard nodded. He looked miserable.

"That's normal. Teens need to separate from their parents, but her need for independence shouldn't hurt your family this much. Maybe you and Jess could learn to speak Lily's language." Richard opened his mouth to protest, but Nora held up her hands. "I'm not defending her. She's breaking the rules, which are important to her safety and well-being. But she won't come around until she believes she'll be heard and respected. She'll just keep pulling away."

"We don't want that. We want our little girl back." Richard's voice cracked.

Nora gave him a sad smile. "That little girl is gone. Your daughter is growing up, and she's trying to figure out what kind of adult she wants to be. It's a scary and emotional journey for her. For you and your wife as well. If you'd like, I can give you several books to help bridge the gap between you two and your daughter. It's not too late to reach her. Part of her is hoping that you'll try — but not by yelling or lecturing her."

"I'm still selling her moped," Richard said, crossing his arms over his chest. "Lily needs to know that her actions have consequences."

"I get that. Maybe I could rent the moped until you're sure about selling it. In the meantime, why don't you finish your coffee while I pull some books for you? Sound good?"

"Yeah. Sounds good." Richard sank back into his chair.

Nora smiled at him. She believed that this man, armed with a bag of books, could change his family dynamics for the better.

Moving to the fiction section, she chose Stephen Chbosky's *The Perks of Being a Wallflower*, *Prep* by Curtis Sittenfeld, Jay Asher's *Thirteen Reasons Why,* and Emily Giffin's *All We Ever Wanted.*

These novels would give Richard and Jess a glimpse of what it was like to be a teen. Next, she added two nonfiction books to the pile. She didn't want Richard and Jess to feel overwhelmed by advice, so she limited the self-help titles to *How to Raise an Adult* by Julie Lythcott-Haims and *Screens and Teens: Connecting with Our Kids in a Wireless World* by Kathy Koch.

"There's a pile of books on the counter by the register," she told Richard when she was done. "Look through them and see what you think. If you decide to read them, you might want to share what you're doing with your daughter. Even if she doesn't show it, it'll mean a lot to her. She knows that you and your wife are angry and disappointed, but when she sees the two of you reading in an effort to connect with her, she'll know that you love her too."

"Thank you." Richard stood up to shake Nora's hand. "Do you have kids? You seem so sure about what to do."

"I've given books to other parents in similar situations."

A customer asked Nora for a copy of Jodi Picoult's *Small Great Things,* and Nora turned to show her where it was shelved. Before she could walk away, Richard put a hand on her arm.

"Sorry, but is there a name for what you do? The way you help people with books?"

Nora smiled. "It's called bibliotherapy. I have no formal training in psychology, but I know books. Words have the power to hurt and to heal. The books I gave you will do both. They'll hurt because they'll give voice to the pain you're feeling. And then, they'll help you heal. That's what the best books do if you're brave enough to read them."

Richard pulled out his wallet and headed to the register.

He was brave enough.

He was ready to read.

CHAPTER 5

You may break, you may shatter the vase, if you will, But the scent of roses will hang round it still.

— Thomas Moore

Buoyed by her bibliotherapy session, Nora called the Inn of Mist and Roses. When Patty answered, Nora asked after Sheldon.

"Poor guy spent the whole day in his room. He's hardly eaten, and the rice bags aren't doing much to ease his pain. I asked if he had medicine, but he said he got in trouble with pills once and won't go there again."

"Could I stop by later?" Nora asked. "My friend knits socks scented with essential oil. I'd like to bring him a pair."

"I'm sure he'd love the company," said Patty. "Lou and I spent another day stripping wallpaper, so we barely saw him. But the inn's official bookings start the first week of June, which means we'll be working night and day to get everything done in time."

Richard had said the same thing about his deadlines at the Meadows. Though he'd used his lunch break talking with Nora about his daughter, he had a sandwich in his truck and planned to wolf it down before he and his crew spent the rest of the afternoon hanging drywall. Nora hoped that he wouldn't be too tired to read when he finally got home.

After a full day, Nora thought she'd be tired too. But the combination of sunshine, robust sales, and a positive bibliotherapy session had her feeling good. She called June and asked if she had a pair of men's socks on hand.

"I do, but they're unscented. I'll have to run home to get the peppermint, which is what your friend needs. I could meet you at the inn later."

Nora used the little time she had to hit the grocery store. She'd just put the last item in her cart on the moving belt when someone placed a bouquet of daisies on top of her box of Raisin Bran. She was about to move the flowers when Jed said, "Ma'am, I paid for these at self-checkout. I just wanted to give them to this lovely lady while I had the chance."

The cashier beamed at him. "Aren't you sweet?"

Jed scooped up the flowers and handed them to Nora. She blushed with pleasure and embarrassment. For over five years, her burn scars had earned her plenty of unwanted attention. Stares and whispers followed her everywhere. And though the scars on her face had recently been repaired by a plastic surgeon, making it hard to tell she'd ever been a burn victim, Nora still felt like one. Inside, she would always be scarred. She would always carry around the heat and flames from one fateful night. And she would always shy away from being the center of attention.

Nora thanked Jed and hurriedly paid the cashier. She wanted to get outside. She reached for her cart, but Jed gave her a gentle shove.

"How will you get all of this on your bike?" he asked, pushing the cart toward the exit.

"I'm walking home."

On the sidewalk, Jed stopped. Nora ran her hand down the sleeve of his uniform shirt. "I'd ask you to come over, but it looks like you're starting another shift. Have you taken any time off this week? And how is

Henry Higgins handling being home by himself?"

Henry Higgins was Jed's dog. Like Nora, the Rhodesian ridgeback was a fire victim. Like Nora, the memory of fire still haunted Henry Higgins. The dog suffered from anxiety, dry skin, a delicate digestive system, a fear of loud noises, and an aversion to strangers.

"I was off this morning," Jed said. "My plan was to stop by the shop with flowers, but Mrs. Pickett's roof leaked last night. The water came down through the attic and flooded her bedroom and kitchen. I moved some furniture and put a tarp over the hole until she could get someone to fix it, but she's pretty upset."

"I thought you were keeping your distance because she has you pegged as husband number four," Nora teased. "Or is it five?"

Jed laughed, and his dimples appeared under the dark stubble covering his cheeks. Nora was tempted to run her fingertips over the bristle, to trace the line of his strong jaw, but there were too many people around. Public displays of affection were not her thing.

"I owe Mrs. Pickett because she's been helping out with Henry Higgins. She feeds him and lets him spend time in the backyard. Henry really likes her. It's been good for both of them."

"It sounds like he's coming out of his shell a little. That must make you happy."

"Do you know what makes me even happier? Being with you." Jed plucked a flower from the bouquet and wove it through the braid in Nora's hair. "Oh, goddess of beauty, books, and coffee, would you join me for dinner this Saturday?"

As he spoke, Jed ran his hand over the curve of Nora's neck. He gazed at her as if no one else existed. As if they were alone in a candlelit room and not standing on a busy sidewalk. Nora couldn't look away from his smiling gaze. She couldn't think of anything else but the feel of his fingertips sliding over her shoulder. Her skin was electrified by his touch, and she wondered if other people could see how her body glowed with a firefly light.

"I'll try to fit you in," she whispered, her eyes moving to Jed's lips. It had been too long since she'd felt those lips on her mouth. On the inside of her elbow. On the tender skin behind her earlobe. On her breasts and belly.

Jed took his hand off her shoulder. He kissed the end of her braid and flashed her a dazzling smile. "My place. Seven o'clock.

Don't bring anything but your amazing self."

As Nora walked home, she raised her lust-warmed face to the breeze sweeping down from the hills. She hoped the air would lower her body temperature, but the scent of wet grass and pine only made her think of Jed more. It reminded her of their first kiss. And of what that kiss had led to. That night, they'd curled around each other like storm winds, reckless and passionate, before parting again the next day. Nora knew that eventually, one of them would blow away for good. She had a feeling she knew which one it would be.

"Come in!" Lou beckoned Nora into a hallway lit with brass sconces. The walls were stripped of all traces of paper, revealing white, pockmarked plaster.

"You finished," Nora said.

Lou grinned. "And we're still speaking to each other."

"Barely," Patty said, entering the hall from another doorway.

Nora ran her hand over the uneven plaster. It felt as solid as time. She admired the elegant curve of the staircase and the scent of beeswax permeating the space.

"I just finished polishing the banister,"

101

Lou said, as if reading Nora's mind. "It was my way of apologizing to Patty, of admitting that heat guns were a good investment. I wish I'd gotten them earlier. I won't be able to lift my arms for a week after this."

"Are you going to paint or paper?" Nora asked, her hand still on the wall.

Patty shuddered. "Definitely paint. *If* we can pick a color. Would you weigh in on our top three shades?"

Lou led Nora to the dining room where three pieces of poster board sat on a square table. The room was outfitted with several tables surrounded by Chippendale-style chairs. An antique sideboard held a fruit bowl, a row of tumblers, and a glass pitcher filled with water. Slices of oranges floated in the water.

"These puke-yellow walls will be painted too," Patty said. "We're leaning toward this sage green for this room. These swatches are for the hall. What's your fave?"

When Nora reached out to take the paint chip, Patty's gaze roved over the burn scars on her hand and locked on Nora's pinkie finger. Or, more accurately, on the space where the rest of her finger should have been.

"I'm sorry," she said when Nora caught her looking. "I didn't mean to stare."

Nora gave her a reassuring smile. "At least you apologized. Most people just pretend they weren't looking, which can be more awkward."

"You and this inn have something in common." Lou made an all-encompassing sweep of her arm. "This lady was burned too. Twice. And she's still standing. Just like you."

"She was the first hotel in Miracle Springs," Patty added. "Built right on what was once known as the drover's road. The accommodations were meager, and the inn was notorious for brawls and robberies. Too much booze and testosterone led to the first fire."

Lou pointed at the window, toward the bookshop. "When the railroad came, this gal was given another lease on life. And she was much grander the second time around. Two stories with high ceilings and formal gardens. The Lattimer family made this their home. They built the lodge and could have lived there, but Muriel Lattimer wanted to raise her children in a normal house. She studied architecture. I was told by my grandmother — she was a Lattimer too — that Muriel designed secret hiding places throughout the house. We've found one so far. A false panel in the back of the closet."

Nora wanted to ask about the second fire, but she was embarrassed by how little she knew of her town's history.

"How did the inn get its name?" she asked instead.

Patty smiled. "Isn't it deliciously gothic? Muriel had one son. Colonel Lattimer. He married Rose Blythe and planted a rose garden in her honor. Legend has it that a morning mist came down from the mountains and rolled over the property. That's when Rose liked to stroll through her garden. Because of the mist and her long skirts, she appeared to float. That's one legend. There's another one, but it's kind of sad."

"I'd like to hear it," Nora said.

Patty gestured at Lou, who took up the thread. "When the Civil War broke out, Colonel Lattimer put the property in Rose's name to prevent it from being confiscated by either side. He then enlisted and died soon afterward from a battlefield injury. Because this house was at a crossroads, both Union and Confederate troops passed it. Rose opened the doors to the wounded, regardless of which side they were on. She ministered many men back to health.

"According to the other legend, the mist is made of the souls Rose couldn't save." Lou's voice was hushed. "They float out from their burial places just before dawn, searching for her. They're cold and lonely. They miss Rose's kindness and the light of her beauty. She was a sister to them. Yankee or Confederate, they were all brothers under this roof."

Lou's words filled the spaces around them like the specters of the fallen soldiers. Nora wasn't a fanciful person, but she believed in the power of stories. This house was a depository of stories. It had seen death. It had been wounded by fire. It kept secrets and survived a war. And its name reflected the beauty and tumult of its history.

Nora looked at the women who now owned it. "Have you seen the mist?"

"We haven't," Lou said, sounding disappointed.

"Sheldon has," Patty added. "He smelled roses too. Just for a few seconds."

The talk of local legends had Nora thinking about Danny. Looking for a distraction, she studied the three blue-gray shades painted on pieces of poster board. Nora preferred the brightness of Blue Lace over the more tranquil Silver Mist. The third was called Rainy Day, which she immediately rejected based on its name.

She was about to share her opinion with Lou and Patty when there was a loud crash from a room at the end of the hall.

Patty hurried off to investigate the source of the noise with Lou right behind her. Nora was compelled to tag along.

"It's got to be the chimney," Patty called over her shoulder.

It was hard to tell exactly what had happened. The empty room was draped in plastic sheeting. Several drop cloths covered the floor. Ladders flanked a stone fireplace and loose stones were scattered on the floor in front of the hearth. Above the mantel were dozens of holes the stones had once filled. Dust hung in the air, and two workmen were staring up at the ruined chimney in bewilderment.

The shorter of the two, a man with a formidable beer belly and a straggly beard, hooked his thumbs under his overall straps and looked at Patty. "It just gave out on us. Tumbled down all at once."

Nora noticed that the plastic sheeting taped over the mantel had been torn. Through the tear, she could see a deep gouge in the dark wood. Lighter wood showed through the varnish like a wound.

Lou glared at the workmen. "That mantel

is original to the house. It escaped a fire and two floods."

"We can fix it," Patty said. She gave Lou a pat on the arm before focusing on the men. "Why did the chimney give out?"

"Couple of reasons," Beer Belly replied. "Mortar's old as the hills and some knucklehead added more stones to this side of the chimney without addin' more support. We took out a few loose stones and that was that."

His partner dusted off his hands. "We'll tackle this in the mornin'. My wife is making fried chicken for supper and she'll have my head if I'm late."

The workmen collected their tools and left. The women stayed in the room, inspecting the ruined chimney and the pile of stones on the floor.

"Was there an earthquake?" came a raspy voice from the doorway. Sheldon stood in the threshold. His eyes looked glassy and his skin was pale.

"More like an innovative method of chimney removal," said Lou with false bravado. "You just pull out the right stones and the whole thing comes crashing down. Sorry about the noise. Anyway, Nora came to see you. If you'd like, I can bring some tea to your room."

"I take mine with milk and arsenic," Sheldon grumbled, and shuffled back down the hall.

Nora followed him. "If you're not up to a visit, I can go."

"You need to see the real me," Sheldon said.

His ascent up the stairs was slow-going. Nora could see the effort it took him to reach the top and lurch toward his room. Once there, he gracelessly dropped on his bed and let out a groan.

"I brought socks," Nora said, brandishing the peppermint-scented knit socks she'd picked up from June. "I didn't know how to gift-wrap a morphine drip."

"I can't bend over to put them on, so hang them on a mantel. The Easter Bunny can fill them with candy."

Sheldon wasn't just grumpy. He was angry. And his frayed emotions were sharpening his words into ice picks.

Nora wasn't touchy-feely and rarely initiated contact with others. Still, she wanted to help Sheldon. Knowing that touch could distract people from their pain, she sat on the end of his bed and pulled off his thin socks. She then gently replaced them with June's.

Sheldon wriggled his toes. "They're soft.

Like rabbit fur."

Nora uncapped the bottle of peppermint oil June had given her and poured a few drops into the small metal bowl she'd brought with her. She then added hot water from the bathroom sink, creating a peppermint-scented steam. Finally, she draped a towel on his lap and put the bowl in the center of the towel.

"Breathe in," she commanded.

"You're a bossy Florence Nightingale."

Sheldon drew in a deep breath. And another. And another. The steam put some color back in his cheeks. His shoulders relaxed. He closed his eyes and kept breathing.

"This is what you warned me about," Nora said. "Your flip side. I couldn't give you a regular work schedule because you don't know when a bad day will come. You'd work when you could and rest when you couldn't."

"In a nutshell." Sheldon's gregarious personality from a few days ago was gone. This Sheldon was dejected, frustrated, and hurting. To Nora's surprise, she found that she liked both of Sheldon's sides. She liked Mr. Hyde as much as Dr. Jekyll. They were equally genuine.

"Why don't we have a trial week?" she

suggested. "You can see if bookstore life suits you and I can see how well I tolerate an employee who begs off work for no good reason."

This earned her a small smile.

"I know you're joking, but people do think that," Sheldon said. "They don't see a shaved head or a wheelchair. I'm not wearing a brace. I don't use a cane or crutches. Which means I'm sitting on my ass, not contributing to society, while my fellow citizens pay for medicine for what is probably a *psychosomatic* illness. If I had cancer, people would pin ribbons to their chests. But fibro and RA? Pffft. Those are in my head."

Nora held up her hands. "Don't get mad at me. I've never worn a cancer ribbon."

Sheldon laughed, causing water from the bowl on his lap to slosh onto the towel. "Don't worry, I won't ask you to help me out of my pants."

"Does anyone?" Nora's voice was gentle. "What I mean is, would you be leaving someone special to move here? Or would that someone move with you?"

"I don't have romantic partners," Sheldon said. "I'm a starfish. Have been my whole life."

"A starfish?"

110

"Someone who isn't interested in sex. If None of the Above were added to the LBGTQ acronym, that would be me. I'd be the N."

Nora had never met an asexual before. "I came across a term for that in a book I read a few years ago. Was it 'Aces'?"

"Aces. Ace of Hearts, whatever." Sheldon rolled his eyes. "I look a bit like the King of Hearts, don't I? Either way, I live alone. Contrary to the norm, I'm quite content by myself."

"Me too," Nora said. She was heading to the door when she spotted a book on the window seat. It was *Circe* by Madeline Miller.

"Do you have a favorite genre?" she asked Sheldon.

Sheldon gestured at the stack of paperbacks on his nightstand. "I read everything. Books push my pain into the background. I read two or three books a week, and I keep a journal of memorable quotes and ideas. On days I don't feel well enough to read, I page through that journal and let the memory of those stories comfort me."

Nora smiled at him. "Sheldon Vega, you're exactly what I need. I've been looking for a person with a heart for books, and here you are."

"Here I am," Sheldon said, spreading his arms in a theatrical gesture. The bowl on his lap overturned, soaking his crotch with warm water.

Nora closed the door on a burst of angry swearing. In Spanish.

Downstairs, she found Lou and Patty in a modern white and chrome kitchen. Large glasses of white wine sat on their farm table.

"It's been a break-out-the-big-glasses kind of day," Patty said. "Care to join us?"

Nora's gaze flicked to the wine. Lit by the clear kitchen lights, it looked like the nectar of the gods. She wasn't even fond of white wine, but she could almost taste its fruity sweetness. She could imagine how it would relax her.

"Another time, thanks. I need to get home," Nora said.

Of course, no one was waiting there. Other than her books. But they were enough. They had always been enough.

"Wait," Lou called before Nora could go. "I forgot to ask if you'd look through the trunks of books we found in the attic. We just want to know if they're trash or treasure. We'll pay you whatever you think is fair."

Nora hesitated. Books that had sat for a long time tended to be badly damaged.

She'd seen hundreds of books ruined by mold, bugs, and water damage. These issues could be treated, but it was rarely worth the time or effort.

"Any idea how long they've been in the attic?"

"Since before the previous owners," Lou said. "They were an elderly couple and never went to the attic. The books are stored in three steamer trunks."

At the mention of trunks, a series of fictional characters flashed through Nora's brain. She saw Harry Potter's trunk being delivered to Hogwarts. Rincewind and the enchanted trunk from Terry Pratchett's *The Colour of Magic*. And Lady Catherine de Bourgh's particular instructions on how to pack a trunk in *Pride and Prejudice*. Remembering this scene brought a wistful smile to Nora's face.

"I'll take a look," she said. "And there's no charge. Just promise you'll come browse the bookshop when you have some free time."

Lou saluted Nora with her wineglass. "We can't wait for that moment."

Nora was vacuuming the shop floor the next morning when someone banged on the back door.

Nora opened it, expecting to greet the UPS driver. But it wasn't UPS. It was Lou.

Lou gestured at the old Volvo wagon idling in the loading zone. The hatchback was open, and Sheldon was bent over, wrestling with one of the trunks.

"I brought the books and your new employee," Lou said. "He was up bright and early this morning, raring to go."

Sheldon lifted a trunk by its handles and lumbered toward the door. "Call me Babe. After the ox, not the pig."

Nora pushed a hand truck over to him. "There's no sense hurting your back when I have this."

Sheldon lowered the trunk onto the dolly and turned to get another.

When her car was empty, Lou waved and drove off.

Leaving Nora to the trunks, Sheldon got busy in the ticket agent's office. He brewed coffee and arranged pastries. Afterward, he tidied the store. When these tasks were finished, he asked if he could fill in inventory and rearrange shelf enhancers.

Nora told him to make himself at home. In the stockroom, she sat on the floor, surrounded by the three trunks. She'd already opened the first, which was the shabbiest. Its leather handles were frayed, its wooden slats were badly nicked, and its metal bore dozens of scratches. When Nora opened the lid, a whiff of old air tainted by honey-scented decay rushed out to greet her.

She saw books. Small hardbacks with black, brown, forest-green, dark-red, and indigo covers. They had been neatly stacked inside the chest. To reach them, however, she had to remove an assortment of personal items. She placed these on the floor and studied them.

There was a pair of satin slippers, a leather case cushioning a pair of wire spectacles, an empty brass picture frame with cracked glass, a watercolor set filled with remnants of dried paint, and a sketch pad with pencil drawings.

Nora turned back to the trunk and pulled out a book. She saw paper sticking out from between its pages and opened the book to find a dried rose. It was brown with age and thoroughly flattened by time and pressure.

The space above Nora's pinkie knuckle began to tingle.

Danger, an inner voice whispered.

Ridiculous. It's just a rose, another voice argued.

Nora reached for another book. It was *The Mysterious Key* by Louisa May Alcott. The cover was in fine condition, but the pages were full of rose blossoms. Though the flowers were sandwiched between sheets of thin paper, moisture from the petals had seeped into the book pages. This kind of damage could not be undone.

A book on European birds was in the same condition, as was a book on constellations, a guide on growing and pickling vegetables, and a dozen works of nineteenth-century fiction. They were all ruined by flowers.

"The petals are all brown now," Nora scolded the unknown owner of the trunks. "They were never going to last. But the books — they could have lasted forever."

Thankfully, the smallest trunk held poetry books and no roses. While Nora was examining a book of poems by Christina Rossetti, a tintype photograph fell out from between the pages. Nora picked it up and was immediately captivated by the image of a beautiful woman in a white dress. The ruffled sleeves of her off-shoulder gown enhanced her smooth, milky skin. Her dark hair had been swept off her face, highlighting delicate cheekbones and full lips. Her hands were folded across her lap in a protective gesture. Her left hand was curled around an oblong-shaped crystal or rock.

Nora was riveted by the woman's expression. She'd been caught on the edge of a smile. There was a naked honesty about her gaze that lent her intelligence as well as beauty and poise. Nora returned the woman's stare and realized there was a hint of defiance in her eyes and in the tilt of her chin.

On the back of the tintype was the name *Rose Blythe Lattimer.* Below this was a date, *1862,* and the words *By sun and candle-light. Forever Yours.*

Sheldon entered the stockroom. He picked up one of the dried roses and sniffed it. "I smelled this *exact* scent at the inn."

"When?" Nora asked.

"I was on the window seat, reading. I woke up just before dawn, and I couldn't get back to sleep. The sky was starting to lighten, and the ground was covered in mist." He reached for the tintype. "I didn't see this beauty walking in it, though. I saw a black man. I waved at him, but he didn't wave back."

Nora's blood had gone cold. "Was he wearing a white T-shirt?"

Sheldon looked at her in surprise. "He was. He moved like he was angry — all tension and tight fists. I was relieved when he was gone. Maybe he comes and goes with the mist."

"Like one of the soldier ghosts in the legend about the inn?"

Sheldon shrugged. "In *Huckleberry Finn,* there's a line about the sound a ghost makes when it wants to tell us something and can't make itself understood. But that's the thing. Loneliness doesn't make a sound. Which is why that man spooked me. He was totally alone. Totally silent."

Nora didn't believe in ghosts.

But as she sat in the stockroom, surrounded by the sickly scent of rotted roses, her pinkie tingling, she thought again of the story about the monster made of rain. Mist was a cloud filled with water droplets. Mist was light enough to hover. It was gauzy. Ghostlike.

The sleigh bells on the front door clanged, signaling the arrival of a customer.

"I'm coming," Nora murmured, suddenly eager to return to the world of books.

CHAPTER 6

Art is not what you see, but what you make others see.

— Edgar Degas

An off-duty Deputy Andrews popped into the bookshop that afternoon. He wanted a new sci-fi novel.

"Is there such a thing as a sci-fi classic?" he asked Nora. "Like the books high school teachers put on their summer reading lists? Not that I ever did my summer reading. I thought books were boring until you gave me *Ender's Game.*"

"Have you heard of Ray Bradbury?" Nora asked.

Andrews said that he hadn't.

"It doesn't matter that you weren't into reading in high school," Nora assured him. "That's the beauty of books. They're always ready. Always waiting. You just need to reach out, and there they are."

Andrews laughed. "You make them sound like lap cats."

"If a book could purr every time a reader opened its cover, I believe it would." Nora found a copy of *Fahrenheit 451* and showed it to Andrews. "In this novel, books are outlawed. They're burned by firemen. People are told to watch TV instead. It's a book about censorship, violence, identity, and courage. I think you'll like it. Unless you have a thing against firemen."

"Cops don't get jealous of firemen. We know we look good in our uniforms."

Nora grinned and handed him the book. She pointed out a few more titles and then asked, "Did Hester tell you about the man in the white T-shirt?"

"Yeah. She said you saw him too."

"And Sheldon." Nora gave a brief summary of Sheldon's experience. "I'm not accusing the guy of anything. He's just . . . it's creepy how he stands and stares."

"Ms. Pennington," Andrews began, and Nora knew by his sudden formality that she wouldn't like what he was about to say. "We're not going to track a man's movements because he acts weird and has a thing for white T-shirts. He hasn't broken any laws. Three people have seen him walking or standing in public areas. That's it. If we interviewed every weird person visiting this town, we'd get nothing else done."

Andrews was right. The man in the white T-shirt might exude menace. He might seem frightening. But his demeanor hardly warranted an official investigation.

"What about Danny? Did you guys find anything at Cherokee Rock?"

"No," said Andrews in dismay. "We have no idea why he left his truck there. If there were clues, they've been washed away by the rain."

Nora had an image of footprints in the mud, slowly filling with water until they disappeared. "Have his lab results come in yet?"

Andrews pulled a face. "I can't talk about that. It's one thing for the sheriff to tell you. Me? I'd get parking ticket duty for a month."

"That wouldn't be too terrible," said Nora. "You could stop by the bakery all the time."

"My pants are already too tight. Hester cracks up when I complain about her making the whole cop/donut cliché worse. She keeps threatening to deliver a dozen pink piggy donuts to the station. Can you imagine McCabe opening that box and seeing those little pig faces Hester makes?"

They both laughed at the thought. Another customer entered the bookshop and headed straight for the checkout desk. Seeing her approach, Andrews thanked Nora and took his leave.

"Do you have books on herbal teas?" the customer asked over the clang of the sleigh bells.

"I'd be happy to help," Sheldon said, coming around the corner of the fiction section. He tugged on his sweater vest and gave the woman a charming smile. "I'm an expert on all things edible. Maybe, after I've helped you find the perfect book, I can entice you to put your feet up and enjoy a cup of our bookstore blend along with a fresh-from-the-oven pastry."

A dreamy expression came over the woman's face. "That sounds lovely."

Sheldon offered the woman his arm and led her deeper into the store.

Later, after selling her two books, an Agatha ChrisTEA, and a chocolate book pocket, Sheldon handed Nora a thick tome listing the healing qualities of herbal teas.

"What's this?" she asked.

"The first of several ideas to expand your menu," he said.

Nora frowned. "It's a good one. Unfortunately, the lodge serves healing herbal teas and smoothies. I really can't compete with them. Besides, I'd rather sell things they don't."

"Do they package their tea? Or is it available only by the cup?"

"I'd have to ask June. She knows every item in their gift shop. Why?"

Sheldon spun around in a Julie Andrews *Sound of Music* circle. His arms were outstretched, and his face glowed. "Books and food are perfect together. They're a power couple. Like Nick and Nora Charles. Elizabeth Bennet and Mr. Darcy. Ma and Pa Ingalls." He lowered his arms. "If we want local readers to view this bookstore as a hideaway from reality, an Aladdin's cave of peace and pleasure, then we should offer them every comfort. Coffee. Tea. Pastries. That's a start. But we could also serve herbal teas based on people's symptoms. IBS tea. Back pain tea. Arthritis tea. Fibro tea. We could sell packets too. The recipes are out there. We just need to put the right blend of herbs into a bag and tie it with a pretty ribbon. Gingham, maybe."

Nora took in this avalanche of suggestions. "Is there enough room in the ticket agent's office to make and store all this stuff?"

"I'd have to do some reorganizing," Sheldon said. "That desk would have to come out. What about expanding the menu? How about *The Grapes of Wrath* fruit salad?"

"That's awful," Nora said, softening the rejection with a grin. "Seriously, though. This isn't a café. I don't want to serve food other than pastries."

He shrugged. "But you're not saying no to the herbal tea idea. Does that mean you're saying yes?"

"I've watched you today," Nora said. "You belong in Miracle Books. You're good with people. You're good at sales. I like having you here, and I love the little changes you've already made. The themes you created on the endcaps are brilliant. I trust your instincts, so I'm willing to let you try other new things."

Sheldon rubbed his hands together with glee. "If you don't need me to close, I'll go back to the inn. I'm going to research herbs tout de suite."

"Why don't you plan to leave at two every day?" Nora suggested. "If you don't overdo it, your body might be more forgiving. And I can't afford health insurance for you."

"I'm not here for health insurance." Sheldon lovingly ran his fingertips over the spine of a book. "I'm here for these. And for the people who need them. I came to this town for help, but it wasn't the funky-smelling springs I needed. It was this place. And you."

Nora smiled at him. She remembered the first time she'd seen a photograph of the old train station that would become her shop. Even in its state of dilapidation, it had called to her. She'd envisioned the building painted a cheerful yellow hue with a periwinkle door and shutters. The front window would be filled with books and there'd be oversized flowerpots flanking the entrance. Inside, customers would wander through a warren of bookshelves. The shop would smell of paper, coffee, and comfort. It would exude quiet and calm in a rushed and noisy world.

Miracle Books was Nora's domain. Nora's sanctuary. But she was ready to share it with Sheldon Vega.

She watched him leave. She liked his jaunty gait. She liked his sweater vest. She liked his waves of silver-white hair and his tidy beard. She liked how comfortable he was in his own skin.

"We're all works in progress," she'd overheard him telling a customer that afternoon. "Except me. I'm a work of art."

The customer had laughed. As had Nora. She laughed often when Sheldon was around.

Now that he was gone, her mind returned to Danny and the mystery of his death. It was a mystery, she decided, because no one understood the why or the how behind it.

While a couple browsed in the unhurried manner of vacationers, Nora tried to puzzle out Danny's reason for driving to Cherokee Rock. Finally, she sent a group text to the members of the Secret, Book, and Scone Society.

Who's up for a picnic? Cherokee Rock? Tonight?

Within minutes, she received replies from her friends. They were all up for an alfresco meal, but they wanted to know why Nora had chosen that spot.

Because of Danny, she replied.

That was explanation enough for all of them, and they agreed to meet behind Miracle Books after closing time. Hester assigned dishes to Estella and June and asked Nora to provide disposable plates, napkins, cups, and cutlery. Since Nora kept a supply of these items at the bookshop, she was ready to go the moment she locked the doors.

June pulled into the parking lot behind the bookstore at a quarter past six. Estella was in the front seat, so Nora got in the back with Hester.

Hester waited until they were underway before asking, "Why do you want to go to Cherokee Rock? The sheriff was already there. What do you expect to find?"

"Nothing," Nora said. "I just need to see it for myself. I found plenty of photos of the symbols online but looking at them wasn't helpful. They don't mean anything to me. I was hoping I'd see something more if they were right in front of me. It's dumb, I know."

"Any excuse for a picnic is fine by me," said June. "Besides, I've been thinking about Danny. And his wife. Maybe we both needed to come here as a way of saying good-bye."

The women were silent for several minutes. Finally, Estella said, "I'm glad it's not raining. Being outside might get me out of my head." She went on to say that it had been another slow day at work.

Nora wondered if Sheldon could come up with some ideas on how to boost Estella's business. She made a mental note to ask if he'd consider taking a look at the salon.

"I've seen this rock a bunch of times," said Estella. "You're not going to look at it and find life-changing meaning in a bunch of old squiggles. I remember being dragged to the site on school field trips. Our teachers went on and on about how the smoke from campfires had nearly ruined the art. But kids don't care about old things. Kids live in the present."

Hester turned to Nora. "I've never been to this rock, but I'm super curious to see what it's like. What did the Great and Powerful Internet have to say about its history?"

Nora smiled. "I might as well have asked Oz because no one knows what the design is supposed to mean. Researchers think it was a stopping point for American Indians traveling to the springs. They discovered the healing powers of the water a millennium ago, so the rock is basically a really old way-point."

"It's a beautiful spot," said Estella. "Unless you're there in the middle of a storm."

The women fell silent, lost in their own thoughts. Fifteen minutes later, June pulled off the highway and drove past a historic marker for Cherokee Rock. The sign included the pictograph's date and its original name, which was Indian Rock.

The camping area was empty, so June parked in front of a site with a picnic table. The four friends decided to view the cliff face before unloading the food and walked over to where the massive rock wall faced the river.

The entire cliff face was covered with graffiti, not ancient art. To see that, Nora had to look much higher up. Shielding her eyes, she stared at the black geometric lines of paint. They reminded her of the maze books she'd done as a child. In addition to these lines was an occasional squiggle. The symbols meant nothing to her. But she wasn't Cherokee. For Danny, this might have been a sacred place. It might have held memories for him. He'd come here the day he died, but Nora had no idea why.

It was beautiful. The river moved in a steady gurgle behind them, vanishing into the unblemished forest. Hawks circled in the waning light while smaller birds searched for shelter in the trees before night fell.

Nora listened to these sounds and felt the same serenity she felt when she was hiking. She was grateful to live in a place that still had pristine views and unspoiled landmarks.

This landmark was hardly unspoiled, however. It had been damaged by centuries of smoke and in recent decades, by graffiti. The vandalism angered Nora. She could appreciate graffiti art when it was done on the proper canvas, but this ancient rock deserved better than someone's initials or a clumsy smiley face.

It was clear that Hester also disapproved. She stared at a set of initials, her mouth set in a thin line of disgust. "What is wrong with people? Why do they do stuff like this?"

Estella moved closer to Hester. "They're just trying to be seen. Or heard. Ages ago, I dated a graffiti artist. He told me that graffiti is a form of protest. It's a way to make people question things. It's supposed to get under your skin."

"They could have gotten under my skin by vandalizing a dumpster instead." June scowled. "Come on, let's eat."

"I'll be there in a sec." Nora gestured at the cliff face. "I need another minute."

June gave her shoulder a squeeze. Though she hadn't seen Danny's body in the water, she'd met Danny. She'd met Marie. She understood Nora's need for a moment of solitude. And because they were sensitive women, Estella and Hester also understood.

Nora tried to view the area through Danny's eyes. She tried to imagine the rain. The swollen river. The muddy ground. After a week of rainy weather, it wasn't hard to do. She could even picture the cliff face, darkened by water, and hear dripping from the wet rocks. She guessed Danny's view had been restricted by poor visibility.

130

What did he want to see? she wondered. *Why did he come here?*

On impulse, she used her smartphone to take photos of the view, the pictographs, and the graffiti. She stood there a little longer, waiting for inspiration. Nothing came.

Disappointed, she rejoined her friends.

Hester had set a table straight out of *Southern Living.* A basket containing Greek chicken salad wraps rolled in wax paper and tied with a pink ribbon took a place of pride on the green-and-white checkered table-cloth. There was also a platter of colorful chopped vegetables accompanied by a creamy dill dip and a bowl of hummus. Finally, there were fruit kebabs made of pineapple, melon, strawberries, and grapes. Estella had topped each skewer with a plump marshmallow.

"This is lovely," Nora said.

June patted the bench on her side of the table. "Tell us how it went with Sheldon today."

Nora was happy for the diversion. As much as she was haunted by the sight of Danny's drowned body, she was even more haunted by the memory of seeing Danny and Marie together. She imagined the initial shock was starting to wear off for Marie.

The pain, the earth-shattering truth of her situation, would be sinking in by now. Marie would realize that Danny's body would never warm their bed again. She'd never cook his breakfast or pour his coffee. She'd never nag him to leave his muddy boots by the back door. Their house would be full of his things. Every time she touched his razor, his favorite shirt, or a piece of his pottery, she'd feel pain. Every time she caught a hint of his scent, she'd turn, searching for his ghost.

"Before I tell you about Sheldon, could we plan a kindness tote session?" Nora asked her friends. "I'd like to put together something for Danny's wife."

Every month, the four friends met to assemble secret kindness totes. Each tote contained a book with a hopeful theme, a spa gift pack, a loaf of Hester's homemade bread, and a pair of June's socks. The women had originally created the bags to help the townsfolk most affected by the Madison County Community Bank scandal. Now they delivered them to anyone facing a difficult time. They dropped them off on front porches or stoops at night, hoping to preserve their anonymity. So far, they hadn't been caught. The paper had dubbed them the Night Angels.

June's expression was melancholy. "What do we give a woman who's lost everything?"

"Books," said Nora.

"And food," said Hester.

Estella pulled the marshmallow off the top of her fruit skewer and held it up. "Something soft. A pair of your socks, June."

"She needs more than socks and a loaf of bread," June said. "A case of whiskey would be more helpful."

"Liquid comfort doesn't last," Nora said, and gestured at Hester. "You're the expert on comfort. How could we deliver something as amazing as one of your comfort scones?"

The women batted ideas around until they were satisfied.

"Can we meet on Friday?" Hester asked. "I can't do Saturday. Jasper's parents are coming to town and he wants me to meet them."

Estella arched her brows. "Sounds like things are moving to the next level. Meeting the parents. Do you think he's going to put a ring on it?"

"No, Beyoncé, I don't," said Hester, trying to hide her blush behind the water pitcher.

"Do you want him to propose?" June gave Hester a playful nudge. "Come on. Tell us.

It's just us girls talking."

Hester pulled a celery stalk apart, one string at a time. "No. Jasper doesn't even know the real me. I haven't told him my secret."

"Hester, that man loves you," Estella said. "Any fool can see that. I'm not telling you what to do, but I believe you can trust him with your secret."

"Maybe." Hester tossed the mutilated celery into the woods. "The thing is, I should have told him months ago. It feels like I waited too long. I hate my parents for forcing me to give up my baby, for treating me like I was the scum of the earth because I got pregnant in high school, but I hate myself for letting the past ruin my future." She sighed. "I've been stalling because Jasper won't look at me the same way after I tell him. I'll be spoiled, like a piece of fruit left out in the sun."

"That's your parents talking," Nora said. "You're not ruined because of an unplanned pregnancy. You were pushed and pulled and forced to do things against your will. When Jasper hears your story, he'll want to protect you."

"I don't need his protection." Hester's eyes flashed.

"Of course you don't," Nora agreed. "But

if you love the man, and no one says that you have to love him, then you should tell him your secret. Secrets and healthy relationships don't go together. Trust me. I know."

"What about Jed? Have you told him yours?"

Hester was clearly trying to turn the spotlight on someone else, and Nora knew why. Jasper was Hester's first serious boyfriend since high school. She owned her own home, ran a successful business, and was smart, pretty, and generous. But she didn't believe in her own worth. Part of her kept hearing her parents whisper inside her head. *You're trash,* the nasty voices would say. *You're a slut.*

Hester's friends tried to shut down the voices with encouragement and praise, but only Hester had the power to get rid of them for good.

"Jed knows about my accident," Nora said. "But the version I told him was abbreviated. I shared all the details with you guys because I wanted you to see the real me. The woman hiding behind the scars. I knew the three of us were forming a connection that wouldn't be broken. I can't say that about Jed. Part of him is here. Part of him is at the coast with his mom."

"Guess I won't be catching your bridal bouquet," teased Estella.

Nora gave her a horrified look. "God, no. Never again."

"What about Sheldon?" June asked. "Is he involved with anyone?"

"He doesn't do relationships," Nora said, repeating what Sheldon had told her.

"Does that mean I won't be able to sweet-talk him into working his magic on my salon?" Estella asked.

Nora promised to broach the subject with Sheldon tomorrow.

The sky had turned a deep plum, and the shadows in the campground were lengthening. It was time to go.

On their way out, Nora glanced at the cliff face. The beams of the setting sun washed over the rock, and the ancient art glowed ember red. Nora thought of the bowl she'd bought from Danny. Despite its imperfection — or because of it — the bowl was important to her. She couldn't give it to Jed. She wanted to use it. She wanted Danny to live on in the clay he'd once shaped.

That night, Nora couldn't sleep. She wandered into her kitchen, which was gilded in moonlight. Danny's bowl sat at the counter. Nora sat on a stool and ran her

136

fingertip around its smooth rim, feeling the chip with each circle. Her thoughts drifted from Cherokee Rock to the tintype of Rose Lattimer to the flower petals pressed into the pages of her books.

Idly, Nora picked up Danny's bowl and turned it over. She looked at the initials and the symbol Danny had scratched into the unglazed clay.

Suddenly, Nora was wide awake. She turned on the lights and looked at the symbol etched next to Danny's initials. It was a bird. She touched it, and the space above her pinkie knuckle vibrated.

Nora had never told anyone of this odd phenomenon. She knew that amputees could feel itching, pain, or pressure from limbs that were no longer there. But the ghost of half a finger? It seemed ridiculous. Preposterous.

On the other hand, Nora knew women who could predict rain based on aches in their hips. She knew men who could forecast snow by sharp pains in their hands or feet.

Nora's tingle wasn't weather related. It was a premonition. A warning.

She looked at the bird again. It seemed familiar. Had she seen it somewhere before? If so, then where?

Her moonlit kitchen held no answers.

■ ■ ■ ■

The next morning, she felt out of sorts. When coffee failed to improve her mood, she put on her hiking boots and grabbed her walking stick. The stick was one of her prized possessions as it had been carved by a local artist and inscribed with a partial quote from *The Little Prince.*

Nora took a trail that wound up into the hills. She didn't run into any other hikers that morning, which meant she could lose herself in the peaceful beauty of her surroundings. As she walked uphill, leaves and small branches crunched under her feet and sunlight fell in slants between the tree trunks.

After hiking for an hour, she descended a hill at the edge of the Tree House Cabins. The road between the cabins built on aboveground platforms took her past a butterfly and bumblebee garden. A bird feeder attached to a pole in the center of the garden had attracted a pair of cardinals.

Nora heard the birds chirp and wondered what kind of conversation they were having. As she walked away, she felt a strong sense of déjà vu.

The bird on the bottom of Danny's bowl, she

thought. *It's supposed to be red.*

After hurrying home, she kicked off her boots in the living room and grabbed her phone from the charging cradle. She pulled up the photos from Cherokee Rock and scrolled through them, not seeing what she was looking for.

Frustrated, she turned to her laptop. After downloading the same photos from the cloud, she clicked on the first in the series and examined the graffiti. She saw initials. A crude heart. The second photo showed more of the same. She'd taken the third photo from a different angle, standing slightly off to the side. There, nestled among a group of black letters, was a small bird. It was red. And it was an exact duplicate of the bird on Danny's bowl.

Nora felt a prickling sensation. It swept over her skin, raising goose bumps along her arms.

She'd found something. But what?

All she knew was that the bird was important. It had been deliberately painted on those rocks, just like the ancient pictographs. It was there to convey meaning to others.

Nora had a powerful sense that Danny had gone to Cherokee Rock because of that bird. She could see him parking his truck at the site, but she couldn't picture him walking to Miracle Springs in the rain. She remembered how the river rushed into the trees, and felt with overwhelming certainty that Danny had never walked away from Cherokee Rock.

He'd died there.

He'd died, and his body had gone into the river.

And the only witnesses had been his killer and a little red bird.

CHAPTER 7

The greatest secrets are always hidden in the most unlikely places.

— Roald Dahl

Nora started work an hour early the next day. After picking up pastries from the bakery, she entered the quiet bookstore and brewed coffee.

When there was enough caffeine-infused ambrosia to fill a mug, she grabbed one off the pegboard. It was green and had black text reading DON'T MAKE ME SUMMON MY FLYING MONKEYS.

Nora grinned, remembering the day she'd found three literary-themed mugs at the flea market. In addition to the *Wizard of Oz* mug, she'd found one with a portrait of Edgar Allan Poe that read POE ME A CUP, as well as one featuring William Shakespeare in sunglasses and the caption HEY GIRL, I HEARD YOU LIKE IAMBIC PENTAMETER.

She carried her coffee to the folktale section. Sitting on the floor, she began pulling books off the shelf and flipping through them. Most of the books contained at least one story about the owl, eagle, raven, robin, hawk, duck, woodpecker, cuckoo, crane, dove, or birds that could talk, like the parrot. None of the stories mentioned the cardinal.

Nora checked the time. She needed to open the shop in a few minutes, which meant she'd have to resume her search later.

Just one more book, Nora thought.

She smiled, knowing this was the same as telling herself, *Just one more chapter* or *I'll stop at the end of this page.*

Luckily, the next book featured tales of woodland animals. The table of contents listed a story called "How the Red Bird Got Its Color." Nora felt a small thrill of anticipation, which was heightened when she read the subtitle: "Adapted from a Cherokee Tale."

Nora opened to the story and was instantly lost in its words.

Raccoon was a trickster. He liked to tease the other animals. The animal he teased the most was Wolf.

Wolf did nothing to deserve this. He

could have bared his fangs or showed Raccoon his sharp claws, but he didn't. He ignored Raccoon. This made Raccoon tease Wolf even more.

One day, Wolf lost his temper. He became very angry at Raccoon. He chased him through the forest until both animals were exhausted.

When Wolf went to sleep that night, Raccoon covered Wolf's eyes with mud.

By morning, the mud had dried into a hard crust. When Wolf opened his eyes, he could not see.

"I've gone blind!" he cried, turning his head this way and that. He howled, crying over his lost sight. He whined and called out for help.

None of the other animals came to his aid.

Finally, a bird landed on a tree branch above Wolf and asked, "Brother Wolf, what is wrong?"

Wolf told the bird how he had gone to sleep with his sight and woken up to blindness.

"I am Brown Bird," the bird said. "I am not big or powerful, but I will help you if I can."

The bird flew down from his branch and began to peck at the dried mud covering

Wolf's eyes.

"If I get my sight back, I will take you to a magic rock," Wolf promised the bird. "You can paint your feathers with the red paint that flows from this rock."

Brown Bird managed to peck off all the mud. Wolf was so grateful to have his sight back that he told the bird to get on his back. "To show my gratitude, I will take you to the magic rock."

When they reached the rock, Wolf used a stick to paint Brown Bird's feathers. When Wolf was done, the bird was bright red and very beautiful.

Red Bird thanked Wolf and flew off to show his family his new feathers. Because of his kindness, his family grew and grew in number. The woods are now filled with red birds. Some call them cardinals.

Nora examined the illustration of the bird and the wolf. The bird's feathers were a vibrant cherry red and the wolf's yellow eyes glowed like full moons in his gray face. His teeth were bared in a lupine smile. The bird was meant to draw the reader's eye, but Nora couldn't stop staring at the wolf. Did his smile look more threatening than friendly?

She closed the book and thought of Danny.

The birds etched into Danny's pot and painted on Cherokee Rock were cardinals. Nora was sure of it. They were North Carolina's state bird. They were cheerful and colorful. But there must be another reason Danny had chosen to etch the bird into the bottom of his pottery.

The only way Nora could learn of Danny's connection to this animal would be to ask Marie.

"How would I explain my sudden interest in her late husband?" Nora asked the book spines lined up in front of her, but they offered no advice.

Nora finished her coffee and unlocked the front door. The shop was open for business and Sheldon hadn't come. When he arrived at half past ten, he made a beeline for the ticket agent's office.

"I'll need to sit more today," he told Nora when she came over to say hello. "I had a bad night. Every part of me aches. Even my earlobes hurt."

"Should you be here at all?" Nora asked.

He waved off her concern. "Just don't ask me to carry heavy boxes and I'll be fine."

Nora looked at the folding chair she used as a desk chair. Sheldon couldn't sit on that

145

all day. It would exacerbate his aches and pain.

"Use one of the reading chairs when you're not serving customers," she said. "At lunchtime, I'll run to the hardware store and buy a cushioned stool with a supportive back. I'll grab us food from the Pink Lady while I'm at it."

Sheldon paused in the act of arranging pastries on a platter. "You sound almost chipper. Hot date last night?"

"I hung out with my friends. Sometimes, that's better than a hot date."

"Amen to that, sister." Sheldon pointed at the fridge. "And forget about ordering from the Pink Lady. I made Cuban sandwiches. If we served sandwiches, I'd call this one the King of Havana after the novel by Pedro Juan Gutiérrez." He smiled. "Let's play a game today. Whoever comes up with the best sandwich and a literary name for it, buys a bag of potato chips for our meal."

In between helping customers, Nora thought of ideas. Old Man and the Sea for a tuna salad sandwich. Sheldon retaliated with One Fish, Two Fish. When he suggested the Godfather for an Italian sub, she fought back with the Conte of Monte Crisco.

"I have a title for a club sandwich," she

told Sheldon later that morning.

"The club?" Sheldon looked horrified. "That's the whitest sandwich ever. It screams country clubs and people named Biff."

Nora wagged her finger. "Not this one. Take the basic club and add wasabi mayo and super-thin cucumber slices and call it the Joy Luck Club."

Sheldon roared with laughter and deemed Nora the winner of the game. She ran out for chips and diet sodas anyway. At half past noon, they sat at the front counter to eat lunch.

Nora bit into her Cubano and moaned. "This is delicious. How did you toast it? It's still warm."

"Panini maker," Sheldon said. "And before you ask, yes, I travel with a panini maker. And bread-baking supplies. You can't just buy Cuban bread at Food Lion. It has to be lovingly made by deft Cuban hands. Or deft, half-Cuban hands. Keep moaning. It pleases the chef."

Nora had no problem acting like she enjoyed her lunch. She gulped it down and snacked on chips while paying bills. There was a lull in business around two, so Nora told Sheldon that she wanted to run down to the hardware store to buy him a stool.

"You can leave as soon as I get back," she added.

"We've been busy all day until now, so I'll stay until three. You're bound to have an afternoon coffee rush. Besides, I need to come up with a vegetarian sandwich name. Just for fun." He tapped his chin. "How about the Beet Queen?"

Nora laughed. "That's awful."

"You're right. What about Princess and the Pea? Snow peas with avocado on pita bread?"

"The princess didn't sleep on mattresses piled on top of a snow pea," Nora said.

"Fine," Sheldon huffed. "Let's see what you come up with."

Nora didn't have the chance to think of a name because she had to help a woman searching for books similar to Jodi Picoult's. Nora suggested that she give Anna Quinn, Jojo Moyes, and Kristin Hannah a try. The woman bought five books, a pewter teapot, and a set of mala beads made of turquoise, rosewood, and clear quartz.

"I'm coming back tomorrow," she told Nora on her way out. "Your coworker promised me the best coffee of my life. Who could resist that offer?"

Nora smiled. She had a coworker. She had someone who loved books, who made cof-

148

fee like a professional barista, who had the courage to wear his happiness and his pain on his sleeve. She had Sheldon Vega. And if he stayed, they would be more than coworkers. They would be friends.

At the hardware store, Nora tested the stool for comfort and told the clerk she'd take it.

"The floor sample's a little scuffed up. I'll get a new one from the back," he said.

Nora lined up to pay. Lou was right in front of her, so she tapped the other woman on the shoulder. Lou started in surprise and then turned and laughed.

"I was miles away," she said. "My to-do list is taking up all the space in my head."

"Is that for the hallway?" Nora asked, pointing at the paint cans in Lou's cart.

Lou nodded. "My arms are still sore from scraping wallpaper. By the time I'm done with paint rollers and brushes, I'm going to need to soak in a thermal pool for a month. Sometimes, I worry that buying that old house will be the death of me. I guess the pull of family was stronger than logic."

Nora was about to tell Lou about the contents of the steamer trunks when Lou's phone rang. She pulled it from her back pocket and examined the screen.

"It's Patty. Do you think the roof caved in

149

while I was in here?"

Uttering a quick apology to Nora, Lou answered the phone. She listened for several seconds before her eyes grew round with surprise.

"Nora's standing next to me. Should I ask if she'll take a look?"

Lou hung up and pocketed her phone. Her movements were slow, and she looked dazed.

"Everything okay?" Nora asked.

"It's not the roof," Lou said. "The chimney guys pulled out another loose stone above the mantel. The stone was covering a hole. It was deliberately carved into the wall. And there was something inside."

Nora knew that Lou was drawing out her story, but she didn't care. She was already captivated by the image of a hidey-hole above the mantel.

"What was it?" she asked as Lou placed her paint cans on the counter.

"A box. Patty thinks it's made of crystal. It's locked, and there's no key in sight. When Patty wiped the box off, she could see what was inside." She paused to pay the cashier and then turned back to Nora. "It's a book."

"What's the title?"

"Patty said that she can't really see

150

through the crystal. She thinks the box might be valuable and doesn't want to damage it trying to force it open. Would you take a look and give us your opinion? We don't know much about antiques."

Nora tried to conceal her excitement. "I'll come right after work. I might be able to help with that lock too. I have a lockpick kit, and I've gotten pretty good at using it."

"It's a date," Lou said.

The word reminded Nora of her dinner with Jed. If she stopped at the Inn of Mist and Roses first, she'd probably be late. But Jed would understand. How could she pass up the chance to examine a book locked inside a box hidden in the wall?

Nora carried the stool to the bookstore and told Sheldon about the walled-up book.

To her surprise, he seemed discomfited by the news. "What if it's a grimoire or something wicked like that? There's a reason somebody locked the thing in a box and stuck it in that hole. A glass box? That's weird too. It's like the book is Snow White, waiting on a prince. I don't like stories where women are imprisoned by sleep or thorns or towers until some guy kisses them awake. They should be fierce enough to *get woke* on their own."

Nora was too fixated on the walled book

to discuss gender bias in fairy tales. She went off to search for shelf enhancers that came with keys. She'd bring all the keys to the inn. If none of them worked, she'd try picking the lock. Many of the vintage items she bought for the shop came without keys, which is why Nora had learned to pick simple locks. She could now open clock cases, old boxes, tea caddies, or a file cabinet.

When Nora had her materials assembled, she told Sheldon to call it a day. On his way out, she handed him a check. "If I don't see you at the inn, I'll see you Monday."

"Wouldn't miss it for the world. Unless I have to." He pocketed the check without looking at it.

Nora smiled. "By the way, I thought of a name for a veggie sandwich. The Lady of Shallot."

"Yes!" Sheldon cried. "Shallots and mushrooms on a baguette." He pointed down the sidewalk. "Oh my. The ugliest Vespa in the world is heading this way. Time for me to fly."

Sheldon wriggled his fingers in farewell and scurried past Richard Kerr.

Richard saw Nora standing in the doorway and waved. This wasn't the haggard, dejected man who'd visited the bookstore a week ago. He looked at ease. Happy even.

"Here she is," he said, and balanced the moped on its kickstand. He touched one of the hot-pink flowers decorating the canary-yellow body. "You can take these off if you want."

"I'm just renting it, remember? Lily might want to reclaim her moped — flower stickers and all — in the future."

Richard entered the store. "We've been talking," he said shyly. "Me, Jess, and Lily. It hasn't all been productive. Or peaceful. But the walls between us have crumbled a bit."

"Which means a little light is coming through."

Richard smiled. His eyes were bright with hope. "Exactly. Jess and I are still reading the books you recommended, but we're making progress as a family. I can't thank you enough for helping us."

Nora thought of her recent fall on her bike and of the damage to her flea market finds, including the bowl Danny made. "You're helping me too. I haven't driven anything with a motor for years."

Richard handed her the owner's manual, bought the last book pocket to eat on his way home, and left.

Nora had just enough time before closing

to scour the Internet for red bird symbols like the ones on Danny's pot and at Cherokee Rock. The image had flitted around in her head all day long. She'd see a flash of red and think of the cardinal. And since her only customer was a mother reading board books to her toddler, Nora felt free to focus on her laptop.

She quickly learned that the cardinal was an important bird to Native Americans. It was a messenger — an animal that could travel between Earth and the spiritual realm. Some tribes believed the cardinal was the daughter of the sun. Others believed the red bird could predict the weather. A symbol of strength, passion, and monogamy, the red bird didn't migrate. It endured the cold, its red plumage a bright contrast to the winter snow and bare tree limbs. Its constancy instilled hope and the promise of spring.

Nora paused her research to ring up the mother's selections of Sandra Boynton's *Moo, Baa, La La La,* Margaret Wise Brown's *Goodnight Songs,* and *Hello Bugs!* by Smriti Prasadam. The toddler was holding *Hello Bugs!* with a death grip and eyes that warned of an impending tantrum. But Nora needed to scan the bar code, so she patted the counter and spoke to the child. "Why don't you sit up here? You can zap your book with a red light. Want to try?"

The boy's mother placed him on the counter and Nora took his chubby fist in hers and gently guided his hand so that the price gun hovered over the bar code on the back of his book. She helped him squeeze the trigger button, and when the register beeped and the price flashed on-screen, the boy grinned.

"Again," he demanded.

Nora cleared the sale and let him ring up all of his books. She then gave him the bag to carry.

"Thank you," his mother said. "We're supposed to meet my husband for dinner, but we're early. I stayed here too long and now Jefferson is hungry, which means he's on the brink of a DEFCON 5 meltdown. Between these books and the Cheerios in my purse, we just might make it through our meal."

Scooping the little boy up in her arms, the woman planted a kiss on his round cheek and walked out.

Nora locked the front door, flipped the OPEN sign to CLOSED, and returned to her laptop.

One website featured the red bird's spiritual characteristics:

If a cardinal is trying to get your attention, ask yourself who might be sending you a message. Cardinals do not appear at random. If one comes close to you, it bears a message from the spirit world. Someone might be trying to communicate with you through the cardinal. Ask yourself what message that person might want to deliver.

Nora remembered the pair of cardinals she'd seen on her hike. The air above her pinkie knuckle hummed.

"Danny's not trying to speak to me," she muttered in annoyance. "We didn't even know each other."

Then why did his death bother her so much? She'd found his body and the experience had been horrible, but she'd faced trauma before. So why was she fixated on Danny's death?

Because he loved his wife, a small voice whispered.

Nora knew this was the truth. She rarely thought about Danny without also thinking of Marie. She kept replaying the couple's interaction at the flea market. Why? Because she'd never looked at a man the way Marie had looked at Danny. And no man had looked at her like Danny had looked at his wife. Nora had dated men. She'd had a husband. But she'd never been in love with a man who was also her friend. She didn't want to admit it, but she was jealous of Danny and Marie. What they'd shared reminded Nora of how much time she'd wasted on bad men.

Now that Marie is alone, there's no reason to be jealous, the small voice whispered.

Shoving the barbed thought aside, Nora locked up Miracle Books and sat on her moped.

"You look like SpongeBob with the pox," she told the vehicle before donning the hot-pink helmet.

The moped was a breeze to drive. The speed limit downtown was twenty-five, so Nora had no problem keeping up with car traffic. She pulled into a parking spot in front of the inn and was taking off her helmet when a woman eased a white sedan into the next spot.

"Cute bike," she said as she got out of the car. Her gaze lingered on the daisy decals.

"It's a loaner," Nora said. Normally, she would have stuck with "thanks" and walked away. However, she wanted to prove to this slim, well-coiffed woman that she had better taste than the moped suggested.

"Lou said that the local lock picker would

157

be coming by after six." The woman shot Nora a quizzical look. "Is that you?"

Nora showed her the lockpick set. "I'm just an amateur. I learned to use this because some of the items I carry in my bookstore come with locks but no key."

"Is Miracle Books yours?" the woman asked, her warm brown eyes shining. "I dropped by this afternoon to see Sheldon. He sold me some fabulous art books, but I'm sorry that I missed you. I'm Georgia Gentry, by the way. That's my husband, Bo." She pointed at the inn's front porch. "Say hello, Bo!"

A middle-aged man lowered his cell phone and waved.

"Nora Pennington."

The women walked up the front path together.

"You've created a fairyland for book lovers," Georgia said. "I could spend every afternoon for the rest of my life in your shop. And I love that you breathed new life into the old train station." She gestured at the inn's façade. "Buildings deserve second chances. Given enough love, even the hopelessly neglected ones can be beautiful again."

"It takes lots of love. Lots of money too," Nora said.

"And a shit-ton of work," Georgia added.

The women shared a laugh.

Nora cast a sidelong glance at Georgia. She was an attractive woman with glossy, dark brown hair and a lean frame. Her clothes were simple and perfectly tailored. Though she and Nora were roughly the same age, Georgia had a confidence and easy affability that Nora had never possessed.

At the approach of the two women, Bo got to his feet. Like his wife, his hair was brown, though it had gone gray at the temples. His tanned and freckled skin, polo shirt, and salmon-colored slacks gave off a country club vibe. He welcomed his wife with a kiss on the cheek before turning a friendly smile on Nora.

"Bo, Nora owns that darling bookstore," Georgia said. "She bought the old train station. Do you remember me talking about boarding trains from that station when I was a girl, and how I worried that we'd find it an abandoned wreck?"

Giving her an indulgent look, Bo said, "If I had a nickel for every time you got all worked up over some old building . . ."

"You'd be a millionaire. I know." Georgia squeezed her husband's hand before turning to Nora. "I'm in the restoration business. It's like running an animal shelter for historic buildings. Instead of saving animals from ruin and placing them in good homes, I save the homes from ruin. And Miracle Springs holds a special place in my heart. The waters saved my granny's life. I came here with her when I was a girl. We spent the summer at the lodge. She could barely walk in June. By the end of August, she could dance."

Nora mumbled something positive and glanced at the front door. She liked Georgia, but she wished Lou or Patty would appear. She wanted to see the book in the box. After that, she wanted to see Jed.

Georgia must have read something in Nora's expression. "Sorry to babble," she said with a self-effacing smile. "What I was trying to tell you — and not doing a very good job of it — is how happy I am that you not only saved the train depot, but you also turned it into a magical place. I'm going to let Bo drag me to dinner now. Good luck with the lock picking."

With a parting wave, Nora entered the inn. The hallway walls were no longer a pock-marked white. They were freshly-painted, and the blue gray was perfectly serene.

"What do you think of the finished product?" Patty asked, bustling in from the kitchen.

"It's really nice," Nora said. "All you need now is some art."

Patty glanced at the bare walls. "Lou wants to hang a big mirror so that we can see what our visitors are made of. You know, spy on them from the dining room." Patty laughed over Nora's evident confusion. "There's an age-old superstition shared by innkeepers that we should all hang a mirror in the foyer if we want to catch a glimpse of a guest's shadow soul. That's what shows in the mirror and lets the innkeep know if they've let a room to a psychopath. The original owners hung a mirror here. It was one of the few items to survive the fire and is somewhere in the attic."

As she talked, Patty led Nora to the library where Lou was waiting for them.

The rubble had been cleared away. The chimney stones had been completely stripped. Fresh drop cloths draped the mantel and covered the floor. The room was prepped for a transformation.

Lou greeted Nora and said, "They'll start rebuilding tomorrow." She ran her hand along the top of the mantel, smoothing out the plastic sheeting. Her touch was filled with affection. "Ever since we bought this place, I feel like it's been trying to tell me something. I just don't know what. This seems like a pretty blatant attempt to communicate."

Nora's gaze was fixed on the hole in the wall. The shadowy niche was about a foot above the mantel and to the right. It silently called to her.

Lou beckoned her closer. "I put the box back where we found it so that you could see what we saw. Well, almost. Patty wiped ten layers of dust off of the box."

As Nora approached the hole, her pulse quickened. Background noises faded, and she felt like she was moving in slow motion.

Lou indicated the stepstool in front of the mantel and Nora ascended it in a trancelike state.

She peered into the darkness and saw a shape inside the wall. A rectangular box. Also known as a coffin box.

Without asking for permission, Nora's hands reached out. Her fingers closed around the box and withdrew it from its dark hole.

The box had been in the wall for decades. As Nora examined it, she guessed that it was more than a century old. Its crystal surface was unblemished, and there was no rusting to the bronze hinges or lock.

The box was smaller than she'd imagined, which meant the book inside was roughly the size of a mass market paperback, though not as thick. It had a brown cover with no obvious title or author.

"Can you get it open?" Lou whispered.

Nora suggested they relocate to the kitchen where the light was better. She put the box on the table, and the women sat down and pulled their chairs close together. After selecting two tools from her lockpick set, Nora inserted a hook with a right angle into the lock. The hook applied pressure while she used her other hand to work the pick. It took her over a minute to spring the lock.

Instead of opening the box she pushed it over to Lou. Lou shot a questioning glance at Patty, but Patty waved for her to go ahead.

Nora held very still as Lou raised the lid.

As soon as the box was open, the air filled with the scent of roses.

CHAPTER 8

Widow. The word consumes itself.
                                — Sylvia Plath

Lou took out the book and laid it on the table. She gently opened the cover, supporting the spine with her left hand in case the binding was fragile.

Nora watched, feeling a rush of admiration for Lou for treating the book with such respect.

The first page was blank. The second page contained a small painting of a single red rose. Directly under the painting, a name was written in neat script.

"It's Rose's diary," Lou said in an awed whisper.

Nora's eyes moved from the book to the coffin box. She'd read about diaries in dozens of books. Anne Frank's *The Diary of a Young Girl, Bridget Jones's Diary, I Capture the Castle, Diary of a Wimpy Kid, The Color*

Purple, *Dracula,* *The Lacuna,* and *Gone Girl*
were just a few.

A diary represented the secret thoughts of
the writer. It was meant to be private — to
be hidden — because it held secrets. Some
diaries were kept under lock and key. Some
had pages filled with forbidden yearnings,
desperate desires, or impossible dreams. To
read someone's diary was to peer into the
crevices of their soul. It was both a trespass
and a privilege. A violation and an invitation. It was as intimate as a kiss.

Lou seemed reluctant to turn another
page, as if she believed that Rose's secrets
should be treated with reverence instead of
being revealed to three women at once.

Nora touched Lou's hand. "If the house
has been trying to speak to you, this might
be how you'll discover what it has to has
say."

With a nod, Lou turned the page.

A dried flower floated out of the book and
landed on the table.

"Is that a rose?" Patty asked. She lowered
her face to the flower and inhaled. "I can't
smell anything."

Lou got up, took a small plate from the
drying rack, and gingerly slid the rose off
the edge of the table and onto the plate.
She then passed the plate to Nora.

Nora knew that she'd be able smell the rose before she even tried. She felt like she'd been haunted by the scent ever since the dried petals had fallen from between the pages of the books kept in the steamer trunks. It was a cloying perfume, a mixture of sweet and rot. And though Nora had never liked roses, she would have given anything to see what this one had looked like in bloom. She could imagine entire bushes of these flowers, glowing like small suns. Bright, resplendent red petals. Cardinal red.

"Are you okay?" Lou asked. "You look like someone just walked over your grave."

That's exactly what Nora had felt, but she didn't want to admit it to people she barely knew. Instead, she slid the plate with the dried rose back to Lou. "The books inside the steamer trunks must have been Rose Lattimer's. They were filled with the same flowers. All roses."

"Isn't that a bit vain?" Patty asked. "To keep so many flowers because you share their name?"

Lou ran a finger over the diary's cover with the same tenderness she'd shown to the library mantel.

Nora didn't believe in the supernatural, but maybe the house was trying to speak to

166

Lou. Maybe it was trying to reach Nora too. Why else could she smell the roses? But what did the house — or Rose Lattimer — want them to know?

"From what I've read about Rose, she wasn't the least bit vain," said Lou. "She was strong, generous, and determined. I think we would have liked her, Patty."

Nora suddenly remembered the woman in the tintype portrait. She was beautiful, of that there was no doubt, but there was far more to her than beauty. There was her intelligent gaze, the stubborn set of her jaw, and her proud bearing. Her youthful face glowed with confidence. And the way she was on the verge of smiling at someone standing to the side of the photographer lent her an air of secrecy.

"I should have brought that tintype with me," Nora told Lou and Patty. "I was in such a rush to get here that it didn't cross my mind."

"There's always tomorrow." Lou placed both hands over the diary. It was a protective gesture. A possessive one too. "We're really grateful. We would never have gotten this open without your lock-picking skills."

"Why don't we repay you with supper tomorrow night?" Patty asked. "By then, Lou will have read the whole diary and she can fill us in on the juicy bits."

Lou agreed and fumbled for her reading glasses, which were once again nesting in her gray curls. She seemed distracted and distant. It was time for Nora to go.

Patty walked her to the door. "Don't mind Lou. She's a sensitive soul and this pile of brick and timber means everything to her. Ever since we met, she's talked about living here."

"How did you end up buying this place?" Nora asked. "Do you have a connection to Miracle Springs?"

"Not me," Patty said, opening the front door. "I'm a Chicago native. Lou's family is from North Carolina. She was born in Chapel Hill but went to college at Cornell. She worked in Manhattan for years and never considered returning to her home state. After her parents died, she started researching her family history. We met at a genealogy convention. We both had this crazy notion that by finding links to our past we could ease our sense of loss. Research was a way of staying connected to our parents and grandparents."

A car horn sounded outside, and Patty seemed to remember that she was holding the door open. "See you tomorrow. Georgia, Bo, and Sheldon will be there too. I'm not sure about Micah. Our young hiker sticks to his room when he's not working off his reduced room rate. Either way, it'll be a nice, cozy party."

Nora wished Patty a good night and drove to Jed's house. She was eager to see him, to spend an intimate evening with him, but she wished she had a few minutes to clear her head first. Thoughts crowded all the recesses in her brain, and without the chance to reflect on them, she worried that they might explode out of her like colored paper from a confetti cannon.

At Jed's, she parked her moped and jogged up to the porch. She knocked and then glanced at her watch. She was nearly an hour late and she hadn't even called to let him know.

"I'm so sorry," she said when he opened the door.

He took her hands in his and looked her up and down. "Is everything okay?"

Nora drank in the sight of him. Jedidiah Craig was a bona fide hunk. He had the toughness, the calloused hands, and the five o'clock shadow of a cowboy from a Western novel, but his tousled brown hair, ocean-blue eyes, and wry smile were reminiscent of Rhett Butler's. His clothes were always casual — flannel shirts, black T-shirts, jeans, work boots. He looked good in his clothes and in his uniform. He would look good in a hazmat suit. Whenever Nora was close to him, she felt like she didn't measure up. Though the burn scars on her face had been repaired, they still existed in her memory. In her mind, she would always be flawed. And Jed was pretty close to perfect.

"It's a long story," she said, leaning in to kiss him hello. "Can I tell you over dinner, or have I totally screwed that up?"

Jed pulled her inside and shut the door. "Nothing's screwed up. The beauty of fried chicken is that it tastes good cold. Besides, tonight isn't about the food. It's about making you smile."

He stopped Nora before she could walk by the living room. "As you know, I don't own much furniture. I only need a mattress and a place to sit and eat, but I feel like I'm not a real adult because I have no sofa, no TV, and the wrong kind of bed for nighttime cardio sessions."

Nora arched her brows. "Are we having fried chicken in bed?"

Jed flashed her one of his brilliant smiles. "No, but I like the way you think. Stay here for a sec. Don't move an inch."

"Where's Henry Higgins?" Nora called after him.

"He has a date tonight too," Jed called back, and Nora assumed that Henry was spending time with his favorite neighbor, Mrs. Pickett.

Jed hurried into the kitchen and returned with a bottle of non-alcoholic beer in each hand. He handed one to Nora and said, "Do you remember when we talked about our favorite kids' books? The only one we had in common was *Curious George.* You said that you loved the scene where George transforms the Man in the Yellow Hat's living room into a jungle. Well, I thought I'd bring that scene to life for you."

Putting his hand on the small of Nora's back, he propelled her forward.

When Nora saw what Jed had done to his living room, all thoughts of the inn and Rose Lattimer vanished. Jed had re-created the scene from *Curious George* down to the last detail. He'd transformed two drop cloths into yellow leopards and draped the cloths over a pair of chairs. The red-and-white giraffe had been fashioned from a stepstool, a sheet, and a broom. A rocking chair covered with another drop cloth was now a zebra. Painted palm trees grew up the walls, and Curious George climbed a tree near the window.

Jed bowed like a courtier. "Madame,

171

would you like to sit on a leopard or a zebra?"

Nora couldn't believe her eyes. "This is so . . . I can't . . . won't you get in trouble for this?"

"Ah, I'll paint over it. My landlord will never know. Or, if you'd like, I could make a scene with that bear you liked so much when you were a kid. The one who lost his button."

"Corduroy," Nora said, and shook her head in astonishment. "You did this for me?"

Jed slipped an arm around her waist and murmured, "We always hang out at your place. You're always cooking for me. When I stay over, you make me the perfect cup of coffee the next morning. Your sheets smell like sunshine and lemons. Your towels are always folded. You never run out of toothpaste. You have fresh fruit on the counter. For once, I wanted you to come to my place and feel as comfortable as I do at yours." He gazed around the room. "I figured that something out of a book would make you feel at home."

Taking Nora's hand, Jed led her to one of the leopard chairs. She sat down and took a sip of beer. The tension knotting the muscles of her back eased. In this colorful, crazy space, she could completely focus on Jed.

She could drink, eat grocery store fried chicken, comment on Jed's work stories, and laugh.

After dinner, Jed produced two cupcakes from the Gingerbread House — double chocolate for him and strawberries and cream for her — and challenged Nora to a game of Life. She hadn't played the board game since she was in junior high, but she remembered it well.

"I'm so going to beat you to Millionaire Mansion," she said, holding up her game piece, which was a blue car.

"Hmm. How could we make this a little more interesting?" Jed rubbed his chin in mock concentration. "I know. Every time one of us spins a six, we both have to take off a piece of clothing."

Nora grinned. "You're on. And if I get cold, I can strip the sheet off the giraffe."

"Poor giraffe." Jed put a hand over his heart as if Nora had wounded him. He then covered the giraffe's broom head with a paper towel. "I don't want him checking you out. Because I have to tell you, my beautiful book goddess, that I'm going to spin a shitload of sixes. Prepare to get naked."

Jed wasn't kidding. He spun a six every time. By the time Nora's game piece had reached the STOP sign indicating marriage, she was already without socks, shoes, or a top.

"It doesn't matter who gets here first," Jed said, pointing at the plastic mansion at the end of the road. "I win either way. Because I get to look at you. I get to see your bare skin. I get to watch your beautiful body move. And here's the best part. The whole time we're playing, I get to imagine what will happen after this game is over."

They didn't make it to the end. They never saw who would become a millionaire and who would have a less comfortable retirement. After Nora added another boy peg to her plastic car, Jed spun yet another six.

He pulled off his shirt with exaggerated slowness, and Nora held his eyes while slowly removing her bra. She dropped it on the floor and watched Jed stare at her body, his eyes dark with hunger. Their ocean blue had become the gray blue of a stormy sea, and when he reached for his game piece, he kept his gaze on Nora's face.

"I think you should make a different move," Nora said. When his brow furrowed in puzzlement, she grabbed his hand and pressed it over her left breast.

He let out a low moan as his fingers

danced over her skin, raising goose bumps. Nora held his stare, letting him see how much she wanted him. The more Jed touched her, the warmer the room got. Nora's heartbeat quickened. Her skin was flushed with heat. She felt like she might burn Jed with her touch. She arched her back, inviting him to come closer, to take control of her body with his hands and his mouth.

Jed read her unspoken invitation and let out a soft groan. The gameboard sat between them, but he swept it out of the way. On his hands and knees, he crossed the rug and grabbed Nora by the waist, roughly pulling her into his bare chest. She felt his muscles rippling under the skin, the drumming of his heart. She wanted to sink into him — for the two of them to melt together like two lit candles.

His mouth found hers. His hands were everywhere. Nora closed her eyes and stopped thinking. She was dying to lose herself in this moment.

There, in Jed's living room of painted palm trees and a rocking chair zebra, she surrendered to the fire that Jed's body ignited in her. She pulled him down on top of her, closed her eyes, and welcomed the burn.

■ ■ ■ ■

Nora didn't sleep over. Jed tried to convince her to stay, but she didn't want to spend the night on his air mattress. She'd done it before, and her middle-aged body had ached for hours afterward. Jed teased her for being soft, but he didn't mean it.

It was after midnight when Nora put her clothes on and gave Jed a long kiss good night. He wanted to drive her home, but she said that she'd be perfectly safe on her moped.

The next morning, she slept in. When she finally shuffled into the kitchen to make coffee, her eyes landed on Danny's bowl. It was Sunday, which normally meant a long hike followed by flea markets and garage sales, but she had something more important to do. She was going to see Marie Amoadawehi.

Nora found Marie's address online and plugged it into her phone. Then, she stood in her kitchen and wondered what Marie needed most right now. In the end, Nora decided that the kindness tote the Secret, Book, and Scone Society had prepared would have to be enough.

It was a liberating feeling to put the tote

bag in the moped's rear cargo basket and drive west. The morning sunshine burnished the hillsides a greenish gold and there was very little traffic. When a car came up behind Nora, she moved over to the shoulder to let it pass. She was in no hurry, and the closer she got to Danny and Marie's house, the more she doubted her decision to visit a woman she didn't know.

Danny hadn't been kidding when he said that he and his wife lived on the side of a mountain. Their small, cream-colored house was very isolated. Trees surrounded it on three sides and a deck jutted out over more trees in the back, making it seem like the branches were within reach.

Nora stood in the driveway for a moment, taking in the scenery. Unlike the woods near her house, this forest was preternaturally quiet. She heard no birdsong or squirrel chatter. There was only the occasional crack, as if the ancient trees were communicating with one another in a language Nora couldn't understand. Overhead, a solitary hawk wheeled in the empty sky.

When Nora glanced back at the house, Marie was standing in the doorway.

"I hope I'm not bothering you," Nora called out. She held up the tote bag. "I came to give you this."

Marie didn't respond. She didn't smile or invite Nora in. It was as if she didn't have the energy for words. She turned and went back inside, leaving the door open behind her.

Nora followed, feeling more than a little nervous.

What would she find inside the house? Would the spaces be permeated with an atmosphere of loss? Would she say the wrong thing to Marie? Would Marie refuse to speak to her at all?

Taking a deep breath, Nora mounted the steps and entered the house.

The first thing she noticed was the light. Because of the surrounding trees, she'd expected dim rooms with shadowy corners. But as she moved into the great room that served as kitchen, dining, and living room, she was struck by the brightness of the space. A bank of windows marched across the entire rear wall, and through them the mountains spread out like a green sea. Sunbeams cascaded into the room, gilding the furniture and area rugs.

"How beautiful," Nora whispered.

"Danny's idea of heaven," Marie rasped. Nora wondered how long it had been since Marie had spoken out loud. "When we bought this place, it was a run-down vacation cabin. Barely more than a shack. They're everywhere here. You can buy one for a song. But it takes more than money or hard work to turn a house into a home. Only love can do that."

Nora put the bag on the kitchen counter and hesitated. She didn't feel like she could join Marie on the sofa without being asked.

"I wish there was a book that taught people what to say when another person's world has been turned upside-down," she said. "All I can think of is that I'm sorry that your husband was taken from you. I'm sorry he's gone."

Marie had been staring out the window. Now, she looked at Nora. "I wasn't ready. I'd never really be ready. But if we were old, I would have expected it. I don't know how to live without him. I don't know who I am. It feels like I'm the one who died. I can't move on. I just float from room to room. I'm the ghost."

"Do you have anyone? Family? Friends? People who won't tiptoe around you. Who will urge you to talk? To eat. To make you go outside? All the stuff you don't want to do. All the stuff that might take you away from pain for a few minutes."

Marie stared numbly at her. "What do you know about pain?"

179

Nora moved to the sofa and pulled up her shirtsleeve. The jellyfish burn on her arm, with its bell-shaped head and puffy tentacles, writhed when she balled her fist. "I lost a husband too. He didn't die. He left me. But part of me died when it happened. I didn't handle it well. I caused a fire. I'm responsible for these scars."

Tears rolled down Marie's gaunt cheeks. They'd sprung suddenly, as if Marie could call up a rainstorm of tears in an instant. "I feel like burning everything. This house. All our stuff. I wish I could. That way, I could disappear too."

Nora sat in a chair across from Marie. "Remember the bowl I bought from Danny? It was meant as a gift, but I couldn't part with it. Once it was in my house, I wanted it to stay there. It's the first thing I see when I walk into the kitchen. Right now, it's full of apples. Granny Smith. The green looks so bright against Danny's brown glaze."

Marie wiped her face with the heel of her hands. "Danny started making utilitarian ware two years ago. Before that, all his pieces were an homage to the original Cherokee pots. But I convinced him to make something for everyday use. I said, what do you think your ancestors did with their pots? They baked with them and

180

stored things in them. Pottery is meant to be handled."

Seeing Marie become animated was encouraging. She clearly was enjoying talking about her husband's craft.

"There's a bird on the bottom of my bowl," Nora said. "Does it mean something?"

"The red bird." Marie turned back to the windows. "Danny's favorite. We have a bunch of feeders filled with a songbird seed blend to attract cardinals. Danny said the birds were in his blood."

Though Nora didn't understand, she kept quiet.

Marie wasn't in the room with Nora anymore. She was far away, submerged in the past. For her, neither the ocean of pine trees nor the wide, clear sky existed. Only her memories.

"The birds are in his blood on his mama's side," she said after a long silence. "Her real name was Cheryl, but everyone called her Red Bird. Her mother was called Red Bird too. Danny said that generations of women in his family have had this nickname." She put a hand over her belly. "He was so excited about passing it on to his daughter. He wanted her to be as strong and beautiful and kind as the women who'd raised him."

Nora couldn't tear her eyes away from Marie's hand. Her belly showed no signs of roundness. In fact, she was alarmingly thin. But her protective gesture was born of instinct.

Marie was pregnant.

Nora moved to the sofa and sat next to Marie. She took the other woman's hand in hers. The slender fingers were cold. Nora gently rubbed them until Marie's skin was warm again.

"You can still call your daughter Red Bird. She'll be everything Danny dreamed she could be. I don't have kids, so I don't know anything about bringing one into the world, but I know this: Expectant mothers need food. Fresh, healthy food." When Marie began to protest, Nora gently shushed her. "I know you're not hungry, but you need to eat. I'm going to rustle up something for you."

Nora expected Marie's refrigerator to be stuffed with Tupperware and casserole dishes. In times of sickness and loss, people made food. Because it was a tangible way to help, people made baked ziti, chicken enchiladas, and stew. They made cake, Jell-O parfaits, and pies. They stuffed the pantry with chips, bread, and tins of cookies. The grieving rarely ate these offerings, but people felt compelled to bring them all the same.

Marie's refrigerator was empty of such offerings. Hadn't anyone stopped by to give her food? Hadn't Danny's family and friends gathered in his kitchen and laid out a spread? Where were all the leftovers?

"I threw everything away," Marie said as if Nora had spoken aloud. "I couldn't stand the sight of it. There was enough food to feed a family. But there's no family. Just me."

Nora spotted a container of cream cheese and checked the expiration date. She then unwrapped Hester's cinnamon raisin bread and opened drawers until she found a serrated knife. She cut two thick slices and popped them in the toaster. After the bread was toasted, Nora spread them with a generous layer of cream cheese and cut each piece into bite-sized squares.

She put the plate on Marie's lap and set a glass of water down on the coffee table.

"Start with this," Nora said.

"My mom used to make me raisin toast when I had a bad day. She'd cut it triangles." Marie's eyes filled with tears again. "But I like the squares too."

She began to eat, and Nora let out a small sigh of relief. When the toast and water were

183

gone, Nora asked if she could make coffee or fix Marie more food.

"I'd offer to take you to the grocery store, but I don't think we'd make it down the mountain on my moped. It's not meant for two people, let alone two people and a very small Red Bird." Nora pointed at Marie's belly and winked.

This earned her a small smile, and she decided that Marie was strong enough to hear her other reason for showing up on her doorstep. "I was curious about the bird on my bowl, so I searched for Cherokee bird tales. I found an illustration that reminded me of a painting I'd seen at Cherokee Rock. The bird on the rock is just like the one on Danny's bowl. I thought this was a strange coincidence considering that's where Danny parked his truck. Do you know anything about the bird at Cherokee Rock?"

Marie stared at her with a mixture of suspicion and surprise, and Nora had the feeling she'd made a mistake by mentioning Danny's truck. But there was no backing down, so she pulled up the photo on her phone and showed it to Marie.

"Do you see the bird? Right above those black initials?"

Judging by Marie's sharp intake of breath, she saw it.

"I don't understand," she murmured. "I've been to Cherokee Rock dozens of times. This wasn't there before."

"I'm sure the sheriff asked why Danny might have parked at the rock and walked into town —"

"He asked, but I couldn't answer," Marie interrupted. "Cherokee Rock wasn't special to us. Sometimes, we'd eat there on the way home from the flea market. It was a pretty spot and Danny liked that his ancestors painted the rock. But I have no idea what Danny was doing there. Or why he loaded pottery in his truck when we'd decided not to go to the flea market."

There was a long moment of silence.

"It must have been dark out when he left," she continued wearily. "I didn't even hear him. Ever since" — she paused to fold her arms over her waist — "I'm only ten weeks, but I'm really tired. I don't remember ever being this tired. Anyway, I didn't hear him leave."

Fearing that Marie might be pulled under by her grief, Nora squeezed her hand to keep her focused. "This isn't your fault. I just wondered if someone had painted the red bird as a sign for your husband. Like they were marking a meeting place."

Too late, Nora realized she should have

chosen her words with more care.

"A meeting? With who? A woman?" Marie fumed. "Are you saying that Danny was messing around?"

It was possible, of course, but Nora didn't think so.

"No," she said. "I saw the two of you at the flea market. Your husband looked at you with stars in his eyes. You were the only woman in his universe."

Seeing that Marie was pacified by this answer, Nora pressed on.

"What if someone had a bone to pick with him? Or was calling in a debt? I have no idea. I just thought you should see this bird. It feels important, but I don't know why."

Marie was silent for a very long time. Finally, she whispered, "I feel it too. That bird was a messenger. Not from the spirit world. It's a man-made message. I don't know what it meant to Danny. I wish I knew. I didn't think he kept secrets from me, but I guess I was wrong. Why else would he sneak out like that? Why wouldn't he stay home like we planned?"

"Maybe he was keeping secrets to protect you. You and his baby."

Marie released a sigh that permeated the room with sorrow and the kind of bone-deep weariness that only the sleep-deprived

186

understand. "He can't protect us now."

Nora stood up. "I didn't mean to upset you. I should go."

"Have you told the sheriff about the bird?" Marie asked.

Nora shook her head. "I thought I should tell you first."

"Would you tell him? I need to lie down now."

"I'll drive straight to the station from here." Nora held up a finger. "On one condition."

Marie looked at her with lifeless eyes. "Yes?"

"After you rest, I want you to take a shower and go to the grocery store. My friends and I are going to check in on you. We're going to be regular pains in the asses. We're going to make you eat. We're going to clean your house. We're going to talk to you."

"Okay."

The word was a puff of air. It was all Marie could manage. She was being engulfed by her pain. Soon, she'd give herself over to it.

Nora produced a business card. "I'm just a phone call away. I'll leave this in the kitchen. Next to the raisin bread."

When Marie didn't respond, Nora showed

herself out.

In the driveway, she glanced around, half expecting to see a cardinal perched on a nearby branch. But the woods were still eerily quiet.

The hawk was gone, leaving the sky empty. It was as if Marie was the only living creature for miles. A lone heartbeat surrounded by trees and grief.

Two heartbeats, Nora thought, and made a silent promise to Danny that she would not abandon his wife.

Even if he had.

CHAPTER 9

Sharing food with another human being is an intimate act that should not be indulged in lightly.

— M. F. K. Fisher

Sheriff McCabe was thrilled to see Nora.

"Have you had lunch yet?" he asked as soon as she stepped into his office.

Nora glanced at the wall clock. It was eleven thirty. "I usually eat around one."

McCabe scooped up a set of keys. "I didn't have breakfast, so I'm ready now. Do your local lawman a solid and come to Pearl's with me."

Nora couldn't refuse a pimento grilled cheese sandwich. "Sure, but no hush puppies for me this time. The owners of the Inn of Mist and Roses are having me over for dinner and I have a feeling that they're going to have a lot of food."

McCabe was interested in the inn's renovations. He asked questions about the building and the owners as he drove through downtown Miracle Springs.

Pearl's was three stops down the tracks, as the locals liked to say, and it was well worth the trip. Nora and the sheriff ate there at least once a month. The food was amazing, and the proprietors were delightful.

The hostess greeted them with a big smile that quickly morphed into a frown. "Pearl and Sam will be bummed that they missed you. They're still at church. The rest of us were at the early service, so you might catch us yawning."

The woman's necklace caught Nora's attention. The pendant nestled in the V of her throat held two charms. A small silver cross and a white dove.

Another bird, Nora thought.

As the hostess showed them to a table, Nora thought of how both cardinals and doves were spiritual symbols. One was a messenger from the spirit world while the other represented the Holy Spirit.

"You haven't opened your menu," the sheriff said after they were seated. "Do you know what you're having?"

"Pimento grilled cheese and a side salad."

McCabe looked disappointed. "No sweet potato chips?"

190

With a laugh, Nora told him to order a basket.

"I'd better not. I'd eat the whole thing and, at my age, it's hard to keep the weight from piling on. If you'd share one with me . . ."

Nora grinned and shook her head. "It's not like I can keep the weight off any easier than you. I didn't hike this morning and I'm eating out twice today."

"It doesn't feel like overindulging if someone else overindulges with you," McCabe said.

"I think that's called enabling."

They were both laughing when their waiter appeared. He took their orders and moved off to check on a couple seated in the bar. When he was out of earshot, the sheriff tented his fingers and said, "I'm guessing that you didn't drop by my office because you wanted a lunch partner."

"I want to talk about Danny." Nora was grateful that she never had to mince words with McCabe. He appreciated directness as much as she did. "I stumbled across something. I felt Marie should hear about it first, so I went to see her this morning. I honestly don't know if it's important, but it feels important. Let me explain."

McCabe listened without interrupting

191

while Nora described the bird symbol on Danny's pottery. She then showed him the photo from Cherokee Rock. "It's the same bird."

"A cardinal," McCabe said.

"The Cherokee call it Red Bird." Nora briefly described the bird's significance in Native American culture. "According to Cherokee lore, this bird is a messenger from the spirit world. If someone painted a red bird on the rock as a message for Danny, it did the trick. He met this person at the rock, and, in my opinion, the meeting was fatal for Danny. I don't have a lick of proof to back up that statement either."

The server arrived with their meals, topped off their water glasses, and returned to the kitchen. During this time, Sheriff McCabe was lost in thought. Even though he'd been anticipating his soul food meal, he made no move to dig into his smothered pork chop or black-eyed peas.

"We've been investigating all angles, including foul play," he told Nora. "There were no clues indicating any kind of altercation at Cherokee Rock. Sadly, Danny's body was head-to-toe lacerations and bruises, so there's no way to tell if he was the victim of violence before he drowned." He held up a warning finger. "That is not to be repeated, especially to his wife."

"I wouldn't cause her more pain than she's already in by filling her head with that image," Nora said, a little stung. "Give me some credit."

McCabe held up his hands. "Sorry, I was out of line. I'm frustrated by this case and I'm taking it out on everyone. Without evidence, I have no choice but to confirm the accidental death ruling. But I don't like where his body was found compared to where he parked his truck. I don't like the way he left his home so early on the day of his death. Nothing is open at that time. Where was he going? What was he doing? His behavior makes no sense." He clasped his hands. "Life is messy. I accept that. But when it comes to sudden death, I need a clear picture. Danny's picture is a goddamn jumbled kaleidoscope."

"I'm sure you interviewed everyone he knew. No one had an idea why he went to Cherokee Rock?"

The sheriff took a bite of his entrée. As he chewed, he seemed to be wrestling with himself. After a drink of water, he said, "Someone inferred that he was meeting a woman."

Nora remembered Marie's reaction to the idea that Danny had snuck out before dawn for a romantic assignation. She considered her own reaction to this suggestion. She'd rejected the idea as firmly as Marie had. Which made no sense. Nora had seen Danny and Marie together exactly once. What did she really know about them as a couple? Why did she want them to be what they appeared to be?

"Your face just clouded over," McCabe said. "What are you thinking?"

"I should know better than to believe what I see. That kind of blindness can be destructive. That kind of blindness is why I ended up in Miracle Springs. I set fire to my old life. I've never looked back, but I guess I can still be naïve. I can still be fooled into believing what I wish was true."

The sheriff put his fork down. "It's not a bad thing to believe the best in people. Sure, they might disappoint you. Then again, they might not."

Nora appreciated that he didn't focus on her past. Instead, he surprised her by saying, "I've been blind too. I'm in the business of dealing with folks who make bad choices, so you'd think I'd know when someone was lying to me. When it mattered most, I didn't know. I didn't see it. That's why Sheila has the house and the dog and I'm here."

Nora caught the flicker of sadness in the sheriff's eyes. "I'm sorry."

He shrugged. "It's been almost four years now. It sounds strange, but I'm a better man for going through that ordeal. The good, the bad, and the ugly helped me learn things. I learned who my real friends are. I learned that I was pretty handy in the kitchen. I learned that I like cats more than dogs. Go figure."

Nora smiled. "Are you a crazy cat lady now?"

"It wasn't in the master plan, but some jackass pitched a bag of kittens in the river and a deputy I used to work with rescued them. He brought them into the station in a box. At the end of my shift, I found myself driving home with Magnum and Higgins."

This made Nora laugh. "Oh man, I loved that show. I don't think there's a woman alive — in my age group, anyway — who didn't have a crush on Tom Selleck."

They fell into an easy conversation about 1980s TV shows. Before long, their food was finished, and the server delivered the check.

Nora tried to pay for her half, but the sheriff refused. He claimed that he'd forced her to accompany him and was therefore duty-bound to pick up the check.

As he took bills out of his wallet, Nora asked, "Before we go, would you tell me who said that Danny might be meeting a woman?"

"Why? Do you want to see if you know the person?"

"Yeah, something like that."

McCabe nodded. "To be honest, I'd like to hear your opinion. I'm sure you know this woman, considering you visit the flea market all the time. Her name's Beatrice."

"Bea's a good egg," Nora said without hesitation. "She's not the type of person to spread malicious gossip. She wouldn't want to hurt anyone either, so I can see her struggling with the decision to tell you about Danny and this mystery woman."

The waiter returned to collect the check and the money. McCabe told him to keep the change. He then focused his intelligent gaze on Nora. "She was pretty reluctant. She was only willing to repeat what Danny said to her. She didn't embellish a word. I wish every witness was like that."

"What did Danny say?"

"Bea bumped into him outside the restrooms. He looked upset, so she asked if everything was okay. He told her that he'd recently met someone and that he couldn't tell if her appearance in his life was a gift or

196

a curse, but he was about to find out. This was the day before he died."

Nora sat with the words for a moment. Eventually, she said, "If this woman was his lover, I don't think he'd talk about her so openly. He obviously didn't want Marie to know about her. But why? If she wasn't his lover, then what was she to him?"

"Someone he couldn't get a read on. A gift or a curse makes me think that she made Danny an offer."

"Beware of Greeks bringing gifts," Nora murmured.

McCabe was puzzled. "Do you have something against Greeks?"

"No. The Greeks bearing gifts refers to the men who tricked Troy into opening its gates to allow entry to their giant horse. I'm sure you know the rest of the story."

"Bloodshed, pillaging, rape."

Nora felt a stirring in her bones. There was something important about this mysterious woman. But without knowing her identity, how could they hope to find her?

"Who was Danny's Greek?" she asked, speaking more to herself than to McCabe. "It sounds like this woman offered him a horse, but he ended up floating in the river. The same river that runs past Cherokee Rock."

McCabe stared off into the middle distance. "Gifts. Red birds. A strange woman." He shook his head. "If not his attention, then what did she want from Danny Amoadawehi? Pottery?"

"Maybe. According to Marie, Danny used to make traditional art pieces. Collector's items. Something you'd put on a shelf and never use. Some of his older pieces could be worth decent money. I don't know the market, so I have no idea what kind of money we're talking about, but it's worth looking into."

McCabe took out a small notebook with a golf pencil tucked into its spiral and jotted down *pottery value* and *red bird.*

"It was good of you to visit Marie," he said, closing his notebook. "She doesn't have people to look after her. Her story is not mine to tell, so all I'll say is that her family didn't want her to marry Danny. They didn't like the idea of their Southern belle tying the knot with a redskin. That's what they called Danny."

"Jesus." Nora was mortified. "What about his family?"

"They never warmed to Marie. They stop by out of politeness, but that's it. She has a few friends. Folks have brought her food. But in my experience, she'll get fewer visitors as time goes by. Unfortunately, death changes a person's social circle. It usually makes it smaller."

"I'm taking the women in my book club to see her," Nora said. "They don't know it yet, but they're going."

McCabe laughed. He then donned his hat and was instantly transformed from Nora's lunch companion into Sheriff Grant Mc-Cabe. "I'll drive over to her place later this afternoon. Looks like she and I have more to talk about."

Nora didn't want to show up at the Inn of Mist and Roses empty-handed. After surveying the books in her Home & Design section, she ambled over to the cookbooks and selected a like-new copy of *Best Recipes from American Country Inns and Bed & Breakfasts.* Flipping through the book, she saw several delectable dishes including London Broil with Mustard Caper Sauce, Grilled Shrimp with Basil and Prosciutto, Baked Apple French Toast, and Brownie Chocolate Chip Cheesecake.

As she wrapped the book in brown tissue paper and tied it with a satin ribbon the color of a ripe pomegranate, she thought of Rose Lattimer's diary and the dried flower that had fallen from its pages. She hoped

Lou would share the diary's highlights with her.

At the inn, Nora ran into Hester taking a bakery box out of the trunk of her car.

"Patty said that you'd be coming," Hester said. "Can I tell you how relieved I was to hear that? I'm awful at dinner parties. I always say stupid things when I'm nervous."

"Really? How did your dinner with Jasper's parents go?"

Color flooded Hester's neck and cheeks. "I don't want to talk about it."

"Okay. But if you're upset —"

"Can we go in? I'm dying to meet Sheldon."

Because Hester's hands were full, Nora rang the bell. While they waited for someone to open the door, Nora asked, "How did you meet Lou and Patty?"

"I haven't met Lou yet. Patty came into the bakery one day to try my cheese biscuits. The day after that, she brought me lunch and we talked food and recipes in between customers. Man, I wish she didn't already have a job because that woman can really cook! Her guests are going to be so spoiled."

"I guess we're about to find out for ourselves," Nora said.

Patty opened the door wearing a purple apron and a smile. "Now everyone's here!

Good. Come in, come in. We're all in the dining room, but Lou is mixing drinks in the kitchen. What's your poison?"

"I'll have whatever you're having," Hester said, handing Patty the bakery box. "I'm sure you made an incredible dessert, but I figured you could always use another one."

"There's no such thing as too much dessert. Thank you." Patty gave Hester a one-armed hug. "What about you, Nora? What'll you have to drink?"

Nora asked for club soda if they had it.

"Club soda it is. Go say hello to the others. I'll be right back," Patty said, and bustled down the hall.

Nora and Hester entered the dining room. The mustard-colored walls were now a bright white. Nora assumed that they'd been primed in expectation of their new sage-green color.

Sheldon, who'd been talking with Georgia and Bo, saw Nora and Hester enter. He excused himself from his conversation and made a beeline for Hester.

"You must be the beguiling baker," he said. "I've heard so much about you."

Hester held out her hand and Sheldon squeezed it between both of his.

"What has Nora been telling you?" she asked.

Sheldon touched one of Hester's corkscrew curls. "That your food is a lovely as you are. And if I succumb to your culinary charms, my arteries will be totally blocked by Christmas."

Hester laughed.

Sheldon turned to Nora. "You got here just in time. I cannot small-talk with Buffy and Biff for another second. I've heard enough about Biff's law firm and Buffy's art gallery. They're friendly enough, but I don't do well with Barbie and Ken types. I'm worried that I'll do something rude like yawn in their faces."

"I'm glad to see that you're feeling frisky," said Nora. "I was hoping you could put your mind to work on behalf of a friend of ours. Her name's Estella and she owns a salon. The business is in trouble. Do you think you could take a look at it?"

Sheldon frowned. "What I know about running a salon could fit in a fairy thimble."

"That doesn't matter. You have an innate ability to size up a business in about thirty seconds and figure out how to improve it."

"Flattery will get you everywhere."

"If you'll stop by tomorrow, I'll bake you a special surprise goodie," Hester said, smiling prettily.

Sheldon's eyes gleamed. "I love surprises.

It's a deal."

Leaving Hester and Sheldon to become better acquainted, Nora headed to the kitchen to say hello to Lou.

She found Lou filling a wineglass with chardonnay. Patty stood by the sink, tossing a salad with a pair of wooden forks.

After greeting Lou, Nora added, "I know you're busy, but I brought Rose's photograph. I thought you might want to look at it without an audience."

Lou put down the bottle of wine. "I would, thanks."

"This is for both of you," Nora said, placing the gift-wrapped book on the table and fishing the tintype out of her purse.

While Patty dried her hands on a dish towel, Lou peeled the layers of tissue paper away from Rose's portrait.

"Oh!" she softly exclaimed. "She's beautiful. Look at that skin." She showed the tintype to Patty. "Were we ever that young?"

"If we were, I don't remember looking like this. That girl's face is smooth as glass." Patty cocked her head. "But she has an older-than-her-years vibe about her."

"I thought that too," said Nora. "She looks smart. And interesting. Like someone you'd want to sit next to at a dinner party."

Lou looked up at Nora. "Thank you for

bringing this. And I'm glad you found me because I wanted to show *you* something. I just hope it doesn't put you off your dinner."

"Nothing does that," Nora joked, and followed Lou into the library.

The crystal casket holding the diary was sitting in the middle of an empty shelf.

"Did you finish reading it?" Nora asked, although she already knew the answer. "The diary?"

"Are you kidding? I couldn't do anything else. Rose Lattimer was an incredible woman. I'll tell you more about her at dinner, but I wanted you to see what happened to the end."

To the end. Not at the end, Nora thought, feeling uneasy. Had the book been damaged?

Lou took the diary out of the box and opened to a section marked by a piece of string. Nora couldn't help herself. She let out an involuntary gasp when she saw that a chunk of pages had been ripped out of the book. The jagged edges of paper protruded from the gutter like spikes on a stegosaurus.

"What a shame," Nora said. She quietly stared at the ruined pages and then pointed at a blob of dried candle wax on the inside of the back cover. "Are there candle wax stains on any of the pages?"

Lou showed Nora a page with several round, oily marks. "Several pages have these."

Nora nodded. "Rose must have written her entries at the end of the day. By candlelight. It's not uncommon to find wax stains on old books. But those torn pages? That's deliberate. And they were torn with haste, violence, or both. The hinge might have been damaged by the action. Did her entry on the previous page hint at why she destroyed the end of her diary?"

"I think she was pregnant," said Lou in a near whisper. "She never says so outright, but she talks about being tired and how her body felt strange. At first, I thought she was worn out from nursing soldiers — this house served as a makeshift hospital during the Civil War — but when she mentioned that certain smells were making her nauseated, I decided that it was more than fatigue."

Lou caressed the cover before returning the diary to the box. "I'll tell you more about Rose while we eat."

Though disappointed that she hadn't been invited to read Rose's diary firsthand, Nora told Lou that she'd finished evaluating the books in the steamer trunks. Lou wasn't concerned about the damage done by Rose's dried flower petals. All she cared about was the small trunk containing what were probably Rose's personal possessions.

"You seem really connected to her," Nora said as they headed back to the dining room. "Is it just because she owned this house or is there another reason?"

"Rose Lattimer was a remarkable woman. She would have done anything for this house and the people in it. I feel the same way." A curtain fell over Lou's features, as if she'd revealed too much. Nora realized that she'd seen the same expression on Lou's face the night she'd first opened Rose's diary.

What does she know about Rose that she wants to keep hidden? Nora silently wondered.

Lou led her out of the room. "Thanks for going through those trunks," she said. The brightness in her voice sounded forced. "Let me know what we owe you for your time."

Nora wanted to wash her hands before dinner. Since the downstairs bathroom was occupied and Lou was filling a water pitcher in the kitchen, Patty told Nora to use the bathroom in her room.

"Until Lou and I move into the carriage

house, we're inhabiting guest rooms. Mine is at the top of the stairs, first door on the right."

My room. Not ours.

Were Lou and Patty a couple or not?

Nora didn't want to invade Patty's space more than she had to, so she walked straight into the bathroom and washed her hands. On her way back through the bedroom, she noticed a pottery vase on the nightstand. It had been incised with geometric swirls, much like the ones painted on Cherokee Rock.

Nora couldn't stop herself from crossing the room and taking the vase in her hands. She knew, even before she turned it over, that she'd find Danny's initials and his Red Bird symbol on the bottom. And she was right.

Unlike the bowl in Nora's house, however, a number was etched inside the bird's body.

"Fifty-four," Nora mumbled. "What does that mean?"

The glaze on the vase was very dark. Instead of the molasses-brown glaze Danny had used on the utilitarian ware for sale at the flea market, this glaze was black. It was the black of a raven's wing. Or a shark eye. It had a slight sheen, as if life were stirring deep inside the glaze where it met the clay.

Nora had never seen a piece like this one at the flea market. The body of the vase was round, like a full belly, and the designs scratched into the clay reminded Nora of water lines on a map.

Putting the vase exactly where she'd found it, Nora left Patty's room and went in search of Lou's. She was being unforgivingly rude. After all, owning a piece of Danny's pottery was hardly nefarious behavior. Danny's pottery probably adorned lots of nightstands, tables, kitchen counters, and bookshelves in Miracle Springs. It made sense that two women who clearly appreciated fine craftsmanship would have purchased his work. Still, Nora wanted to know if Lou and Patty had one piece. Or more.

Nora found more blackware in Lou's room, which was obviously Lou's based on the collection of paint chips, books on North Carolina architecture, and a spreadsheet showing the estimated cost of the renovations.

Moving quickly, Nora walked over to a wide-mouthed vase and turned it over. The number forty-one was etched inside the red bird. The designs on the vase were more elaborate than Patty's. The glaze was as dark and glossy as onyx.

Replacing the vase, Nora approached two

more pieces sitting on a candlestand in the corner of the room. One was a footed bowl and the other looked like some sort of smoking pot or pipe. The birds were marked with the numbers thirty-seven and twenty-two.

Four pieces. Lou and Patty are clearly fans of Danny's work, Nora thought.

Collecting the work of a local artist wasn't at all unusual, and Nora decided to ask about the vase in Patty's room over dinner. She was curious to hear about the interaction between Danny and her hostesses. How long ago had they bought the pieces from him? Had they heard of him before moving to Miracle Springs or met him at the flea market?

I don't remember seeing pieces like theirs at the flea market, Nora thought.

On the stairs, she encountered a young man with walnut-colored skin and shoulder-length dreadlocks. Small shells were tied to some of the locks and they made soft clicking sounds when he moved. He paused on his step and glanced up at her.

"Hey," he said. "I'm Micah."

Nora introduced herself. Micah raised his hand in a wave and Nora noticed a small compass tattoo on his wrist.

"Does it point to someplace special?" she

asked, gesturing at the tattoo.

He touched it with his fingertip. "Nah. I want to explore in every direction. I don't care where I go. I just want to keep moving."

"I'm guessing that your dream job doesn't involve a desk or a cubicle."

"Does anyone's?" After flashing her a shy grin, Micah said that he was going to his room to read and resumed his ascent.

Nora smiled and continued down the stairs.

In the dining room, several tables had been pushed together to form one long table. A flower arrangement in pastel hues sat on a lacy cloth. The sideboard had been laid with an array of sumptuous-looking dishes.

"Pile your plates nice and high, folks," Lou told her guests. "Patty always makes enough to feed an army."

Nora deliberately delayed in order to be the last guest in line. She dropped a scoop of potato salad on her plate when Lou got in line behind her.

Nora passed her the serving spoon. In a low voice, she casually asked, "Have you and Patty met Danny Amo-adawehi? The Cherokee potter?"

Lou scrunched her lips in concentration.

"The name isn't familiar, and that isn't an easy one to forget. Why do you ask?"

Nora shot a glance at Lou. Didn't she read the paper? Hadn't she heard the townsfolk talking about his death? Could she truly be oblivious that the man who'd died during the rainstorm had made the blackware pieces in her bedroom?

Lou didn't wait for Nora to reply. Instead, she made a point of turning away to ask Patty if all their guests had enough to drink.

She's lying, Nora thought.

She couldn't focus on the food in front of her. She put things on her plate without paying attention to what she was doing.

Why did Lou lie?

Suddenly, Nora heard her cell phone ring. Though she'd left her purse in the kitchen, she knew it was hers. Her ringtone was an instrumental song from *The Lord of the Rings.*

"Sorry, I forgot to mute that," she told the room at large. She left her plate on the sideboard and hurried out of the room.

"Manners, Galadriel!" Sheldon called after her.

By the time Nora got to her kitchen, her phone had stopped ringing. Her screen showed a string of texts, all from June. The missed call had been from her too. Without

211

reading the texts, Nora dialed her friend's number.

"Nora!" June's voice was breathy, panicked. "I need help!"

Nora's blood froze. She'd never heard June sound so scared. No, not scared. Terrified.

"Are you at home?"

"Yes. Hurry."

"I'll be there in five minutes."

Nora sprinted down the hall and out the front door. Without bothering to strap on her helmet, she fired up the moped, backed out of her spot, and drove away.

As she sped off, she saw a woman's figure darken the inn's doorway.

It was Lou.

Nora could feel the other woman's eyes on her, but it didn't matter. Her thoughts were entirely trained on June.

She willed her moped to go faster, faster.

Four minutes later, she pulled into June's driveway and gasped in horror.

Someone had painted a word across the front of June's house.

Someone had committed a hate crime.

CHAPTER 10

Hate is like a swordfish,
working through the water invisibly
and then you see it coming
with blood along its blade.
— Pablo Neruda

Tearing her gaze from the painted letters, Nora looked around for June.

She knocked on her friend's front door. She waited. Knocked again. No one answered. The house was dark and still.

Dread crept up Nora's spine, raising gooseflesh on her arms and the back of her neck.

"June!" she called, turning this way and that on her friend's front porch.

There was no reply.

Nora walked around the entire house. Her footfalls sounded too loud in the silence. She saw shadows move on the edge of the yard. They were quick and low to the ground.

Cats, Nora thought, releasing a held breath.

Cats. But no June.

Nora returned to the driveway where she finally spotted her friend.

June was sitting in her car, her hands gripping the steering wheel. Her shoulders shook, and Nora could hear her friend's powerful sobs before she even opened the passenger door.

"I'm here," she said, sliding her arm around June and pulling her close. "It's okay. I'm here."

June buried her face in Nora's shoulder and cried. She didn't speak. She just poured out her feelings in guttural sobs and hitches of breath.

Nora made soothing noises while rubbing gentle circles on her friend's back.

After a time, June's body shook less. Her cries weakened and dissolved into sniffles.

When she sat upright and began to dig around in the door pocket, Nora broke the silence.

"Can you tell me what happened?" she softly asked.

June kept rummaging. "I know I have napkins in here. I know I do. I always keep napkins in here."

Nora waited while June found what she was looking for. After her friend had wiped her face and blown her nose, Nora repeated her question.

"Lord, I haven't cried like that in years," June said. "But look what I came home to." She gestured at the house with a limp flick of her wrist. "I can't tell you what happened. I don't know why. I don't know who. I just came home, and there it was."

"Okay. Let's try to figure things out. First of all, when do you think this happened?"

June's eyes strayed to her house. "When I was at work, I guess. It wasn't there this morning, which means somebody did this in broad daylight."

The angry red letters glared at them. Each one was painted on a slant, and every brushstroke looked aggressive. Combative. Thin streams of extra paint had dribbled down the siding. The overall effect made Nora think of blood. Of violence.

"No one's called me that godforsaken word since I was in elementary school," June said. "I remember the last time like it was yesterday. It was a boy on my bus. We were both from the same neighborhood. It was a rundown, rough neighborhood. His family was white, but my family owned a

215

car. It was a junker, but it ran. That wore on this kid — that we had wheels and he didn't. One day, as we were getting off the bus, he pushed me into a seat and whispered, 'What does a nigger need a car for anyway?' "

Nora heard the pain in June's voice. The memory might be old, but it had left its mark. The words had scarred. Everyone had old wounds that never stopped hurting. For June, that wound had been ripped open, exposing her to fresh pain.

"The day on the bus, I didn't say a thing to that boy," June went on. "I wish I'd given him what for. I wasn't scared. I was just too shocked to move. He cut me into a million pieces in a few seconds." She gestured at the red letters again. "When I drove into my driveway and saw this on my house, I was that girl again. I was on that bus, shocked into helplessness."

Nora was furious on June's behalf, but June didn't need her anger. She needed a friend.

"What can I do to help?" Nora asked. "Have you called 911? Do you want me to?"

June shook her head. "What's the point? What can they do? Take pictures of my house? Ask the neighbors if they saw anything?"

"They can find out who did this. You know the sheriff. He'll take this seriously. This is a hate crime."

"*You* know the sheriff," June snapped. "He's *your* friend. *I* don't have lunch with him. I've never even been to that soul food place you two are so crazy about. I'm just another citizen with a problem he needs to fix."

Nora didn't shrink away from June's anger. She'd rather see June irate than defeated. Anger meant that she'd be willing to fight for justice. However, it wasn't up to Nora to make decisions for her friend. Not in this case. She couldn't begin to understand how the racial slur made her friend feel. She couldn't know the lacerating shock of seeing it painted across the front of her house in bold letters. And because she couldn't know, she sat in silence and waited for June to decide what to do.

"I keep wondering who I pissed off," June said after a few minutes. "Someone from work? A guest I interacted with at the pools? A salesperson at a store? A teller at the bank? I can't come up with anything. If I did something to offend someone this much, I didn't realize it."

Nora said, "No one did this because of an unintentional slight. This is . . . rage."

217

An image of a man pressing down so hard on the button of the spray paint can that it left a round indentation on his index finger appeared in Nora's mind. Before she could think about why she'd automatically pictured a male, June let out a heavy sigh.

"Make the call," she said. After a heartbeat, she added, "Please."

Nora called Sheriff McCabe's cell phone.

After listening to her summarize what had happened, he told both women to stay put.

"I'm getting in the car now. Be there in ten minutes."

He got there in eight, and he wasn't alone. A second car, driven by Deputy Fuentes, pulled in behind the car carrying Sheriff McCabe and Deputy Andrews.

The three men directed flashlight beams around the yard before regrouping on June's front path. They stood, hands on hips, and stared at the word painted on her home.

"Be right back," Nora told June, and got out of the car.

Andrews swiveled toward the sound of the car door closing and marched across the lawn to meet Nora. "Where's Ms. Dixon? Is she okay?"

Nora saw the genuine concern on his face and wished June could see it too. "She's in the car. And no, she's not okay."

"Physically, I mean. Is she hurt?"

"No. She's rattled. Who wouldn't be?" Nora fought to keep the anger out of her voice as McCabe and Fuentes joined them. "She has no idea who did this. She hasn't had any altercations — not so much as a harsh word with a coworker, a neighbor, or a stranger. She just came home to *that*."

They all glanced at the word.

"I saw this kind of shit on a daily basis where I used to live, but this is the first time I've seen it here," Fuentes said. His brown eyes were dark with anger.

McCabe put a hand on his deputy's shoulder. "We need to make sure this is the first and last case."

While the sheriff and Andrews spoke to June, who refused to leave her car, Fuentes took photos of her house.

The camera flash illuminated the bushes lining June's front porch and startled a handful of cats from their hiding places. They dashed across the yard, heading for the area of clumped bushes and trees separating June's property from her neighbor's.

From somewhere behind the house, a cat started meowing. The sound was shrill and plaintive, like the cry of a hungry baby. Nora wished it would stop, but the cat's wail quickly infected the other cats, and before

219

long, a chorus of dissonant yowls filled the night.

"This is some spooky shit," Fuentes muttered. His camera flash increased in intensity, as if he wanted to finish his task in a hurry.

Having no role to play, Nora stood in the driveway and watched the goings-on. She could feel the force of the red letters. They seemed to throb on the wall behind her, but she refused to turn and look at them.

Eventually, she walked to her moped, took out her phone, and called Hester.

"What the hell, Nora?" Hester's whisper was filled with censure. "Why did you bolt out of here like that? Lou and Patty don't know what to think!"

"Can you come to June's? Right now? She could use a friendly face. And a place to stay."

Nora quickly explained what had happened. She'd barely finished when Hester said, "I'm on my way," and ended the call.

Seeing that June had exited her car, Nora headed over to where she stood. June was speaking to McCabe and Andrews, and as she talked, tears slipped down her cheeks. She dabbed at them with a wadded napkin.

Nora put a hand on June's back, offering her wordless support. The sheriff tried to coax the names of possible suspects out of June, but she kept shaking her head and telling him that no one came to mind.

"Do you have a place to stay tonight?" McCabe asked June when he'd run out of other questions.

"She does," Nora said, pointing to the car pulling into the driveway. She smiled to see a second car pull in behind Hester's. Estella had come too.

June wasn't pleased. "You called Hester? She was at that dinner."

"You matter more than some dinner," Nora answered.

She then stepped back to allow Hester to race straight up to June and throw her arms around her in a fierce embrace.

"I'm okay, baby," June whispered, as if Hester was the one in need of comfort.

Hester had clearly called Estella on her way, and Estella didn't wait for Hester and June to separate but threw her arms around them both. The three women stood there for a long moment, like football players in a huddle, until June beckoned for Nora to join the circle.

Estella made room for her and the four friends held one another. Their touch said, "I love you," and "I'm here for you," more powerfully than words ever could.

A man cleared his throat and the women slowly broke apart.

Hester immediately rounded on Andrews. "You need to find out who did this! This is *sick*. June is the sweetest, most generous . . . well? What are you going to do?"

Andrews, clearly startled by Hester's anger, opened and closed his mouth like a fish. Feeling sorry for him, Nora put a hand on his shoulder as if to remind Hester that he was a good man. She then looked at the sheriff. "When can she paint over that?"

"Give us twenty-four hours," McCabe said, turning to June. "I'm sorry that this happened to you — that we live in a place where someone isn't afraid or ashamed of committing such a heinous crime. We're going to start working this case right now. In the meantime, what can I do to make you feel safe?"

Though June seemed to appreciate the question, her eyes were dull with sorrow.

"There's nothing you can do," she said. "As long as we live in a world where people feel the need to do this to other people, there is no safety."

Behind the sheriff, Deputy Fuentes dipped his chin in agreement.

McCabe and his men checked every room, closet, and dim corner inside June's house before making another sweep of her yard. The cats became even more agitated, and Nora was sure that the whole block could hear their cries of distress.

"It's all right, you crazy beasts." June tried to hush the cats as she stepped out of her house, carrying an overnight bag. "I'm okay, you hear me? But you're on your own tonight. So watch your backs. Whoever did this won't think twice about kicking you."

During this short speech, the cats had gone quiet. And the moment June opened her car door, they began to disperse. Smudges of gray and black darted across the lawn and dashed into the woods. Only one cat moved in the opposite direction. A big, mangy, orange tom ran straight up to June and rubbed his body against her calf. His movements were filled with nervous energy.

"Go on, now," June said, trying to shoo him away. "You take care of the others. I'm telling you. I'm okay."

The tom glanced up at her with an expression of pure adoration before trotting off toward the street.

"I'm going to be up all night worrying about those miserable animals," June grumbled. "I never wanted a cat, but here I am, surrounded by them. Too bad they didn't claw the bastard who did this to my house. If I had dogs hanging around instead of these cats, that jackass would be in jail. Or the hospital. Either one would be fine by me."

Nora took June's bag and put it in the back seat.

"Thanks for coming," June said.

Embracing her, Nora whispered, "Whoever did this is a coward. You're not. You've worked hard to find peace in this town. And in this house. Don't let anyone take that away from you."

"I'll try not to," June whispered, and got in the car.

With her friends gone and the sheriff and his deputies already knocking on neighbors' doors, there was nothing for Nora to do but go home.

She didn't want to go home. She wanted company. Not the kind of company that ended up with her naked on Jed's mattress, but the company of a friend. She called Estella and asked if she wanted to meet at the Pink Lady.

"I know it's after eight, but I haven't eaten yet."

"I'm in," Estella said. "I don't really want to be alone right now, anyway. Hester will make June some tea and the two of them will snuggle up on the couch. That leaves the two of us."

"I'll snuggle with you," Nora said, going for levity. "As long as you let me eat."

Because Estella had a car, she beat Nora to the diner by several minutes. Sitting in her favorite booth at the back of the diner, she was so caught up in her conversation with Jack Nakamura that she didn't see Nora come in.

"Hey," Nora said, and slid into the seat across from Estella.

Jack smiled at Nora. "Estella says you're here for a late dinner. I'll make you anything you want. Just name it."

"I'd love a Pink Lady breakfast sampler," Nora said. "There are times when only breakfast can make a girl feel better."

Jack smoothed his white apron. "Crisp bacon and rye toast buttered in the kitchen, right?"

"You always remember."

"I remember everything about my favorite customers," he said, and flashed Estella another hundred-watt smile before heading into the kitchen.

A waitress appeared carrying a strawberry milkshake. "Here's your shake, sweetie. Jack said to put extra cherries on top, so I gave you seven. That's my lucky number."

The waitress bustled off to clear dishes from another table.

Nora looked at the cherries sitting on a pillow of whipped cream. "Are you sure that you and Jack are just friends?"

"Yes. Let's focus on June, not me."

Nora rubbed her temples. "Sorry. I'm wound pretty tight. Seeing that word on her house really pissed me off. I feel so helpless, and it didn't happen to me. *I* wasn't the victim of a hate crime. Who would do this to June? She's one of the finest people I've ever met."

"She honestly has no clue?" Estella asked.

"That's what she said. She hasn't been in any arguments. She didn't offend any guests at the thermal pools. She didn't even flip off the guy who almost forced her off the road because he was texting."

"I would have given him the bird with *both* hands," Estella said before popping a cherry into her mouth.

At the mention of a bird, Nora's thoughts shifted to Danny.

The waitress returned with Nora's decaf and a promise that her food would be out shortly. Nora waited for her to leave and then told Estella about her visit to Marie. When she was finished, she showed Estella the photo of the red bird at Cherokee Rock.

226

"I don't remember seeing that before," Estella said. "All the times I've been to that rock, you'd think I'd recognize it. I do know someone who could tell us if it's new. Mr. Buckley, my high school history teacher. He's retired, of course, but whenever I see him around town, we stop for a chat."

"If you'd give him a call, I'd appreciate it." Seeing Jack heading their way with a breakfast platter, Nora spoke quickly. "I asked Sheldon to swing by the salon tomorrow. He can't promise a miracle, but he'll take a look."

"I hope he can help. I'm getting desperate. I figure I have three months and after that . . ." She shrugged. "Making women beautiful is all I know how to do. It's what I was born to do. I don't want to spend my life doing a job just to pay the bills. That doesn't sound like living. It sounds like a very slow death."

Jack caught the end of Estella's sentence and his smile wobbled. He served Nora and asked if he could get them anything else.

They both said, "no, thanks," but he remained rooted to his spot.

"More cherries?" he asked Estella.

"Only if they're stuffed with arsenic," she muttered.

When Jack's face creased in concern,

227

Estella reached out and squeezed his arm. "Don't mind me. I'm in a mood. Nora will talk me down from the ledge."

Taking the hint, Jack returned to the kitchen.

While Nora ate, Estella talked about organizing a painting party for June.

"We could enlist people from the lodge and from June's church. People can paint, bring food, or buy supplies." Warming to her idea, Estella continued. "I could hand out flyers to my customers too. We could plan the party for this weekend. June will have to stay with Hester for a few days, but I don't think she'll mind."

Estella finished her milkshake and Nora paid the bill. They left the diner full of ideas on erasing the word on June's house as a community. Despite Estella's enthusiasm, Nora had to wonder if a word like that could truly be erased? Wouldn't June see the ghosts of those hateful red letters every time she walked up her front path?

"We can fix the damage done to June's house, but what about the damage done to June?" Nora asked. "How do we help her recover?"

Estella glanced at the pedestrians on the sidewalk. Her gaze passed over an elderly couple strolling hand in hand, a father pushing an empty stroller while his wife carried their baby, and a group of teenage boys with their hands shoved in their pockets.

"We let her know she's not alone," she said. "We remind her that this is her home. Her community needs to rally around her. That's the only way she can see that most people aren't like the bastard who wrote that on her house. Most people are better than that."

Nora looked down the street. At the far end of the block, the windows of the Inn of Mist and Roses glowed like candles in the darkness.

She thought of how she'd run out on Lou and Patty's dinner. She'd have to call them and explain her behavior.

Not tonight, she thought. *I don't want to talk anymore.*

Nora walked over to her moped and dug out her keys.

Estella burst into raucous laughter. "Is that yours? It looks like a My Little Pony with wheels. If Princess Peach from Mario Kart had a moped, it would be this one."

"It's on loan." Nora scowled. "If I end up buying it, I'll peel off these stupid flower decals."

"That's no fun. Seriously, if Lisa Simpson had a scooter, this would be it. It's so *not* you that it's like having a secret identity."

Nora donned her helmet and turned on the engine. Raising her visor, she said, "It's tough to keep an identity secret when you're riding something that looks like the offspring of the Pink Panther and Tweety Bird."

Estella patted a handlebar. Her eyes were dancing with humor. "Thanks for asking me to meet you. I feel better than I did an hour ago."

Nora covered Estella's hand with hers and smiled.

With a playful flick, Estella used her other hand to snap Nora's visor shut. She waved and walked toward her car.

Nora waited until her friend was safely inside before driving away.

At home, she washed up, put on pajamas, and turned on the TV. After an hour of channel surfing, she gave up and went out to the deck. She sat at her little café table and stared up at the starry sky.

It was a perfect night. A wind drifted down from the mountains, and Nora drew her legs into her chest for warmth. In the distance, she heard the lonesome call of a train whistle. At this hour, it would be a freight train, bound for Asheville or Blacksburg.

Tomorrow, the passenger train would arrive carrying a fresh group of visitors to Miracle Springs. That meant potential customers for Nora's bookshop, Hester's bakery, Estella's salon, and the thermal pools June managed.

Had a train also delivered a killer to Miracle Springs? Had Danny been murdered by a stranger? Someone who'd already come and gone?

And what of the person who'd painted angry red letters across the front of June's house? Had a train delivered that person too? Or was it a neighbor? Someone they passed in the street on regular basis?

Nora stayed on her deck until the train rumbled by.

It was a long one, holding over two hundred containers. Nora caught flashes of color. Blue, white, orange, red. She saw glimpses of words, but it was too dark for her to read any of them.

The blurred words and logos on the containers were an accurate reflection of Nora's mind. She was filled to the brim with words and images. Facts and details. Theories and questions. They were all unreadable. And they kept racing away from her, as intangible as smoke from a locomotive.

■ ■ ■ ■

When Nora woke the next morning, she felt dazed. Unrested. After a cup of coffee, she rallied. She sat in her kitchen, looking at Danny's bowl, and decided to take control of her day. She would change the display window. Create something colorful. Something irresistible to book lovers. Something to make people feel good.

She walked to the dollar store and purchased several kites, a few green plastic tablecloths, and a bunch of flower-shaped placemats. She stuffed what she could into her backpack and carried the rest in a plastic bag. She could have taken the moped, but she needed the exercise.

As she walked the final blocks through town to the bookstore, she noticed people milling about on the sidewalk near her shop, but not directly in front of it. Some were pointing. Others shook their heads. Nora saw surprise on their faces.

Nora increased her pace. Fear made her move fast.

When she reached her block, she understood what was wrong with the scene.

She saw triangles of glass on the sidewalk. A jagged hole in the center of her display window. A brick sitting in the middle of her toppled books. More splinters of glass, as dazzling as winter ice, were sprinkled over the books.

Nora stared at the hole, the glass, the brick. To her, they spelled a word.

That word was HATE.

CHAPTER 11

Every face, every shop, bedroom window, public-house, and dark square is a picture feverishly turned — in search of what? It is the same with books. What do we seek through millions of pages?

— Virginia Woolf

Nora entered the bookstore by the back door and immediately called Sheriff Mc-Cabe.

"Have you touched anything?" was his first question.

"I read crime novels. I know better than that," Nora said, surveying the damage. When she'd first seen the broken window, she'd been scared. Now, she was angry. "I doubt you'll find anything useful. It's a brick."

McCabe was annoyingly calm. "Is there anything written on it?"

Nora hadn't had the chance to look. "I

don't know."

"We'll check it out. Be there in five," McCabe said. "And Nora?"

"Yeah?"

"Make yourself a strong cup of coffee. Bricks through windows are not a nice way to start the day."

For the first time, Nora wished she had a security camera. She'd love to pull up the feed and see the face of the brick-throwing jackass. But she didn't even have a security system. She had smoke and carbon dioxide detectors. Fire extinguishers. But theft prevention? She couldn't afford that.

How much does a plate glass window cost?

Worried and angry, she reached out to the row of spines on the fiction shelf. Her fingers came to rest on Austen's *Northanger Abbey.*

"Coffee," she murmured, heading for the ticket agent's office.

She was scooping grounds into the filter when Sheldon called out, "Nora? Where are you?"

"Here!" she shouted. It felt good to shout. To raise her voice and bellow. It also felt good to have Sheldon in the store. She'd left the back door unlocked for McCabe, but she was far more comforted by Sheldon's arrival.

Suddenly, he was standing in the ticket agent's office window. Jerking his thumb toward the front of the store, he asked, "What the hell is that?"

Nora thought of the toppled books. Of the glass fragments on the sidewalk. Of the jagged hole. Her beloved shop had been injured. Deliberately damaged. Her thoughts jumped to the word on June's house. Were the members of the Secret, Book, and Scone Society being targeted?

Sheldon came into the office and opened his arms wide. "Come here, you."

Nora accepted the invitation. Sheldon smelled like wool and peppermint. He smelled like her grandfather — the one who'd passed away when she was a young girl. His arms felt like her grandfather's too. They were soft but strong.

Sheldon held her in his fierce bear hug for a long time. When he finally released her, he gave her one more squeeze and said, "There. That's better."

Nora didn't think she'd ever had a better hug. She told him as much.

"That's the nicest thing anyone's ever said to me. Now, go." He shooed her out of the office. "The cavalry will want coffee. Oh, and I picked up the pastries on my way over. I put them in the stockroom because I was in too much of a hurry to give you that hug."

Before Nora could reply, she heard Sheriff McCabe's voice. "Ms. Pennington?"

Not Nora, she thought. *I'm a citizen today. A case number. A victim.*

Nora was done with that role. Once, she'd been the victim of her ex-husband's deceit. Before that, she'd been the victim of her own blindness. As she'd lain in bed in the burn ward, she vowed never to be a victim again. She would be in control of her life.

A brick through her window was the opposite of control. It was chaos.

The sheriff and a female deputy entered the shop through the back door. Nora led them to the front. The woman immediately started photographing the scene. McCabe silently waited until she was done. He then pulled on a pair of disposable gloves and reached for the brick.

As he examined its underside, his face darkened. He shot a quick glance at Nora before dropping it in the evidence bag the deputy held open.

"What does it say?" Nora asked.

The deputy, whose badge identified her as Officer Wiggins, answered, "One word. The definition of a female dog."

The sheriff told Wiggins to take the bag to the car.

While he continued to examine the damage, Nora tried to remember all the people she'd spoken to over the past few days. There hadn't been any negative interactions. There'd been a few flat exchanges with customers. Some had ignored her altogether. But that was normal. Not every customer cheerfully responded to her greeting. Not every customer found what they needed in her store. Nora's feelings weren't hurt when this happened. That was life in retail.

"I'm going to sound just like June, but I have no idea who did this," Nora told the sheriff. "I haven't argued with anyone. I don't think I've offended anyone. And the last person I upset was Marie."

A glint of curiosity showed in McCabe's eyes. "During the visit you told me about?"

Nora nodded. "When I showed her the bird. The possibility that her husband might have been unfaithful came up. Naturally, she got upset. But she didn't throw a brick through my window."

"No," McCabe agreed. "I dropped by to see her after you and I met at Pearl's. I wanted to learn more about Danny's pottery. Turns out your hunch was right. His older pieces have skyrocketed in value. Marie said that traditionally crafted Cherokee

238

goods are trendy right now. Interior designers have been buying them like crazy. All the pieces that had been gathering dust in his studio are now sold."

Momentarily forgetting about the window, Nora asked, "Did she mention selling pieces to the owners of the Inn of Mist and Roses?"

"No."

Just then, Deputy Wiggins approached the sheriff. "I'd say, based on the thickness of the glass, that whoever threw that brick was really strong."

"Or really angry," Nora muttered.

Wiggins shook her head. "A senior citizen denied health insurance could throw that brick with all their might and they'd barely dent the glass. Whoever broke your window had a football or baseball player's arm."

Nora gestured at the evidence bag. "Do you think the vandal is male?"

"No," said Wiggins. "Both genders use the word written on the brick. As a feminist, I'm offended by any woman calling another woman a bitch. As for men, they should never say it. I can tell you how many times a coworker made the mistake of using it on me." She raised her index finger. "Once. I'm a sixth-degree black belt in karate and I gave that guy a very location-specific kick."

"Do you think a woman can throw as hard

239

as a baseball or football player?" Nora asked.

Wiggins said, "I do." She looked at the sheriff. "I'd be glad to take this on, sir. Somebody vandalized this woman's business. Yesterday, somebody vandalized a woman's home. If it's the same perp, and if there's a chance he's targeting women, I want to be the one to take him down. Or her," she quickly added.

"The case is yours," McCabe said, and focused on Nora again. "Let's start with your statement. We'll question the neighboring merchants afterward. Some open an hour earlier than you, right?"

Nora rattled off the hours of every business on her block. "Can we continue this in the back?" she asked. "Sheldon makes amazing coffee. We also have pastries."

"I love this place," Wiggins said, her eyes moving hungrily over the books. "I can't wait to come back the next time I'm off-duty. I moved here from Arizona three weeks ago, and I'm still dealing with paperwork from last week, aka the week of hell. I've never seen that much rain in my life."

When they reached the circle of chairs, Sheldon came out with three Cuban coffees. He introduced himself before returning to the ticket agent's office to plate three book pockets.

"I didn't know you'd hired someone," McCabe said to Nora.

"I'm on trial," Sheldon answered. "Not in a *12 Angry Men* or *To Kill a Mockingbird* way. In a let's-see-if-I-still-like-you-after-a-week way."

Nora raised a hand. "Stop. You know I like you, but I'd like you more if you could wave a wand and magically fix my window."

Sheldon flashed her a coy grin. "Actually, I have an *amazing* idea for that window. A lemons-into-lemonade idea."

Nora promised they'd talk later, and Sheldon asked the sheriff if he could sweep up the glass.

McCabe gave his permission and even offered to help, but Sheldon insisted that he be allowed to do it alone. "This is my way of showing Nora that I care."

Nora smiled warmly at him and then excused herself to call her insurance company. During one of the many lengthy holds she was subjected to, she tried to figure out who might be angry with her. Angry enough to destroy her property.

Is the vandalism somehow linked to Danny?

Other than the bowl Nora had bought from him, there was nothing to connect her to Danny. But then she realized that there

241

was another connection. She knew Lou and Patty.

The pottery in their bedrooms. Lou's lie. She pretended that she'd never heard of Danny.

Nora wasn't able to pursue this train of thought because an agent finally came on the line. "How about that hold music?" he joked.

Nora wished she could put her hand through the phone and slap him. "Clients call you because something bad happened to them. Do you really think 'Walking on Sunshine' or 'Good Vibrations' is what we want to hear in the middle of a crisis?"

The agent was instantly defensive. "According to the research of a *famous* neuroscientist, those songs make people feel *happy.* When you're dealing with an *unfortunate* event, don't you want something to make you feel better?"

"The Beach Boys won't make victims of a violent crime feel *better.* A little sensitivity and a lot less time on hold would be a good start."

After releasing a sigh rank with disapproval, the agent launched into a well-rehearsed speech on the forms Nora needed to complete, along with the police report, estimates from two glass companies, and photographs of the damage.

When he was done, Nora asked, "Once you have everything, how long will it be before I get a check?"

The agent cheerfully replied that her claim could take five to ten days to process.

Nora bit back the harsh words that were locked and loaded on her tongue. Instead, she thanked the irritating agent and hung up. It would have been cathartic to throw her phone against the wall, but she couldn't afford another expense.

After vowing to cancel her policy after her window was replaced, Nora sent a group text to her friends. She told them about the window and warned Hester and Estella to be vigilant.

Estella was the first to respond.

I don't get it? Why would someone come after us?

Hester's text came in seconds later. OMG, are you OK?

Nora assured her that she was.

June's working and probably won't see this until lunch, Hester wrote. Do you need anything? Are you worried about staying at your place tonight?

Nora wrote that nothing would stop her from sleeping in her own bed.

Want to grab a drink? Estella asked.

Impromptu SBSS meeting at my house?

243

Hester suggested.

YES! Estella wrote.

I'm game for a girls' night. Can I bring anything? Nora replied.

No, Hester answered.

Don't forget to send Sheldon my way, Estella wrote.

For a moment, Nora was annoyed with her friend. Last night, June had been the victim of a hate crime. Nora's store had been vandalized. It seemed selfish for Estella to focus on her salon, considering what was going on.

But Nora couldn't be angry with her friend. The salon was everything to her, just as Miracle Books was Nora's everything. Estella was fighting for the survival of her business and would go to any length to save it. Since Nora would behave the same way, she told Estella that Sheldon would drop by the end of the day.

Returning to the front of the store, Nora saw that the glass was gone, and all the books had been removed from the window display. Sheldon was placing the last one in the Fiction section.

When he was done, he handed Nora a piece of paper. "I want to surprise you with my idea, but I need you to buy a few things before I can get started. I made a list."

Nora scanned the items.

Black duct tape, 3 rolls
A piece of clear sheeting or acrylic (big
 enough to cover the hole)
4 plastic table cloths. They <u>must</u> be orange.
Chicken wire or barbed wire. Enough to
 stretch across the whole window.
That magical baked good Hester promised
 me

Knowing the bookstore was in good
hands, Nora pocketed the list, grabbed her
purse, and headed out. She sent Hester a
text saying that Sheldon was expecting a
treat today. No doubt, her friend would
bake something amazing.

Nora drove to the dollar store first to get
the tape and tablecloths. The store was an
explosion of pink, yellow, and green pastel.
Everywhere Nora looked, she saw Easter
baskets, hats, candy, decorations, crosses,
and figurines.

With all the recent craziness in her life,
Nora had forgotten about Easter. She had a
handful of Easter items for sale in her shop,
but a few vintage bunnies and chicks hadn't
exactly transformed it into a springtime
paradise for book lovers. Based on Shel-

don's list, he wasn't designing an Easter scene. Though she didn't think he was going to use the barbed wire to capture the Easter Bunny, she had no clue what he planned to do with it.

Nora quickly found the tablecloths, but the duct tape wasn't right. All the rolls had decorative patterns. She picked up a roll and stared at the smiley faces and hearts. "What do people do with this?"

She hadn't directed her question to anyone, but the woman standing next to her said, "My kids tape their binders with it. They don't have lockers anymore. Because of all the school shootings, they have to carry everything in their big binders. The things are totally wrecked by Christmas break. Instead of buying new ones, the kids repair them with duct tape. It's kind of creative."

"It is," Nora agreed.

She thought of Harry, the boy who came to her shop on a regular basis. He was in middle school this year and had a sister in elementary school. Nora didn't want those sweet children to worry about school shootings. The worst violence any student should experience at school should be in a dodgeball game.

Feeling glum, Nora bought the tablecloths

and drove to the hardware store. Here, she found the duct tape, two acrylic panels that had been sitting in the stockroom for years, and a roll of chicken wire. When she asked the clerk if he had any barbed wire, he shook his head.

"Gotta go to Tractor Supply for that. We keep the chicken wire because folks have chickens. I don't know what they'd need barbed wire for, but people have a right to their privacy. It's their God-given right."

Maybe they need protection, Nora thought, recalling the word painted on June's house.

"Want this added to your account?" the clerk asked.

Nora said that she did and turned to leave. On her way out, she was inexplicably drawn to the paint swatch display.

She remembered bumping into Lou when she'd come to buy Sheldon's stool. Lou, who had a secret. Lou, who'd lied about knowing Danny. Even if she hadn't met him, she must have heard of him. His pottery was displayed in her bedroom. In Patty's bedroom. Those women knew something. But what?

As her thoughts raced, only to loop back on the unanswered question, Nora stared at the labels of the red paint swatches. Bull's Eye. Chili Pepper. Blood. Scarlet Fever.

Lava. Dragon Fire. Red Hot Meltdown. Volcanic. Fire Brick.

She'd never noticed how these names implied heat, energy, and violence. She found a swatch called Cardinal and held it for a long moment, thinking of the birds on Danny's pottery and the red bird at Cherokee Rock. Turning the swatch over, she noticed the sentence, ALSO AVAILABLE IN RUST-PROOF SPRAY PAINT, GLOSS, 12 OUNCES.

She glanced around for the shelf of spray paint and found a can of Cardinal Red. Carrying it to the checkout counter, she said, "Could you add this to my account?"

The clerk took the can and scanned its bar code. "This red sure is popular."

Nora's heart almost stopped.

"Oh? Have you sold a bunch of Cardinal Red lately?"

The clerk shrugged. "Two or three over the last week or so. But we don't usually sell red this time of year. Maybe folks are refreshin' the paint on their garden benches or yard gnomes."

Nora smiled mechanically, though her mind flitted between the red letters on June's house and the red bird at Cherokee Rock.

"Do you remember who bought the other

cans?" she asked.

A veil fell over the clerk's face. He'd already made his opinion on privacy quite clear and here she was, asking him to divulge information about his customers.

"Sorry. Forget I asked." She quickly backpedaled. "Guess I'm still a little frazzled. Someone threw a brick through my store window last night."

The clerk's mouth fell open. *"No."* Recovering, he shook his head in disgust. "Never thought I'd see the day. Blatant vandalism in downtown Miracle Springs. Think it was kids? They dare each other to do dumb things. Like shopliftin'."

Nora had wanted to find out if the hardware store had security cameras, and the clerk had just given her the perfect opening to raise the subject.

"Have kids stolen from you?" she asked, making the crime about the clerk, not the store.

He folded his arms across his chest. "You know them multitools? The ones with the knife, pliers, bottle opener and such? Three kids pinched a multitool each. I saw them with my own eyes. I didn't get the law involved. No, ma'am. I took them in the back room and called their folks. I got some free labor out of those hoodlums. The way I

249

see it, I did them a favor. Not one of those boys knew how to do a decent day's work before I showed them."

"You must be very observant," said Nora. "I assumed you had some fancy security system."

The clerk guffawed. "Don't need one. We all keep an eye on things. It's cheaper than cameras. More effective too. We know when folks are up to no good and when they need our help. You gotta know how to read faces in our line."

Nora gave the clerk another forced smile and left.

She returned to the shop, driving one-handed while hugging the roll of chicken wire against her chest with the other. When she passed the fire station, she realized that she hadn't called Jed to tell him about her smashed window.

With a prickle of guilt, she thought, *He should have been the first person I thought of.*

But he hadn't been. Nora had reached out to her friends first. With Sheriff McCabe handling the investigation, her friends helping to calm her frayed nerves, and Sheldon overseeing the cleanup, there wasn't much for anyone else to offer.

Perhaps she hadn't called because she didn't want Jed to assume the role of her protector. He'd want her to sleep at his place or insist on sleeping at hers, and Nora refused to make changes because she'd been vandalized. She didn't want to give in to fear. She wanted to sleep alone to prove that she was stronger than the person who'd thrown that brick.

Inside Miracle Books, Nora delivered the items to Sheldon. He inspected each one and then rubbed his hands with glee. "You were probably hoping for a window bursting with springtime books. Floral covers. Pretty pastels." He shook his head. "I'm not doing that."

"I trust you," Nora said.

"Good. Now, go away. I want this to be a surprise. Stay behind the counter. Read something. You need to take a long mental health break. If someone wants coffee, I'll handle it. You focus on relaxing and taking people's money."

Nora sent up a silent prayer of thanks for Sheldon's appearance in her life. She hoped he was as he seemed. Flawed and loveable. She didn't think she could take it if it came out that he'd been hiding some terrible secret from her — something that would keep him from working at Miracle Books. She didn't think this was the case, but then again, everyone had secrets.

Again, Nora thought of Lou. What was she hiding? Was she ashamed of an event in her past, just like the members in the Secret, Book, and Scone Society? Was she protecting someone? She'd lied about Danny, and Danny was now dead. That had to mean something.

Nora decided to type up the steps for removing candlewax from book pages as an excuse to pop by the inn after work. She was interrupted a few times by customers looking for recommendations or others who were ready to check out, but business was slow. The broken window had scared off lots of potential shoppers.

At lunchtime, Hester appeared. She had a takeout bag from the vegetarian restaurant in one hand and a white bakery box in the other.

"I hung my BACK IN 5 MINUTES sign, which means I have three minutes left to give you a hug, your surprise lunch, and Sheldon's treat."

"Did I hear my name?" Sheldon called out from behind a bookshelf. He came around the corner and saw Nora and Hester embracing. "Is this a free hugs session? Because I love hugs."

Hester released Nora and opened her arms to Sheldon. He slowly curled his arms around her, humming as he squeezed her.

"Wow. You're an amazing hugger," she said when they separated. "Your treat is on the counter. It's a comfort scone."

Sheldon's eyes went big. "I've heard about those scones. They're, like, a local legend."

Hester blushed, said that she had to run, and left the shop.

Sheldon winced at the sound of the sleigh bells banging against the door. "Can we — ?"

"No." Nora opened the takeout bag. "I'm not very hungry. I shouldn't have eaten that chocolate book pocket so close to lunch. If I take the lentil soup, do you want the entrée?"

"Depends what it is."

"Gnocchi Arrabiatta."

Sheldon made a gimme gesture. "I've never met a dumpling I didn't like. I'm going to eat while I work, so is it okay if your book keeps you company?"

"Always," said Nora.

By midafternoon, Nora's only real accomplishment had been completing her insurance forms and getting an estimate from the area's only glass company.

The shop was dead. Nora worried that it would stay dead until the window was fixed. Unless Sheldon could perform a creative miracle, people would look at the bookstore and feel uneasy. A broken window wasn't charming. It didn't evoke visions of reading and relaxing. It evoked a lack of security, which was never charming.

"I'm taking a scone break," Sheldon announced. "Want to have a cuppa with me?"

Since Nora had had her fill of coffee, she made herself some herbal tea.

Sheldon warmed his scone and joined Nora at the circle of chairs. He raised his plate to his nose and inhaled. Tears instantly sprang to his eyes.

Gently, Nora asked, "What is it?"

"It's a Nutella Scone. How did she know?"

Sheldon took a bite. He chewed, swallowed, and began to cry in earnest.

Nora grabbed some tissues from the ticket agent's office and knelt beside Sheldon. She rested her hand lightly on his knee and waited for him to cry it out.

"I'm okay," he said after a while. He took the tissues and wiped his blotchy face. "My parents — they weren't good together. They were like your broken window — all sharp edges. They threw things. They called each other names. They fought over what their god wanted for me. The Jewish God versus the Catholic God. My mom would accuse *his people* of worshipping humans. She was

254

referring to the saints. My papa would accuse *her people* of killing Jesus. They took turns shoving Hanukkah and Christmas traditions down my throat. Yom Kippur and Easter. In the end, I rejected both faiths. They both sulked about this until they went to their graves. They died within weeks of each other. It was their final fight. Who'd get to heaven first."

"Why didn't they just split up?"

"They didn't believe in divorce. They cohabitated in misery for nearly fifty years. The only thing that they could agree on — that only thing that brought peace to our house — was Nutella. They were wild about it. So was I. That's why this scone reminds me of our best times. Nutella was my Hanukkah and Christmas. It was my temporary heaven. Nutella wasn't big in America back then, but my mom shopped at an international deli that imported it. It was an extravagance — my parents fought over money several times a day — but they never argued about Nutella. That chocolatey hazelnut miracle spread was, and always will be, my comfort food."

Nora squeezed his hand. "This is Hester's magic. Like all magic, it's fickle. But when it works, it really works."

"Speaking of magic, do want to see some

of mine?" Sheldon asked with a smile.

"Of course."

Sheldon finished his scone and took a sip of coffee. He then dabbed his mouth and stood up. Helping Nora to her feet, he said, "Allow me to channel Melissa Etheridge by saying, *Come to my window.*"

CHAPTER 12

The important task of literature is to free man, not to censor him.

— Anaïs Nin

Sheldon made Nora promise not to look at the window until they were outside.

"I want you to see it like everyone else will," he explained. "I'm pretty sure no one will pass by this window without stopping. They won't be able to help themselves. It's like seeing someone with head-to-toe tattoos. You have to look."

Nora closed her eyes and allowed Sheldon to lead her out into the balmy April afternoon. She inhaled the scents of cut grass and the tulips and hyacinths in the pots flanking her front door. She felt the sunshine falling on her face.

Sheldon pivoted her by the shoulders. "Open your eyes."

The large piece of acrylic Nora had bought

at the hardware store covered the hole in the glass. A swath of chicken wire stretched across the bottom half of the window and columns of black duct tape were placed at regular intervals across the glass and the piece of acrylic. Nora felt like she was looking into a prison cell. When she saw that the books were draped in prison orange, she understood that Sheldon had created a jail scene. In the center of the window, directly behind the hole made by the brick, was a sign reading,

ARE YOU BRAVE ENOUGH TO BUY A BANNED BOOK?

The books on display represented every genre. Under each book, Sheldon had affixed a sign indicating why the title had been banned. Nora was familiar with most of the books, but she was surprised by the inclusion of certain titles. For example, a used copy of the *American Heritage Dictionary* was on display. The sign hanging below the reference tome read, BANNED FOR OBJECTIONABLE ENTRIES.

"A dictionary?" she murmured in astonishment before her eyes fell on another shocker. "*Charlotte's Web*? Seriously?"

Sheldon followed her gaze. "A parent

258

group in a Midwestern state complained because the animals could speak. These folks took issue with animals being elevated to the same communication level as humans. In their eyes, this was sacrilegious."

Nora kept looking at the books. "I've heard lots of reasons for the Harry Potter series being banned. Do you know how many people became book lovers because of that series? And the idea of banning Anne Frank's *The Diary of a Young Girl* because it's heavy and depressing is ridiculous. If all books without a happy ending were removed from the shelf, younger readers wouldn't be prepared for the inevitable moment when their real lives disappoint them."

"Disappointment happens," said Sheldon. "Anyway, there's more. Watch what happens when someone buys a book."

He rushed back inside and removed *James and the Giant Peach* from its display shelf. With the book gone, a sign was revealed. It read, FREED BY A FEARLESS READER.

Sheldon was beaming when he returned to the sidewalk. "See? The hole in the glass amplifies our message that banned books need to be freed. We can fill a table with more banned titles for the sidewalk sale and another table can feature springtime titles."

Nora grabbed Sheldon's hand. "This is

incredible. Thank you."

"You're welcome," he said. "I'm shooting for employee of the month."

"I have an idea too." Nora hooked her arm through Sheldon's and led him back into the store. "Imagine you've just entered the shop for the first time. You're taking in all the books. The colors and signs. The shelf enhancers. You hear soft music. You smell coffee. You're already relaxing. You're also feeling a bit peckish. You follow the coffee scent trail until you reach the ticket agent's office. You read the menu. The book pockets sound tasty, but they might not be substantial enough. Then, you see another item listed below the book pockets."

"Which is?" Sheldon asked, his eyes sparkling with curiosity.

"The Shel Silverstein. Nutella on toasted bread. Cuban bread."

Sheldon clapped his hands in glee. Suddenly, he stopped clapping and frowned. "Wait. Shel Silverstein is *not* Cuban. Did he even like Nutella?"

Nora shrugged. "It doesn't matter. This treat is named after you, and it's the only way to use your name while sticking to our literary theme. And I'm sure Shel Silverstein loved Nutella. He wrote about all kinds of food. Chocolate, peanut butter, toast, sandwiches. We'll just say this was the mystery sandwich in the 'Cookwitch Sandwich.' "

" 'I heard that Katrina the Cook was a witch,' " Sheldon recited a line from the poem.

" 'Make me a sandwich, and ZAP — she did'!" continued Nora.

Sheldon smiled at her. "I'm honored. Thank you."

"Excuse me?" a woman called from the front of the store.

Nora gestured for Sheldon to sit. "I've got this. You take a break. That's an order."

She walked to the front of the store where a middle-aged woman in a bright blue blouse and black dress pants was examining the banned books display.

"Hi," Nora said. "Can I help you with anything?"

The woman pointed at the window. "I was walking by, and I stopped to look at your display. I was shocked to see that *The Color Purple* was repeatedly banned for sexually graphic and violent content. That book changed my life. It gave me courage. It gave me wings. It told me to fly away from an abusive situation, and I flew! It hurts to see it in that window." She touched her chest. "It hurts right here."

261

The woman was on the brink of tears. Nora grabbed a box of tissues from the checkout counter and offered them to the woman. She took the box and held it between her hands.

"I volunteer in a shelter for victims of domestic violence. I want to give *The Color Purple* to every one of these women. I want *this* book to be *their* wings. Do you have more copies?"

"Let me check my inventory," Nora said. "In the meantime, why don't you take the one in the window? I think you'll like the message you find behind it."

Nora's inventory included two used copies and three new copies of *The Color Purple.* The woman bought them all and ordered several more. She also selected a dozen mala beads and added them to her book pile.

"Would you like a cup of coffee or tea for the road?" Nora asked. "It's on me. A thank-you for helping other women. Sheldon is a brilliant barista. He'll make whatever you want."

The woman left her purchases on the counter and headed to the back.

As for Nora, she spent a long moment staring at the window. Sheldon's banned books display had shown her that she could use an act of vandalism to the shop's advantage. She could rise above the attack against her, against the word used against her. Like the books in the window, she could still have a positive effect on others. She could still thrive.

Nora grabbed the topmost book in the box Sheldon had set aside for the sidewalk sale. It was *The Catcher in the Rye,* and the sign accompanying it read, BANNED FOR PROFANITY, REFERENCES TO PROSTITUTION AND PREMARITAL SEX, ALCOHOLISM, AND MORE.

Nora stroked the red horse on the book's cover, recalling the first time she'd met Holden Caulfield. Like the book's hero, she'd been an angsty teen during her inaugural read and had understood Caulfield's frustrations. When Nora revisited the novel in her late twenties, she identified with the hero's love of books and his ability to truly value the special people in his life. In her thirties, Nora read the novel with fresh eyes and was grateful to Salinger for writing about the importance of taking the time to notice the world's beauty.

"You have so much to offer," she told the book as she tenderly placed it on the empty display shelf. "I hope you stay on high school reading lists until the end of time."

By this point, *The Color Purple* customer

had returned with her coffee. Steam escaped from the opening in her take-out cup, curling like a question mark.

"I'm going to take a picture of your window. I want my students and fellow teachers to see it in person. Art should make us think. It should make us question. It should make us feel. Your window is all that and a bag of chips."

Nora said, "We're going to have a table full of banned books during the sidewalk sale. If the staff or students from your school make a purchase, they're entitled to a half-price beverage."

"It's a good thing you don't serve Frappuccinos," the woman said on her way out. "You'd have a line out the door."

After the sleigh bells stopped clanging, Sheldon joined Nora by the checkout counter. "Do you think we should start —"

"No," Nora answered. "No caffeinated milkshakes allowed. No blender will ever disturb the peace of this store." She patted Sheldon's arm. "Besides, you're doing more than enough already. I don't want you burning out because you have more ideas than energy."

Sheldon feigned offense. "I bet Estella won't dim the light of my star. I'm stopping by her salon on my way home." He paused at the door. "Speaking of homes, I need to find one. If you hear any murmurs about a cute cottage hitting the market, call me."

"That's the kind of thing Estella would know," Nora said.

By closing time, Nora was worn out. It had been an emotional day. She hadn't heard from the sheriff and though she had complete faith in Deputy Wiggins, she didn't expect her to solve the case. Someone had thrown a brick through the window in the dead of night. Nora didn't have a security camera. Neither did the other businesses on her block. Even if the traffic signal at the end of the street had captured footage of the vandal, the man — or woman — had probably worn clothing to obscure their face.

Nora had just finished locking up for the night when the sheriff called.

"I wanted to touch base," he said. "Deputy Wiggins is working hard, but I don't want to mislead you. There's not much to go on."

"What about June's case?"

"Same goes for hers, I'm afraid." McCabe sighed. "I keep coming back to the idea that these aren't random acts of violence. You and June are friends. The word painted on Ms. Dixon's house. The word painted on the brick. They're full of anger. Every letter

265

looks angry. This person wants to scare both of you."

"It worked," said Nora. "But not completely. Not permanently. I'm nervous, but even more than that, I'm determined not to give in to fear. If I do, whoever threw that brick gains power over me, and I won't allow that."

The sheriff chuckled. "You're a fierce and wonderful woman, Nora Pennington. I'll call you tomorrow with another update."

Grinning like a fool over McCabe's compliment, Nora reached out to hit the light switch. Just then, someone knocked on the front door. She heard a dog bark. It was a friendly bark. It sounded like Henry Higgins. Following this bark was a second one. Nora didn't think it came from the same dog because it was deep and wary.

Nora peeked out to find Jed standing on the sidewalk. He wasn't alone. Deputy Wiggins was there, holding the end of a leash tethered to a gorgeous Doberman pinscher.

Unlocking the door, Nora tried to push aside a rush of guilt. She'd meant to call Jed after Sheldon left for the day. But then Sheriff McCabe had called, and their conversation had ended with her smiling. Pressing her lips together to hide the grin, she threw open the door. The force of her movement caused the sleigh bells to bang louder than ever.

"Sorry," she said, seeing the dogs' ears twitch. She quickly put her hand over the bells to stop the vibrations.

When the noise had died to a hum, she gave Jed an apologetic look. "I was going to call you on my way home." She waved at the deputy. Wiggins waved back. "Do you have news?"

Jed pointed at the window. "This is about me. I just wanted to make sure you were okay — to see you in person instead of hearing everything through the work grapevine. I feel like the whole town knew about what happened to you except for me."

Deputy Wiggins moved away from the front door, giving Jed a little privacy.

"Did you call your book club friends?" he demanded. "I bet you did."

"Yes. I needed to warn them to be careful," said Nora. "I wasn't picking them over you. After what happened to June, I was worried that Hester or Estella could be targeted next."

Judging by Jed's rigid stance and the way he chewed on his lower lip, Nora's response didn't make him feel better. He was angry.

"I wasn't going to let the day end without

talking to you," she said.

"Well, I've seen you in person. You're obviously okay," Jed said in a tight voice. He began to turn away.

Nora didn't want Jed to leave in a huff, so she pointed at the Doberman. "Who's that good-looking fellow?"

Jed glanced at the dog. The Doberman's coat reflected the glow of the streetlamps and his caramel eyes sparkled with intelligence. "Atticus. He and Henry are being trained to help the sheriff's department. They're learning to bring down a fleeing suspect or detain a perp until an officer can make an arrest. Officer Wiggins thinks some of Henry's anxiety will go away if he's given a purpose. Like humans, dogs need to be needed. They can be playmates, exercise buddies, full-time companions, therapy dogs, or working dogs. But they need an identity."

Nora could see the wisdom in this. "How is Henry taking to it?"

Jed's jaw relaxed. "He loves it. I haven't seen him act like this since before the fire. He's getting better around groups of people. As long as Atticus is close by, he's not on edge like he used to be. These two have really bonded."

Nora looked over Jed's head at Deputy

Wiggins. "Is he named after a famous Roman or Atticus Finch?"

"*To Kill a Mockingbird* is my favorite book," said Wiggins. "My daddy read it to me when I was a kid. After we were finished, I told everyone to call me Scout."

Nora smiled. "You remind me of her. You both have a stick-to-your-guns spirit."

Wiggins was clearly pleased by the compliment. "I told Jed that he might have to call me Scout from now on. We won't hear the end of it when our coworkers realize that Angela Wiggins is training Henry Higgins."

Nora laughed. "Wiggins and Higgins. Sounds like a law firm."

"I'd make a lousy lawyer. Too much desk time," Wiggins said. "Speaking of work, I'd better get going. I want to get back to your case bright and early tomorrow."

Taking the hint, Jed said good night to Nora and issued a soft command to Henry Higgins.

Nora watched the foursome walk away, their shadows stretching out behind them. She wasn't sure exactly what had just happened between her and Jed, but she felt like something had been lost.

At home, she took a quick shower and put on a pair of clean jeans and a gray cardigan.

Estella would tell her to add a pop of color, but Nora was in a gray mood. Her mood worsened when she realized that she hadn't offered to contribute any food to their impromptu supper.

She called Hester before starting up her moped.

"I didn't make anything for tonight," she said.

Hester told her not to worry. "I picked up some Perrier for you," she added. "I noticed that you've been avoiding alcohol lately, which is cool. Sometimes, a cinnamon roll and a good book are better than booze, anyway."

"You're very wise for your tender years," Nora said, brightening a little.

Hester laughed. "Tell that to Jasper. He's so worried about me being alone at my house that he wants to park his patrol car in my driveway and sleep there."

"Why doesn't he just spend the night in your bed? What better protection could you get?"

After a brief pause, Hester said, "Um, he's on duty."

Nora had a feeling that this wasn't the whole truth, but she didn't press the issue.

"I have to drop something off at the inn,

but I'll see you soon," she said, and hung up.

The moment she pulled into a parking space in front of the inn, Bo and Georgia materialized on the front porch. The couple appeared to be waiting for Nora.

Their grim expressions contrasted with the warm light shining through the inn's windows and the perky pink and purple phlox lining the front path. Nora quickened her pace, anxious to learn why the Gentrys had taken a sentinel position on the porch.

"Hi," she said, glancing first at Georgia and then at Bo.

Georgia returned the greeting while her husband managed a brief wave. Neither of them smiled.

"We're sorry," said Georgia. "But if you came to see Patty or Lou, this isn't a good time."

Nora immediately thought of her broken window. Had the inn been targeted too? "Is everything okay?"

"It's Micah." Georgia laced her fingers together and squeezed hard enough to cause the veins on the back of her hands to swell. "He left yesterday to go on a hike. We all saw him at breakfast, but none of us noticed if he came back. We don't eat dinner together and everyone's busy during the day,

271

so breakfast is the only time we all really see each other. Bo and I spent the day at the folk museum. That's why we didn't know that Micah never came back."

Looking grim, Bo picked up the narrative. "Lou and Patty were working, so they didn't realize it either. Not until they knocked on his door late this morning. When he didn't answer, they went in to tidy up. They saw that he'd taken his hiking gear but had left other things behind."

Nora thought of the young man with the soulful brown eyes she'd bumped into on the stairs. Patty and Lou had described Micah as humble, sweet, and shy. He was a modern-day Thoreau — searching for life's greater meaning by immersing himself in nature.

"I'm surprised he didn't hit the Trail before now," said Nora. "Doesn't he plan to hike the whole thing? That takes months."

Georgia nodded. "He wanted to repay Lou and Patty for their kindness before he set out again." She gestured at the flowers. "He planted all of these. He's also aerated, seeded, and fertilized the lawn. Yesterday, over breakfast, Patty told Micah that he'd done more than enough and should hit the Trail when he was ready."

"Maybe he took her advice and continued

on his way," said Nora.

"According to Lou and Patty, he wouldn't have left the items they found in his room. I guess Micah told them that they were important to him. I don't know what they are, but Lou and Patty are very upset. They've called the sheriff and are expecting him to show up any second now."

There was nothing Nora could do but say that she hoped Micah was okay and that someone would hear from him soon.

"You don't have to tell Lou and Patty that I stopped by," she added. "They have enough on their minds, and I was just saying hello."

Georgia unclasped her hands. "Thanks for understanding. Bo and I hope to see you tomorrow. Sheldon told us that you have some collectible books and we can't resist old things. I especially like books that have been signed and dated by their owner. I love those personal links to the past. Those links can define us."

Nora gave the other woman a friendly smile. "I can already think of a few books you'd really like. See you tomorrow."

A few minutes later, Nora pulled up to Hester's house, a pale pink Victorian-style cottage with an abundance of latticework, gingerbread trim, and board-and-batten shutters painted a whipped cream white. Purple hydrangea bushes and beds of spring flowers completed the fairy-tale look. The cottage reminded Nora of a teacake.

Stepping into Hester's cottage was like entering her bakery. It was warm and cozy and always smelled good. Tonight, it was too quiet. The sounds of laughter, conversation, and the clank of flatware were absent. Hester, Estella, and June were gathered around the kitchen table, and Nora could tell by their frightened expressions that something dreadful had happened.

"You were right to warn Estella and me," Hester said as soon as she saw Nora. "Guess it was my turn."

Estella patted the empty chair next to her. "You'd better sit down."

After Nora was seated, Hester pointed at the sink. "There's a dead bird in my sink. The string I use to tie my bakery boxes is wrapped around its neck. I found the bird in my mailbox."

Nora pressed her fingers against her lips to keep an exclamation of shock from escaping.

Another bird!

"No sense holding anything back," June told Nora. "We all freaked out together. Go

274

on and let it out if you need to."

"Jesus," Nora whispered. "When did you find it?"

"Five minutes ago. I already made our soup and salad and I have a fresh baguette keeping warm in the oven, so supper was pretty much handled. I knew I had plenty of time to get the mail. June and Estella had just pulled up to the curb when I opened the mailbox. They heard me scream."

"I'm so sorry, Hester."

Estella covered Nora's hand with her own, as if telling her that none of this was her fault. Nora shot Estella a grateful look and turned back to Hester.

"You called Andrews?"

June answered before Hester could. "Not only is her man on his way, but he came by during his lunch break. Turns out he hid a few cameras around the place, just in case his woman was the next target. The camera in the birdfeeder was recording the front yard. If we're lucky, we'll find out who this sicko is before our soup gets cold."

Andrews arrived with a squeal of tires. The women heard him slam his car door shut. They heard his tread on the gravel path leading to the kitchen door. He entered the house and, without saying a word, pulled Hester out of her chair and took her in his arms. He murmured into her hair and held her as if he wanted to shield her from the world's hurts.

That's what love looks like, Nora thought. She was happy that Hester had found such a good man.

After a moment, Hester pulled away and led Andrews to the sink.

As he stared down at the bird, his fists curled and uncurled. Finally, he clenched them so hard that his knuckles turned the color of bread dough.

"Let's find out who did this, so I can pay him a visit," Andrews said, his eyes on Hester. "If I plug my phone into your laptop, we can watch the feed on your screen." He glanced at the rest of the women. "It's probably the same person who targeted you two, and Ms. Sadler could have been next. That makes this very much your business."

Everyone relocated to the living room. June joined Hester and Andrews on the sofa while Nora and Estella pulled their wing chairs closer to the coffee table.

Andrews connected his phone, pushed an icon, and logged into an account. The screen flashed and, a second later, four views of Hester's yard appeared on screen. Andrews used the laptop's keyboard to select the birdfeeder view. Next, he clicked the play button.

At first, the feed moved in real time. They all watched in nervous anticipation until Andrews grew impatient and pressed another button. The feed moved twice as fast, and they saw a man walking a dog, a kid on a bike, and a woman jogging. No one stopped at Hester's mailbox. Now and then, a car would pass by. During the course of the afternoon, the only person to touch Hester's mailbox was the mailman. He opened the door, shoved in a stack of envelopes, and moved on.

"If the bird had been in the mailbox, he would've reacted," Estella said. "It must have been empty then."

Andrews pointed at the time stamp. "It's only three forty-seven. Let's keep going."

At twenty past five, the daylight had lost its vitality. It wasn't dark, but there was a softening of the light. A subtle surrender.

Four minutes later, a man appeared on the screen.

His T-shirt was white. Not the dazzling white of bleached sheets hanging out to dry. The front was dingy, and it was soiled under the arms and around the collar. A baseball hat was pulled low over the man's brow, throwing his face in shadow.

"It's him," Hester said.

The rain monster, Nora thought, watching the man place the bird into the mailbox. Then, he closed the door and walked away.

The camera could only follow him so far. No one could tell if he turned left or right at the end of Hester's block.

Andrews rewound the footage and zoomed in on the man's face. He hit the pause button and glared at the image filling the screen.

It was impossible to distinguish the man's features. His hat hid his eyes and nose. No one could tell if he had freckles or a scar. Nora stared at the cruel curve of his lips and shuddered.

"That's him. The man in the white T-shirt," she said to Andrews.

The deputy didn't look away from the screen. "I'm going to find him." He put his hand on Hester's. "I won't sleep until I do."

CHAPTER 13

In order to see the birds it is necessary to be part of the silence.

— Robert Lynd

Though he searched for the better part of the night, Andrews didn't find the man in the white T-shirt. After sharing the bad news with the Secret, Book, and Scone Society, he entreated them to avoid being alone, especially after dark.

Shortly after receiving this warning, June called Nora.

"I'm off today. Should we take a kindness tote to Marie? She's been on my mind."

Nora leapt at the chance. "Anything to avoid thinking about the man Andrews can't find."

While waiting for June to arrive, Nora packed the tote with a box of cookies and a loaf of bread from the Gingerbread House, a relaxation spa package from Estella, a hand-knit blanket from June, and a selection of books on grief.

Choosing books for Marie hadn't been easy. Usually, Nora could assemble titles for the grieving without much difficulty. But the suddenness of Danny's death, coupled with Marie's pregnancy, complicated the process. Nora kept taking books off the shelf, only to replace them an hour or two later. These exchanges continued until she felt like half of her inventory had traveled between the shelves and the checkout counter.

In the end, she decided on two nonfiction books and three novels. The nonfiction books were geared toward young widows. The image on the cover of the first book, *Widows Wear Stilettos,* reminded Nora of Marie's strength. The second book, *I'm Grieving as Fast as I Can,* took an honest look at the emotional grenade created by an untimely death. One of the things Nora liked most about this book was its short passages and chapters. Marie didn't have the energy to wade through a twenty-page chapter. Not yet, anyway.

Finding the right novels was also a challenge. Nora didn't want to shove themes of healing or remarrying down Marie's throat. Marie was light years away from even considering either idea. In Marie's mind, there would never be healing — only existing. Her love for Danny was still as real as it had been on the day of his death. She couldn't imagine loving someone else. The very thought would be a betrayal to his memory and to the memory of their shared life.

Nora wanted Marie to use fiction as a distraction. A temporary escape. She also wanted subtle messages of hope to curl around Marie's shoulders like a warm shawl, which is why she packed up *Dream a Little Dream* by Susan Elizabeth Phillips and LaVyrle Spenser's *Morning Glory.* Both books featured Southern settings and widows with children. Nora chose these books because they would invite Marie into another world — a romantic, dreamy world — for a little while.

The last book Nora had added was *The Love of My Life* by Louise Douglas. Like Marie, the novel's main character loses her husband soon after discovering her pregnancy. Like Marie, the main character doesn't have close ties to family. It was Nora's hope that a meaningful line or passage from Douglas's book would encourage Marie to reach out to someone — whether that person was a member of her family or

Danny's — and that her attempt to connect would be accepted.

In addition to the goodies contributed by the Secret, Book, and Scone Society, Andrews had taken up a collection at the station and used the money to buy a grocery store gift card. June had also passed the hat at the thermal pools. She'd collected enough cash to buy Marie a pregnancy massage package as well as a prenatal gift basket filled with vitamins, creams, and snacks.

With so many goodies to deliver, Nora was grateful for June's car. She was even more grateful for her company. Leaving Miracle Books in Sheldon's hands for an hour or so, Nora met June in the parking lot.

"I drove by your window," June said as Nora settled into the passenger seat. "It's pretty amazing."

"Sheldon's pretty amazing."

June turned onto Main Street. "Apparently, Estella thinks so too. We drove to Hester's together last night. Because of that damned dead bird, Estella never got to talk about her meeting with Sheldon. But I can tell you that she's feeling optimistic for the first time in months. Sheldon said that there wasn't a thing wrong with her salon. It's classy and clean. Her prices are reasonable. He said that since her reputation was responsible for her financial problems, she has to do all she can to make people see her in a different light. And she needs to do it fast."

"Estella doesn't think she should pretend to be anything other than what she is," said Nora. "And I don't blame her. None of us should have to wear a mask to succeed."

June grunted. "She shouldn't change, but she *could* dial it down a bit. You and I both know that she provokes the women who whisper behind her back. She needs to stop playing their game and turn the whole game on its head. No more antagonizing the church ladies and PTA moms by batting her eyes at their men. She needs those women as clients, not enemies."

"That's part of owning a business in a small town," Nora said. "Having to be friendly to people you don't like."

June shot Nora a glance. "But if that business is the reason you get out of bed, then you do whatever it takes to make it thrive. That's the point Sheldon was making. He suggested that Estella host a pro-women event — something that would let her bond with the local ladies and allow her to show another side of herself to the community."

"Like a charity event?"

"You got it," June said. "She's planning a

Go Pink Day to raise money for women battling cancer. She'll give free cuts to anyone donating their hair to be used as wigs for cancer patients. She'll have specials on pink mani/pedis, pink hair color, a pink grapefruit body scrub, or pink peony facial. Jack is cosponsoring the event. He's donating food and pink champagne."

Nora smiled. "It's brilliant. Estella will be seen as a caring community member." After a pause, she added, "I worry about her relationship with Jack, though. She says that he's totally fine with being good friends, but I call bullshit. Have you seen the way he looks at her?"

"Yeah." June's tone was mournful. "The boy's got it bad."

"I want Estella to succeed, but not at the price of Jack's broken heart."

June clucked her tongue. "It's not up to you, hon. Even if you think you can spare Jack a whole lotta pain, you shouldn't. He won't stop loving Estella because you warn him off. Real love isn't that weak. It gets down in your bones, kind of like —"

"A disease?" Nora joked. She wanted to change the subject. Any talk of love reminded her of her awkward exchange with Jed.

June was too busy merging onto the

highway to respond to Nora's wry comment, and after going around a painfully slow tractor trailer, she asked if there'd been any news about Danny's case.

"Not that I know of," said Nora.

"I read in the paper that his death was ruled an accidental drowning. Will the sheriff keep looking at different angles now? Especially with this white T-shirt fool running around."

Nora felt defensive on the sheriff's behalf. "McCabe has integrity. So does his team. They won't move on and forget about Danny just because it's convenient."

June grunted again, somehow managing to inject doubt into the sound.

Nora didn't want to spend the rest of the drive talking about the sheriff. Instead, she told June about the pottery she'd seen at the Inn of Mist and Roses.

"You're saying that Danny's older pieces are worth some money?"

"Real money. His utilitarian stuff sells for under a hundred bucks, but his traditional pieces, especially the blackware, are selling for thousands of dollars. The pottery Patty and Lou own is worth at least five grand in total."

June whistled. "You can't spend that kind of money on art without knowing the artist's name. Did you ever get the chance to ask Patty or Lou how they knew Danny?"

"I think Lou lied to me when she said that she's never heard of him, so I was going to ask Patty next. I stopped by the inn on my way to Hester's, but Patty and Lou were too upset about Micah to see me." She filled June in on the details. "Once Micah is found, I'll go back over. I want to find out if Lou and Patty bought the pottery outright or if they came by it another way."

"Like they struck some kind of deal with Danny?"

The Bronco dipped into a deep pothole on the gravel road leading to Danny and Marie's house. Nora waited for the truck to stop rolling like a boat in a storm before responding. "I'm hoping Marie can answer that one. If she feels up to talking."

"If she doesn't, we won't push her," June said firmly. "She's not in any shape to go through your Jessica Fletcher treatment."

"Me, as Jessica Fletcher? I take that as a compliment. *Murder, She Wrote* was one of the best television shows ever made."

June dismissed this remark with a flick of the wrist. "That old bat can't hold a candle to my Luther. I'll take Idris Elba over Angela Lansbury any day."

At Marie's house, June parked the Bronco

as close to the road as she could. "That drop makes me nervous," she said as she gathered up the gift basket.

Nora looped the tote bag over her arm and rang the doorbell.

It took over a minute for Marie to respond. Finally, Nora and June heard a click of a deadbolt. The door was cracked open and Marie's wan face peered out at them.

"Hi," said Nora. "I hope you're up to visitors. We brought you a few things."

Marie opened the door a little wider. Her movements were listless, and her expression was blank.

Nora placed the tote bag on the kitchen counter and gestured for June to leave the basket there as well.

"You look like you've been eating," Nora said to Marie. "That's good."

Marie's hand fluttered to her stomach. "Only because of her. I want her to be healthy."

After introducing herself, June gestured at the gift basket. "That's full of stuff to help you with that."

Marie nodded. She made no move to come into the kitchen. She stood in the hallway, her arms crossed over her middle.

"Marie, I saw some of Danny's pieces at an inn in town. Could we sit down and talk about them? I could make coffee first if you'd like."

"No coffee. Herbal tea is better for the baby."

June smiled. "I'll make it. You two go on and get settled."

In the living room, Nora was amazed by the view all over again. Dust motes danced in the bars of light streaming through the windows and everything in the room seemed infused with a golden glow.

"Have you ever been scared?" she asked. "Living on the edge like this?"

Marie shook her head. "The posts are buried real deep. And sunk in concrete. If they give way and the house drops down into the trees — I'd be fine with that."

Nora didn't want Marie to be pulled under by her grief. Not yet. She was being selfish, she knew, but she needed to understand the connection between Danny and Patty and Lou. At first, she'd wanted the answers to these questions for her own sake. But now, she wanted them for Marie even more.

"I've been learning a bit about traditional Cherokee art," she said, and saw a glimmer of interest in Marie's eyes. "I watched a video of a Cherokee woman working a loom. She was making a blanket. While I watched, I thought of how different the blanket would look without one of its colors. Like blue. The pattern wouldn't make sense without the blue. That's how I feel about your husband's passing. Something is missing. Something that keeps us from seeing the pattern."

"The sheriff calls every day," Marie said in a near whisper. "He says that he's still working on the case, but there isn't any news right now. I think he's giving up. Everyone is. Except me."

Nora was stunned. "Did you tell the sheriff about the blackware? Or about how much Danny's traditional pieces are worth?"

Marie nodded.

"I searched around online, looking for pieces like the ones I saw at the Inn of Mist and Roses. Have you ever heard of the inn? Or of the owners? Patty and Lou?" Nora was talking too quickly. She was also invading Marie's personal space. Marie shrank back.

"Teatime," June announced, placing a tray with three cups of tea and a plate of Hester's honey buns on the coffee table.

Nora shot June a grateful glance. She moved away from Marie and quietly sipped her tea. June followed suit.

Marie didn't reach for her teacup. She

stared out the window, her forehead furrowed in concentration. She was deep in her mental file cabinet, sifting through conversations and images.

Slowly, she turned to Nora. "Can you describe the pieces at the inn?"

"I can do better than that." Nora took out her phone and put it on the coffee table. A blackware vase filled the screen. "These aren't Danny's, but I found photos of pieces that looked like the ones I saw at the inn. Keep swiping to the left to see the rest of them."

Marie moved through the photos quickly. "It's been years since Danny made those shapes. But a few weeks before . . . he . . ." Unable to complete the thought, she moved on. "We were in his studio and he was unwrapping some of his older pieces." She pointed at Nora's phone. "They looked just like those."

"Go on," Nora gently prodded.

"After they were unwrapped, Danny made notes in his inventory book," Marie continued. "When I asked if he'd sold the pieces, he said he expected to sell them soon. To someone he'd met at the flea market. I don't understand why he packed them all in his truck that . . . that morning. Was he trying to sell them that day? If so, why? And why meet at Cherokee Rock? Who was the buyer?"

Patty or Lou, Nora thought.

"Did you always work the flea market together? If the two ladies from the inn spoke to Danny, would you remember them?"

Marie shrugged. "I wasn't always there. I volunteer at a soup kitchen two Saturdays a month. I help with their baking."

June told Marie about her experience working in a homeless shelter in New York while Nora considered who else might have seen Lou or Patty talking to Danny. Another vendor? Beatrice?

She carried her teacup into the kitchen and washed it. Her phone, which she'd put back in her pocket, buzzed to tell her that she had a new message. Because she needed to be sure that all was well at Miracle Books, she read the text.

The message from Sheldon had nothing to do with the bookshop. It was a grainy photo, taken in dim light. Nora squinted at it but didn't recognize it as the bookstore. A second message popped up. Sheldon's text read, Patty sent me the pic. They just pulled down the library shelves and found a secret door where the shelves were. Behind the door is a ladder going to the second floor. Do you see the carving on the wall?

Nora moved closer to the sink and tilted the phone to let the natural light fall on the screen. She studied the image again. A wood panel — the door — had been pushed inward to reveal an opening in the wall. It wasn't as wide as a regular doorway. In fact, it was quite narrow. A person could squeeze through, but not easily.

"What carving?" she murmured, zooming in. The more she zoomed, the fuzzier the image became. She saved the photo to her camera roll and used a brightening filter to banish some of the shadows. A ribbon of sunlight fell across her screen and, for a second, she thought she saw a shape etched into the hidden wall.

A bird.

Nora returned to the living room and held up her hand, signaling for June to stop talking.

"Could there be a connection between Danny, or Danny's family, to the inn?" Nora asked Marie. "It's an old building."

Marie was baffled. "I don't even know which inn you're talking about. There are three or four in town." Her voice turned shrill. "Why are you asking? What's this about?"

Nora sat down next to Marie. "The house

292

— which is now the inn — has secret hiding places and passageways. This morning, one of the library bookcases, which wasn't original to the house, was pulled down. Behind a door made to look like part of the wall, they found a narrow space with a ladder going upstairs. *This* was carved into the wall of that space."

She showed Marie the image, zooming in on the bird. The second Marie saw it, she reeled back like a rabbit dodging a snake strike.

"That's Danny's bird. His mama and grandma's bird." Marie's stare was accusatory. "It's the same bird someone painted on Cherokee Rock. What's going on?"

"I don't know," Nora said. "I wish I did. But there must be more to this bird than a family nickname. When I get back to the shop, I'll research the inn. There must be a clue somewhere that can explain why a symbol used by your husband's family marks a secret ladder leading to the second floor. Who used that ladder? Why was it hidden?"

Marie stared out the window again. She was shutting down. June shot Nora a warning look.

Taking Marie's hand, Nora said, "This is a lot to take in at once. It must feel like it's crushing you. Don't let it. Help me figure this out."

Marie met her eyes.

Nora took this as a sign of assent. "Can you try to search for a link between Danny's people and that house? A scrapbook, a pile of letters, a diary? Even if you have to ask his family members, will you do it?"

"I'll try," Marie whispered.

"You're stronger than you think," June said. She walked over to the sofa and wrapped her arms around Marie. Marie let out a little sigh and hugged June back.

June held her for a long time. She then squeezed Marie's shoulder and said, "Take care of yourself. We'll see you soon."

When she and June were back in the car, Nora said, "I want to stop by that rock on the way home."

"I was thinking the same thing." June glanced in the rearview mirror as if she could see Danny and Marie's house behind them. "I feel like I need to stand where Danny stood. Maybe I just want to tell him not to worry because we'll be looking in on his wife."

Nora held on to the ridiculous hope that June would notice something everyone else had missed. She was good at that. She was amazing at reading people. Occasionally, she caught a vibe about places too.

"I'm going to call Sheldon and the sheriff on the way," Nora said, taking her phone out. "I can't just show up at the inn and demand answers from Patty and Lou. I'll have to leave that to McCabe."

Sheldon answered Nora's call right away. He told her that everything was peachy keen and that she didn't need to rush back. Relieved, Nora raised the subject of the secret space.

"Were you there when they found it?"

"No. I was on my way to work." Sheldon sighed happily. "Lawd, it feels good to say that. I feel like a normal, functioning adult."

Nora told him that she hoped he'd never be normal. Then, before he could go off on a tangent, she asked, "How do Patty and Lou feel about the discovery?"

"The ladder led to Patty's room. Hers is the one overlooking the garden. She never saw the trap door in her closet because it's pretty dark in there. Anyway, it gave them something else to think about for a bit. They're really worried about Micah."

Nora's stomach twisted. What was Micah's story, anyway? Was he truly a naturalist taking a very long hike or was he running from something? The Trail had always been a place where people could drop off the radar for months. Or forever, if that's what they wanted.

"I'm sorry that he hasn't been found yet," she said. "Did you get to know him at all?"

"Not really. He seemed like a good kid. He was quiet and polite. Very introspective for his age. The books he left behind were all philosophy books. I think he wanted to find his way in the world by getting lost in the wilderness. A male version of Cheryl Strayed's *Wild*."

"Was Micah an experienced hiker?"

Sheldon said that he had no idea and that he had to run because a customer needed his help.

Nora called the sheriff next. His cell phone rang and rang, so she disconnected the call and dialed the station. The desk sergeant informed her that Sheriff McCabe was tied up and put her through to his voicemail. After leaving a brief message about the value of Danny's blackware pottery as well as the discovery of the bird scratched into the inn's hidden wall, Nora hung up.

"He's not there," she told June. "He might have joined the search for Micah, the missing hiker."

"Or he's looking for the creep in the white T-shirt," June said, turning onto the road

296

leading to Cherokee Rock.

Nora remembered the way the man had stared at her through the rain. The rigidness of his body. The intensity of his gaze. She felt a sudden chill. It was the same sensation she'd felt the night she'd seen him standing across the street from the diner. The air above her missing pinkie finger had vibrated then. It was vibrating again now like the silent thrum of a rattler's tail. Like a whispered phrase.

Get away. Get away.

Covering her right hand with her left, Nora wondered if there was a clue at Cherokee Rock. Something they'd all missed. A line to help connect the dots.

She hurried over to the cliff face and stared at the pictographs for a long time. They told her nothing. Next, she examined the much newer, much more vibrant painting of the red bird.

"Whoever did this is a good artist," June said, coming to stand next to Nora. "It can't be easy to make a thin line with spray paint."

"It's not hard. There are step-by-step instructions on YouTube on how to make a skinny needle cap for a standard spray paint can. I looked it up after I saw a bottle of Cardinal Red spray paint in the hardware shop."

June reached out to touch the bird. "Do you think the person who bought that red paint made this?"

Looking at the bird, at the proud tilt of its beak, its bright plumage, and the spark of life represented by a dot of white paint in the center of its black eye, Nora wasn't sure. "I saw the paint on the brick thrown through my window. I'd swear that it was the same shade used on your house. And to make this bird. They were all done in Cardinal Red."

June covered her mouth with her hand as she took all of this in.

"The man in the white T-shirt," she whispered, as if mentioning him too loudly might make him appear. "Could he be Danny's killer?"

"According to a flea market vendor, Danny was meeting with a woman. White T-shirt could have an accomplice, but what's his motive? Why kill Danny? Why bully us? There's no profit in these acts. So what does this man want? Fame?"

June grunted. "I hate to say this, but Danny's death is yesterday's news. By now, there's a fresh batch of shock and awe stories in the paper. If the killer wants celebrity status, he'd use social media. It's worth mentioning that idea to the sheriff."

Though it was time to get back to the bookstore, Nora was reluctant to leave. She and June were alone in the peaceful place. The soft rustle of leaves in the woods surrounded them. Birds and squirrels moved in the tree branches. Beyond the trees, Nora could hear the rhythmic rush of the river.

The river.

Nora thought of how Danny's body had floated in the same river.

If I look at it now, without the muck and debris, would that help me see Danny as he was at the flea market? Would I see his smile or how lovingly he gazed at his wife?

Nora started walking toward the river. June followed her.

Green had invaded the forest. The leaves on the hardwood trees were grasshopper-green. The pine needles were a dark emerald. The immature cones looked like prickly pears. Weeds rose from the soil like crocodile heads breaking the water's surface. Even the light filtering through the trees was tinged with a lime hue.

Because she was enveloped in green, Nora didn't notice the olive-green backpack off to her right. She was too focused on the river, too lost in the vision of Danny being carried away in its watery arms.

"Nora."

June's voice wasn't the mountain cold of river water. It was sepulcher cold.

Nora turned toward her friend. Which is when she saw the backpack. A black hoodie covered in leaves. A hiking boot pointing skyward.

Finally, she saw the hand.

The fingers were curled into stiff commas. Ants paraded over the dirty skin. A centipede crawled across the compass tattoo.

Nora closed her eyes, but the darkness behind her lids couldn't erase what she'd seen. The image had been burned into her retinas.

That rigid hand.

That tattooed wrist.

They'd found Micah.

CHAPTER 14

Stand at the top of a cliff and jump off and build your wings on the way down.

— Ray Bradbury

June called 911. Though Nora heard her friend speak, the words didn't penetrate the bubble of shock enveloping her. She stood completely still, staring down at Micah's body.

He was on his back. His torso, legs, and face were covered by leaves and pine needles. It was clear that someone had tried to bury him under a layer of leaves, scooping them from around his body and piling them over him. But errant winds had swept down from the mountain, shifting the leaves and exposing Micah's boots and backpack. And his right hand.

His resting place was the base of an enormous tulip poplar. The lichen-covered trunk was as wide as Nora was tall. It grew straight and proud, like a soldier at attention, and was crowned with dense, light-dappled branches. The yellow-green flowers nestled among the leaves were just beginning to open. Soon, blooms shaped like tulips would cover the entire tree.

Nora wondered if Micah had looked up at the beautiful canopy before he died. She hoped that he'd seen the sun shining through the leaves before the darkness came. She hoped that he hadn't been afraid.

Despite the sunshine, Nora felt chilled. She crossed her arms over her chest and shuddered.

Suddenly, June was there. She put an arm around Nora's shoulder and leaned over until her cheek rested against Nora's cheek. June's skin was warm. Nora smelled her coconut lotion and drew comfort from her familiar scent.

"You're cold," June whispered. "Do you want to wait in the car?"

"After McCabe comes. I feel like . . . like . . ."

June squeezed Nora tighter. "Like we need to watch over him?"

"Yes. He's so young. Just a boy."

The two women held each other as they looked at the mound of leaves. Tears slipped from their eyes.

Neither one spoke for a long time until June said, "One of my coworkers used to belong to a hiking club in New Mexico. Their leader was part Navajo. Before they set out for a hike, he always said the same thing."

June took Nora's hand and led her closer to Micah. Then, in the soft, quiet voice of a mother tucking a child in for the night, she said:

" 'With beauty before me, may I walk.

With beauty behind me, may I walk.

With beauty above me, may I walk.

With beauty below me, may I walk.

With beauty all around me, may I walk.

Wandering on the trail of beauty, may I walk.' "

Nora could see Micah walking among the trees, his pack bobbing on his back, a contented smile on his face. She tried to focus on this image. She didn't want to wonder why his body was so close to Cherokee Rock. She didn't want to think about him spending the night here, alone, or about how the air above her pinkie knuckle had tingled when she'd touched the red bird on the rock.

Danny.

Micah.

Why them? Why here?

The sound of an engine broke the still-ness. Nora and June turned to see two figures exit a truck with an official seal on the driver's door.

The men weren't from the Miracle Springs Sheriff's Department. They were park rangers.

More green, Nora thought, noticing their uniforms.

The rangers approached the women and calmly asked if they required medical as-sistance.

"She could use a blanket," June said, pointing at Nora.

Nora shook her head. "I just need to sit down for a minute. I'll go wait in the car."

The older ranger said that he had water and blankets should Nora need either. The younger ranger tipped his hat. His face was solemn, and his gaze kept straying toward the lump of leaves covering Micah's body.

"We didn't touch anything," June assured the rangers. She and Nora walked to the Bronco with their arms around each other.

Nora had no idea how long it took for the sheriff to tap on the passenger-side window with his index finger. She lowered the win-dow.

McCabe saw the dazed look on Nora's face and said, "You ladies don't need to stay. You should get something hot to drink and take it easy. I'll get your statements when I'm back in town."

"I can tell you now," Nora said. She might not be feeling well, but Micah was dead. He'd been out in the woods for hours. She didn't want him to be kept waiting a minute longer.

The sheriff glanced at June.

"She needs to do this," June said.

Nora nodded gratefully. "June and I went to see Marie this morning. On the way home, we decided to stop here and look at the red bird. That bird. It keeps coming up. It's at the inn too." She showed McCabe the photo Sheldon had sent, pointing out the bird in the wall. "Micah was staying at the inn. Now, he's dead. I called you earlier to tell you about the Cardinal Red paint. Red paint. Red birds. Two young men, gone. I don't understand any of it."

McCabe's gaze followed the progress of two figures carrying a stretcher into the woods. His eyes were grave. "Ms. Dixon? Would you like to add anything?"

"Just that we were drawn to the river," June said. "We were wondering if Danny went into the water here. It's because of Danny that we found Micah. I'm glad we did. That boy needs to be taken someplace safe and warm. He needs looking after."

Nora gave June's arm a squeeze. Although she hadn't spoken to Tyson, her only son, in more than a decade, June's maternal nature was part of her personality. She was a genuine, generous, and openly affectionate woman. She was also fiercely protective, and Nora knew that her friend wanted to protect Micah. Even now, when it was too late.

"We'll take very good care of him," Mc-Cabe said. "You have my word."

When Nora showed up at Miracle Books, Sheldon took one look at her before steering her to the circle of reading chairs. After serving her a steaming cup of Cuban coffee and Nutella on toast, he covered her with a throw blanket.

"It was that bad? Seeing Marie?"

Nora looked at Sheldon's gray and red argyle sweater vest. His yellow bowtie. She took in his waves of silver and gray hair. The warm brown eyes behind his glasses. She saw the concern in those eyes and reached for his hand.

"I'm so sorry, but Micah is dead," she said. "June and I found him near Cherokee Rock."

Sheldon reeled back. His hands flapped like startled birds. "Oh, no. That poor boy.

That poor, poor boy. What happened? Did he fall? Was there an accident?"

"I don't think so."

"What do you mean?"

Nora was grateful for the heat coming from her mug. She couldn't seem to shake the chill she'd picked up in the woods. "His body was covered with leaves. They'd been piled on top of him. It was a hasty job, but it kept him hidden until June and I came along."

"Are you sure it was Micah? Did you see his face?"

"I saw his tattoo. The compass on his wrist."

Sheldon grabbed Nora's coffee cup out of her hands. He gripped the handle and took a fortifying sip.

Nora twisted her empty hands in the blanket and gave Sheldon time to absorb the awful news. He finished her coffee in silence. When he got up to make a fresh cup, Nora said, "We need to talk about Lou and Patty."

"I don't want to."

While Sheldon steamed milk, Nora ate her Nutella on toast. The hazelnut chocolate on buttery toast was blissful. Nora felt her strength returning with every bite.

"I like Lou and Patty," Sheldon said, put-

307

ting Nora's cup down with a thud. "They're good people. Look how they took me in when all the other inns were full. It was like Bethlehem the night Jesus was born, but they made room for me, for Micah, and for Georgia and Bo. With all they have going on, they made up rooms and fed us. They treat me like I'm family."

"I like them too," said Nora. "I like their devotion to the inn. I like their kindness. I like their colorful reading glasses and how they want to keep Rose Lattimer's books even though they have no monetary value. But there's something off about them. Why did Lou lie about knowing Danny? Why won't they let me read Rose's diary? Why is that bird carved into the wall of that secret nook?"

Sheldon put his hands on his hips. "Really? They own a few pieces from a local potter who died in a storm. So what? Lou decided to keep a piece of family history to herself. So what? Just because they keep some things close to the chest doesn't mean that they're murder suspects."

"When you put it that way, it does sound ridiculous. But who else had a connection to both Danny and Micah?"

"Puh-lease. We don't know Micah's whole story. He could be Danny's third cousin twice removed and we wouldn't know it." He frowned at Nora. "I'm tired. I'm sad. And I'm leaving."

By the time Nora got out of her chair to apologize — not for doubting Patty and Lou, but for wanting to talk about them right after sharing the news of Micah's death — Sheldon was gone.

After work, Nora went to the station to provide an official statement. When she was done, she asked to see the sheriff. McCabe wasn't available, so she left.

It was a lovely night. A breeze scented with cut grass scattered white petals from the ornamental pear trees onto the sidewalk. Nora raised her hand to catch a petal. It landed on her palm like a snowflake, only it didn't melt.

Nora didn't want to go home. She wanted to talk to someone who cared about her. She called Jed, but her call went straight to voicemail. Without thinking about what she was doing, Nora drove to his house. The windows were dark, and his Blazer wasn't parked in his driveway. Feeling deflated, Nora got back on her moped.

As she paused at the stop sign near the diner, she saw an EMT rig parked next to the building. She turned into the diner lot and found a spot near the dumpster. Her heartbeat quickened as she imagined walking into the Pink Lady and scanning the room. She imagined seeing Jed at a booth. He would look up and their eyes would meet.

Would he be happy to see her? She didn't know how he'd react, but she wanted to make things right with him. Even if he was on duty, she only needed a few minutes with him. She wanted to touch his arm. To say that she was sorry for leaving him out of the loop. To confess that she was coming to him now because she needed him. She needed his smile. His tenderness. His arms to close around her. The comfort of gentle words and featherlight kisses.

Nora never made it inside the diner. She saw Jed through the front window. He was sitting at the counter, working his way through a burger platter and a chocolate shake. Another EMT was on his right. Jed's partner was busy talking to a fireman. As for Jed, he was having an animated conversation with another person in uniform. It wasn't an EMT. It was Deputy Angela Wiggins.

As Nora watched, Jed threw back his head and laughed. Angela joined in, her face turning a pretty pink. Jed said something else and the two of them covered their mouths, as if trying to keep their laughter from bursting out. Then, Angela balled up her napkin and tossed it at Jed. Still smiling, they focused on their food. Jed's dimples showed as he chewed, and Angela's eyes sparkled with merriment. The energy between them crackled like a summer storm.

Nora turned away from the window and came face-to-face with Estella.

"Hey!" Estella exclaimed happily. "Fancy bumping into you. I was just heading to your place. I know you don't like unannounced visitors, but I figured you might give an unannounced visitor bearing tortellini and steamed broccoli a pass."

"I'm really glad to see you," Nora said. She pointed at the takeout bags in Estella's hands. "Where'd you get the pasta?"

"Jack made it. We had a quick meeting about my event during his break. Between you, Sheldon, and Jack, I might pull off this reinvention."

Nora offered to take one of the food bags. "You just needed a push in the right direction."

Estella smiled. "Oh, and I finally got in touch with Mr. Buckley, the teacher I told you about. He's been on a cruise. Missed the whole week of rain. Anyway, he was positive that the red bird at Cherokee Rock is new. Brand-new. He even stopped by to check. He wasn't happy. He kept grumbling about hoodlums and stiffer fines."

Nora shifted her hold on the food bag.

"Should we go inside?" Estella asked. "We can eat at the counter."

"No," Nora cried. Jerking her head toward the window, she said, "Jed's in there and he's kind of mad at me. Besides, he's having a good time with his friends."

Estella peered through the window. "Oh. So he is."

She gestured at the entrance to the memorial garden. "Madam, allow me to show you to your table."

The women shared a bench overlooking the river of stones. Each of the small, smooth stones bore the name of a loved one who'd lost their life to cancer. In the shadowy twilight, the white, gray, or blue stones seemed to ripple.

"Why are you alone while Jed's inside flashing those dimples at that cute deputy?"

Nora told Estella how she hadn't called Jed after someone had thrown a brick through her window. Next, she told her about Micah.

"Poor kid. I never met him. Danny either. I'm really out of the loop." Estella raised her hands. "I'm not trying to make this about me. I'm saying that I've been so wrapped up in my own stuff that I haven't been a very good friend. I'm sorry for being so self-absorbed, and I'm here for you, June, and Hester. All that's good in my life comes from knowing the three of you."

Nora rewarded her with a warm smile.

"You and Jed are at the crossroads." Estella speared tortellini with her fork. "Every couple gets to this place. It happens when other people start asking when you'll met the parents, or move in together, or get married. Jed is probably happy with how things are, but those commitment questions have him second-guessing your relationship."

"We'll never end up at an altar. Jed knows that." Nora chewed a piece of broccoli and wished she had a glass of red wine. "You said '*probably* happy.' You saw him in the diner. That's what his happy looks like, and he's not with me."

Estella put her fork down. "You didn't think to call Jed when you were upset. You reached out to the people you trust. The people who make you feel safe. June, Hester, and me. Not Jed. Something's missing between you two. He knows it, and I think you do too."

Nora shrugged. "Because we're just dating. It's a casual relationship."

"There's no casual after you reach the crossroads. Either you follow the road Jed wants to travel, or you let him go."

"And here I thought you were going to say 'two roads diverged in a yellow wood.'"

Estella grinned. "Frost knew what he was talking about. You can't see what's waiting ahead of you. All you can do is listen to your gut. What does your gut say about your future with Jed?"

"I guess I can add that to my list of worries. That list started with Danny's death, but since then, I've added Patty and Lou, the man in the white T-shirt, the word on June's house, my window, the bird in Hester's mailbox, and now, finding Micah's body." Nora pushed food around. "I haven't even started this week's book pick."

Estella laughed. The sound bounced off the bell hanging above the stone river, creating a soft hum. Both women gazed at the river. As they listened, the hum ebbed and swelled. It was as if the stones had voices and were singing a song to honor the dead.

When the sound faded, Estella took a blank stone from a bucket and handed it to Nora. "Cancer didn't kill Danny, but you could still add his name to the river. It seems like a good place for him. Who wouldn't love the view?"

Nora glanced up. The sky was peppered with stars.

She didn't take the stone, though. If anyone should write Danny's name, it was Marie.

"You're heading to a crossroads too," she said to Estella. "Jack is your friend because that's what you want. But it's not what he wants. He wants all of you. Your whole heart."

Estella's lips curved into a secretive smile. "I know what he wants. He made that very clear. After he told me what he was feeling, he gave me a tin of heart-shaped marshmallows. In that moment, I knew I loved him too."

Nora looked closely at her friend. Her cheeks glowed. Her eyes were shining with joy. "Oh my God, you mean it."

Estella blushed like a teenager and Nora laughed.

"I'm so happy for you. This" — Nora pointed from Estella to the diner — "makes *me* happy. In the middle of all the crap that's been happening, you go and fall in love. And with the nicest guy in town." She gave Estella a puzzled look. "What was in those marshmallows, anyway?"

315

It was Estella's turn to laugh. "In Japan, there's an unofficial holiday called White Day. Women give men gifts on Valentine's Day, and men give women gifts on White Day. The traditional gift is marshmallows. Mine were homemade, of course."

"White Day?" said a familiar voice. "What? White folks don't have enough holidays?"

June stood on the garden path. Hester was a step behind her.

"It's a Japanese holiday," Estella explained. "White stands for purity and happiness."

"Does it now?" June teased.

Opening her voluminous handbag, Estella withdrew a white satin box tied with a pale pink ribbon. "Come here and try one of Jack's marshmallows."

June and Hester each took a sweet, but Nora hesitated. "Are you sure? Jack made these for you. They're special."

"So are you," Estella said before turning to June. "How'd you find us?"

June sniffed her marshmallow, popped it in her mouth, and chewed. After gushing over how good it was, she said, "Jack said that you'd been in the garden earlier. We hoped you'd still be here. And we hoped Nora would be with you. We already looked

316

for her at home."

Estella spread her arms. "Here we are."

Hester finished her treat and smiled at Estella. "Jack definitely loves you. It's not just the heart shape of his marshmallows. He mixed love into them. I can taste it."

Estella responded with a shy smile.

"Lord have mercy. You feel the same," June cried in astonishment.

Hester spoke before Estella could answer. "Who said the words first?"

"I'll tell you if you promise not to ask more questions. I haven't felt this way in a long time, and I want to keep some of these feelings to myself."

After recounting the story she'd shared with Nora, Estella watched June and Hester beam with pleasure.

"Your turn," Estella said to Hester. "You never told us about meeting your dashing deputy's parents. We all know that something happened. What was it?"

Hester shoved her hands into her jeans pockets. "Jasper's mom was talking about her grandson when she suddenly asked me if I liked babies. I wasn't able to put my poker face on in time and she gave me this sweet, concerned look and, boom! I burst into tears. Now Jasper knows that I've been keeping a secret from him. Normal people do not burst into tears because someone mentions babies in the middle of dinner."

"Why haven't you told him?" June asked.

"You know why. Because I love how he looks at me now. If I tell him the truth, he'll look at me like I'm damaged goods. The girl who got knocked up in high school. The girl who's already had a baby. That's how he'll see me."

Estella packed up the takeout containers and stood up. "You're not giving that boy enough credit, Hester. He loves you. He wants you, warts and all."

June squeezed Hester's hand. "I get it. I feel a physical pain every time someone asks if I have kids. What can I say? Yes, I have a son. But I don't know him anymore. I'll love him until I die, but he hates me and never wants to see me again."

Hester turned to her. "Something can still bring you two together. Don't give up."

June's lips quivered. "I won't. Don't you give up either. Be straight with your man. Tell him while you're all snuggled up in bed and he's holding you close."

When Hester didn't reply, Estella's mouth fell open. "You haven't made it to the bedroom, have you?"

Hester's face blazed with color. "I've tried. And Jasper has been so patient. I just freeze up when we get to a certain point. I go all stiff and —"

"*He's* supposed to be stiff, not you," Estella said. "Listen to me, sweetheart. Your past is keeping you from your future. Give yourself permission to kiss your guilt and shame goodbye. Have your man kiss you all over instead."

"You're our resident Dr. Ruth," June said to Estella. "Can you help our girl?"

Estella held out her hand. "Come with me, Hester. I'm going to loan you some goodies."

Hester gulped. "Right now?"

The rest of the women laughed at her stricken expression.

Nora wished this moment could go on and on. There, in the peaceful garden with her friends, she'd been able to forget about death and grief and all the questions that had no answers.

But it was time to go home.

Estella said good night and led Hester out of the garden. June watched them go before focusing on Nora. "Are you going to be okay?"

"Yeah. You?"

June nodded. "I used to think of rain as this purifying element that washed the world clean. Pollen. Dust. Dirt. The water washed it away. But the rain we had? I feel like it brought something with it. Something toxic."

Nora felt the weight of June's words. And the truth of them. So much had changed with those days of endless rain.

"If the rain was toxic, we need to help find the antidote," Nora said. "If we don't, people are going to keep dying."

On her way back to her moped, Nora glanced into the diner. Jed was gone. So was Deputy Wiggins.

Driving through the starlit town, Nora thought about Jed's Curious George living room, and of all the effort he'd put in just to please her.

The moment she was home, she called him.

Jed answered on the third ring, and Nora was immeasurably relieved to hear his voice. "Hey, stranger," she said. "I'm sorry about the other day. I'd really love to see you. If it's okay with you, I'd like to talk about . . . us. Do you feel like coming over?"

There was a pause. It felt interminable to Nora. Holding the phone to her ear, she couldn't help but wonder if Jed had company.

"Yes, I want to come over," he finally said.

As Nora let out the breath she didn't know she'd been holding, Jed asked, "Should I bring anything?"

"Just you," Nora said softly. "You're all I need."

CHAPTER 15

Bookstores remind me that there are good things in this world.

— Vincent van Gogh

Saturday dawned, bringing clear skies and mild temps. Ideal conditions for a sidewalk sale.

Downtown Miracle Springs was festooned in color. Shop stoops featured flowerpots of impatiens and daffodils. Silver pinwheels spun in every pot, refracting the sunlight and throwing rainbows onto the sidewalk. Flags with dogwood tree designs flew from the lampposts. Bouquets of pink, blue, and purple balloons danced in the breeze.

Sheldon met Nora at the bookshop at nine. He was dressed in an old-timey, black-and-white prisoner costume. It took ten minutes and every ounce of his charm to convince Nora to don a matching costume.

"We want to sell tons of books, but we

also want to raise awareness about banned books," he said, smoothing the front of his costume. "Horizontal stripes are not flattering. Ever. But we must make sacrifices for the sake of literature. Climb in your jumpsuit and get ready to do what you do best: matchmake books with readers."

Nora indulged Sheldon because he needed a pick-me-up. Micah's parents had driven up from Atlanta to identify their son's body, and they'd made it clear that they wouldn't leave until his death was thoroughly investigated. Micah's parents were both politicians and they'd placed phone calls to all their influential friends to put a rush on their son's lab tests.

Nora felt sorry for Sheriff McCabe. Between pressure from Micah's parents, Danny's wife, the media, and the locals, he was probably running on fumes.

Plus, there was still the matter of the man in the white T-shirt. The hunt for him had proved fruitless and would likely take a back burner until the department resolved all questions surrounding Micah's death.

Despite her ridiculous jumpsuit, Nora was looking forward to the sidewalk sale. She welcomed the chaos and color of the festival atmosphere. By ten o'clock, the streets were crowded with shoppers. Local organizations like the Scouts, the Masons, and church groups had erected tents in the park. They offered children's games and gave away trinkets or candy.

Folk music tripped out of the grandstand speakers. The merry sounds of fiddles and banjos floated in air scented with fried dough and the sugary sweetness of cotton candy.

Nora's costume and the banned books displayed in the window and on tables along the sidewalk drew a crowd. People stared at the covers and turned to one another in shock. They purchased titles out of loyalty, feeling the need to defend their favorite books, while others wanted to find out for themselves why certain books were contro-versial.

To serve her customers as quickly as pos-sible, Nora raced from the sidewalk to the checkout counter all morning long. Sheldon couldn't help because he was making coffee as fast as he could. With all the book, shelf enhancer, and beverage sales, Nora knew that it was going to be a banner day.

Dashing outside again to man the tables, Nora took a moment to gaze back at her beloved store. She decided to spend some of today's profits repainting the front door and shutters and installing new outdoor lighting.

It was a pleasant respite to imagine how Miracle Books could be improved, but it was even more delightful to spend the morning talking about books, recommending books, and selling books. Each time Nora placed a book in a reader's hand, she felt like she was giving them a door to a magical realm. In her mind, librarians and booksellers were the human equivalents of C. S. Lewis's enchanted wardrobe. They could transport people anywhere, just by handing them the right book.

Lunchtime came and went, and Nora was fantasizing about grabbing some food from inside when a teenage girl with long, lustrous blond hair approached the banned book table. Nora gave her a brief smile before turning to help a customer looking for a copy of *A Wrinkle in Time.*

"My daughter hasn't read this yet," the woman said. "It was one of those books that introduced me to the idea of reading for pleasure. For the first time, I'd found a book about a girl who loved science. I felt like I'd made a new friend. Meg was a nerd, like me. And she was a hero."

The woman laughed, and Nora told her that she completely understood what it felt like to fall in love with a book. "Lots of us have a first book love. We never forget those books. The first book your daughter falls in love with might not be *A Wrinkle in Time.* It's worth a try, but it might be something completely different."

"Probably," the woman said. "I'll be happy just knowing that it's in her room."

After fetching the book, Nora left the woman to browse.

"What's up with the stripes?" asked the blond girl. She was still there, hovering near the end of the first table.

Nora wondered if she'd come by to take advantage of the half-price beverage deal for high school students and faculty. "It's the vintage jail look," she said. "My co-worker thinks it's cooler than *Orange Is the New Black.*"

The girl smiled and ran her fingers over the cover of Robert Cormier's *The Chocolate War.* She seemed like she wanted to ask a question but wasn't sure if she could get the words out. Nora knew she'd either ask her question or walk away. There was nothing to do but wait.

At that moment, a clown rode by on a bicycle. He tooted his horn and waved at the kids. The little dog in his bike basket barked with unrestrained joy.

Nora said, "That dog's cute, but all clowns

make me think of Pennywise."

"That creepy clown from *It*?" the girl asked. At Nora's nod, she kept talking. "The movie was crazy scary. But it was kind of fun being scared."

Nora jerked a thumb at the bookstore. "The book was way scarier."

The girl gestured at the display window. "This is cool and all, but I'm looking for something else. I'm not sure how to . . ." Trailing off, she fidgeted with the row of hair ties on her wrist.

"It's not always easy to figure out what you're looking for," Nora said. "This might help: Think of the last book that stayed on your mind days after you finished reading it."

"*The Hate U Give*," said the girl without a second's hesitation. "I read the book *and* saw the movie. I want another book like that. You know, where a white girl is friends with a girl of color. And sometimes, she doesn't know what to say to that friend. Like, is she insulting her friend without meaning to? Or does she not talk at all because she doesn't want to sound racist? All the weird stuff keeps them from being close friends, which isn't what the girl wants."

"Yeah, there are more stories like that,"

said Nora.

"I just want one for now. I'm pretty busy. But Gabriela and I have been friends since kindergarten, and things have gotten awkward between us. I'm not sure what to do."

Nora tapped her finger against her lower lip as she sorted through a mental catalogue of book titles. "I have an idea," she said. "Follow me."

In the Young Adult section, Nora found a used copy of *I Am Not Your Perfect Mexican Daughter* by Erika Sánchez.

"It doesn't matter if your friend is Mexican or not," Nora said, handing the girl the book. "This could be about any young Latina woman. It could be about anyone your age who's dealing with the expectation to act a certain way because of culture and customs. You'll like the main character. She's sassy. She fights for what she believes in. Even when her family disapproves."

The girl took the book. "I know plenty about that. Disapproving parents come in every color."

Nora had to laugh. "True. But as bad as it might be now, there *will* come a day when you understand each other again. In the future, you might even see your parents as your friends."

"Maybe," the girl said, sounding unconvinced. "You gave my dad some books a while ago. Things have been better." She pulled a credit card from a case attached to her cell phone. "I'm Lily."

"I hope it's okay that I've been using your moped."

Lily rolled her eyes. "I don't know what I was thinking with those pink flowers. Anyway, I don't want it back. I don't want to go back to being the person I was when I rode that thing." She held up the book. "How about a trade? This for a moped."

Nora shook her head, but Lily stuck the book in her bag, said a quick "thanks," and left.

Back on the street, Nora caught a glimpse of shiny blond hair. Lily had her phone pressed to her ear as she jogged over to the park. Lou and Patty passed by her, heading in Nora's direction.

Since she didn't want to be caught staring, Nora began to straighten books on the table. She was incredibly pleased by how many banned books had been purchased so far, and she loved filling in the holes on the table with fresh titles.

By the time everything was nice and neat, Lou and Patty had arrived.

"We said we'd make it to your shop one day," Lou said.

Both women looked tired. Their eyes were puffy and their smiles felt forced. Sadness rolled off their bodies in invisible gray waves.

Nora briefly touched each woman on the arm. "I'm so sorry about Micah."

Tears sprang into Lou's eyes and she glanced away.

"They found drugs in his system," Patty said, a note of anger in her voice. "We don't believe it. We told the sheriff that Micah was obsessed with avoiding chemicals. His food, his soap — everything was organic. He was trying to be as close to nature as possible. There's no way he'd poison himself with drugs."

Nora thought of the compass tattoo on Micah's wrist. "If he wanted to discover something about himself, maybe —"

Lou cut her off. "He wouldn't do it that way. The whole point of his journey was to cleanse himself of the taint of the modern world by escaping into the wilderness. He wasn't looking for a shortcut. He *wanted* to take the long road."

"What drugs were found in his system?"

Patty shook her head in disgust. "Something called GHB. I looked it up online. It's trendy for teens to make their own liquid ecstasy and use it to decrease stress. As a prescription drug, it's used to treat narco-

330

lepsy. It seems obvious to me that if GHB was in Micah's system, someone put it there."

"Deputy Fuentes said that GHB is similar to Rohypnol. But why would Micah deliberately take a date-rape drug? It's ridiculous." Lou waved off the notion. "We don't believe it. His parents don't either. They're adamant about Micah having no history of drug, tobacco, or alcohol use. He always avoided addictive substances. He wouldn't even use aspirin."

"We told the sheriff to search the inn from top to bottom," Patty added wearily. "They even brought in a dog, but they didn't find anything."

Lou pressed her fingers to her temples. "Let's stop talking about this. We came out to try to enjoy the day, remember?"

Patty went inside while Lou moved off to examine the banned books. Nora rang up a customer waiting at the checkout counter. Then, she wandered around the store until she found Patty paging through a book on regional gardening.

"I'd like to restore the inn's rose garden," she said without looking up. "Lou would love that. Especially if I could grow something that looked like Rose Lattimer's rose."

"Speaking of Rose, those candle wax

stains from her journal can be removed. If you're willing to part with it for a few hours, I'll do it for you."

Patty clearly didn't feel like she could accept Nora's offer. "That's really nice of you, but I'd have to ask Lou. She's really protective of anything to do with the inn or the Lattimer family. It's her heritage and her life. I'm just the best friend, happily sharing in her dream."

Nora decided that it was time to be direct. "Do you remember the night of the dinner party? You let me use your bathroom?"

Patty slid the book back into its place on the shelf. "Sure."

"When I was leaving your room, I noticed a piece of pottery with black glaze. Do you know the one I'm talking about?"

"Of course. I would have gone with something more colorful, but Lou said that the potter was local and that his pieces belonged in the inn." With a shrug, she selected another book from the shelf. "Decorating is Lou's forte. I'm all about the food. As long as I have dominion over the kitchen, I'm happy."

"So you didn't know that Danny made that pottery?"

Patty paled. "The man who drowned?"

Whatever secret Lou is keeping, she didn't

332

share it with Patty, Nora thought.

"Yes," Nora answered. "Danny sold his pieces at the flea market."

"That's so sad," Patty said, lowering the book she'd been holding. "His work is beautiful, and now, there won't be anymore."

It hadn't been Nora's intention to bring Patty down. She and Lou were still reeling from Micah's death, but Nora needed to learn how Danny's valuable pottery had ended up in their possession.

"I think Danny will live on forever through his pottery, just like Rose Lattimer will live on in your garden if you can grow her roses. You and Lou are already preserving the past by restoring the inn. You're keeping memories alive."

This earned her a small smile from Patty. "Thank you for saying that. Other than Georgia and Bo, we haven't met many people who understand our vision. Everyone else says that the inn will bleed us dry. But we saved her. She'll take care of us and travelers will rest under her roof."

Patty spoke of the old building as if it was a family member, and Nora liked her for it.

"Did you know that the bird carved into the hidden wall in the library is the same bird Danny etched into the bottom of his pieces?"

Patty gaped. "But he couldn't have seen our bird. The bookshelves covered that secret doorway for decades."

"Maybe someone else in Danny's family saw it. Or even made it. Did Rose mention the bird in her diary?"

Patty hugged the gardening book to her chest. "I'll ask Lou about it, but not now. She's too upset about Micah. I am too."

"Danny's death bothers me just as Micah's death bothers you and Lou," Nora said in a hushed voice. "At first, I wanted to know what happened to Danny to put my own mind at ease, but now I want to help Marie. She's Danny's wife, and she's having a really hard time."

Patty bit her bottom lip to keep her emotions in check. "Find me after work. I'll give you the diary. If it can make sense of any of this madness, we need to share it. Rose would want me to give it to you. She devoted her whole life to helping others."

"Maybe she's not done yet," Nora whispered.

As she passed the Local History section, she caught the faint scent of roses. She paused and took in another breath, but the air smelled of coffee and books. The hint of rose perfume had vanished.

■ ■ ■ ■

After Lou and Patty left, Nora snuck behind the checkout counter to finish the second half of her lunch sandwich. She was too busy eating to notice June setting up a small card table on the sidewalk next to the bookshop's front door.

When the sandwich and a Honeycrisp apple were gone, Nora returned to her outside duties.

She grinned when she saw June. "When did you get here?"

"Twenty minutes ago. Thanks again for letting me have my little pop-up shop for the afternoon," June said, straightening her checkered tablecloth. "Since I knit when I'm stressed or can't sleep, I've been doing a lot of knitting."

The table was covered with June's colorful, scented socks. Their soft fabric begged to be touched and few passersby could resist the urge. A woman ran her hand over a pair of purple, lavender-scented socks and said that she wanted them for herself. She also bought a pair of yellow socks with orange cat faces on the cuff for a friend.

"These smell like a summer in Florida," she said, holding the cat socks to her nose.

June bagged the socks and said, "Oranges, sunshine, and hugs."

The woman smiled. "I love this town. Everyone is so nice. I came here to try the hot springs. The waters are good but other things have made me feel even better. A scone from the bakery. A walk in the woods. The chance to sit and do nothing for a few days."

"And the heart of this magical place is the bookstore! Why not come inside?" Sheldon gestured at the open door.

"Why not?" The woman grinned at Sheldon and practically danced into the shop.

Sheldon gave Nora a nudge. "Time to trade spots. I need vitamin D and some quality time with Ms. June."

Nora was more than happy to get out of the sun. She went straight to the ticket agent's office and drank a big glass of water. She then cruised around the shop, putting away strays, collecting dirty coffee cups, and pointing customers toward their genre of choice.

As she put a book called *Lights to My Siren* back on its shelf in the Romance section, she thought about last night. And about Jed.

Jed had shown up with raspberries and blackberries and a can of whipped topping.

"I brought dessert," he'd said.

The berries were bright as jewels. They'd reminded Nora of the first time she'd wanted to touch Jed. She'd been picking wild berries when he'd suddenly appeared. There, at the edge of the woods, surrounded by fireflies, she'd watched him pluck berries off the bushes and drop them into her basket. She'd watched his lips move as he spoke. She'd wanted to silence them with a kiss.

Last night, she and Jed had talked about that memory.

"You looked like a fairy queen," Jed had said as they sat on Nora's deck. "And you smelled like honeysuckle and blackberries. Whenever I smell either of those things, I think of you."

Over bowls of berries and whipped topping, they'd talked. Nora told Jed that she didn't always know how to convey her feelings to him. Jed had talked about his mom, and how Henry Higgins's training was coming along. He mentioned Deputy Wiggins a few times, but Nora hadn't been jealous. Jed liked and respected Angela, just as Nora liked and respected Grant McCabe.

They'd talked for hours, under a dome of stars, until Nora could no longer hide her yawns.

"Stay with me," she'd told Jed when he

got up to leave.

Jed had stayed. He'd held Nora, lightly rubbing her back or running his fingers through her hair. For the first time since she'd seen Danny in the river, Nora had felt truly comforted. And when she'd woken in the middle of the night to find Jed beside her, she'd curled against him like a cat, seeking warmth from his body. He'd stirred in his sleep and put an arm around her waist. They'd stayed like that until morning.

Nora's memories of last night were interrupted by a soft cry. A young man had dropped his coffee cup. There were shards of ceramic and a puddle of coffee on the floor.

The man headed for the napkin dispenser at the ticket agent's window, but Nora intercepted him.

"I'll get that," Nora said. "I have a rag."

Though the young man offered to pay for the mug, which had a golden crown design and the text BOOK QUEEN, Nora told him not to worry about it. Later, when she rang up his purchases, she noticed that he'd added another book to the pile of paperbacks he'd originally selected.

"I know why you're grinning," June said when she came inside for a bathroom break. "Because you hired Sheldon. I only have four pairs of socks left, and I started with sixty! That man could sell swampland."

"He's the Wizard of Sales."

"A half-Cuban Dumbledore." June's laughter trailed after her as she rounded the corner of the Fiction section.

A few minutes later, she returned to the front and approached the door. The moment she opened it, angry shouts erupted from outside. A man dashed past the sidewalk tables.

This was followed by more shouting. Shrill and urgent. It took a second for Nora to hear words among the cacophony.

"Stop him!"

"He stole the cash box!"

"Get him! That man in the white T-shirt."

Nora's muscles went rigid. She couldn't move.

As the noise outside escalated, she finally made it to the door. She and June stood in the threshold, shoulder to shoulder, watching the man cut through the crowd.

"He just took it and ran!" Sheldon cried, catching sight of June and Nora. "I'm *so* sorry."

There was a commotion farther up the street.

A voice cried, "They got him!"

Nora and June gravitated toward the ring

of people gathered in the middle of the street. They saw two deputies. Andrews was crouched over the man in the white T-shirt. Fuentes was darting glances between the man on the ground and the circle of observers.

"Stay down," Andrews commanded. "Don't make any sudden moves."

Fuentes motioned for the crowd to back away. His eyes kept returning to his partner and the man sprawled in the middle of the street.

"Place your hands on your head," Andrews ordered. "Slowly, now."

Cursing angrily into the pavement, the man complied.

"He stole that lady's cash box," one bystander told another.

Andrews cuffed the man's hands. Then, he and Fuentes hoisted the man in the white T-shirt to his feet. Keeping a firm grip on his arms, the deputies propelled him toward a patrol car.

Nora and June stood directly in their path. Both women were transfixed by their proximity to the man who'd vandalized their property. Who'd tried to color their lives with red paint and fear.

Nora took in the dark stubble covering half of his face, his wild, hate-filled gaze, his dirty clothes, the untied laces of his bedraggled sneakers. She'd never seen the man before.

She turned to June. Her friend's face was shiny with sweat. Her eyes rolled in their sockets and she swayed. Nora grabbed her by the arm and gently lowered her to the ground before she could pass out.

"My baby."

Nora raised her hand to block the sun from landing on June's face. Her skin was a sickly, ashen hue.

"What?" Nora whispered.

June opened her mouth, but nothing came out. She pointed at her throat, as if trying to say that a dam of words was caught there.

She cried. Tears streamed down her cheeks, fast-flowing rivers of agony.

Nora held her friend and looked at the man being herded their way. The man with the venomous stare.

June had called him her baby.

Nora stared at him, her heart banging like a drum as the truth hit her.

The man in the white T-shirt was June's son.

CHAPTER 16

Just as one candle lights another and can light thousands of other candles, so one heart illuminates another heart and can illuminate thousands of other hearts.

— Leo Tolstoy

Nora knelt on the ground with June's head in her lap. She stroked her friend's hair and softly murmured to her.

Suddenly, Jed was there. He knelt beside June and asked, "What happened?"

"She almost fainted. I think she's in shock."

Jed spoke to his partner and together, the two men carried June to a shady spot in the park. After putting her down in the grass under a tree, Jed coaxed her into drinking a little water. His partner put an ice pack on the back of her neck.

June took hold of the ice pack. "You don't have to fuss over me."

"It's an honor to fuss over you," Jed said. "You're going to be my favorite customer today. You're my first patient who didn't eat too many funnel cakes."

The ashy color ebbed from June's face. She looked more like herself.

"I'm better now. I just want to sit for a few minutes."

June leaned back against the tree trunk and stared at the children in the playground. Her eyes were dark with grief.

Nora took June's hand and enfolded it between her own.

Jed closed his kit and stood up. "Leave that ice pack on for a few more minutes and keep hydrating. I'm putting Nurse Nora in charge."

June didn't reply, but Nora mouthed a "thank you."

Jed gave his partner a clap on the back and the two men walked away.

The women sat in their oasis of grass and shade. The noise and endless movement of the crowd didn't seem to reach them.

"Did you know?" Nora asked. "Before today?"

June let out a weary exhalation. "Yeah. When we watched the video at Hester's. I could spend fifty years apart from my boy, and I'd still know him. The way his ears stick out. The shape of his mouth. His long fingers. I saw the way he moved on that video. Like a cat. That easy, slinky stride. It had to be my Tyson. I called him my little black panther when he was a kid."

Nora made June drink more water.

"What does he want?"

"All I know is that he came here, looking for me." June's voice wavered. "My baby's here. In *my* town. He's angry. He's up to no good, but he's *here.* I can *look* at his face. I can *talk* to him."

Nora understood why June hadn't told anyone about recognizing Tyson. She didn't want to miss her chance to connect with her son — a chance she'd been dreaming about for decades.

"I figured he'd get caught, and that was okay," June went on. "If the sheriff brought him in, my son would be off the streets. He'd have a roof over his head and a bed to sleep on. He'd have food. You saw him, Nora. He's too skinny. He's dirty. My boy is lost."

Tyson Dixon was no child. He was a man in his thirties. A man who'd denied his mother's existence and moved to California after she was sued for risking the well-being of her elderly charges by taking them to a carnival.

344

June never stopped reaching out to her son. She sent him money. She sent care packages and letters, but everything came back unopened. She'd even hired a private detective who tracked Tyson to a club in LA where he worked as a bouncer. The club was a popular hangout for drug dealers. June had called the club many times, but Tyson refused to speak to her. Tyson wasn't on social media. He had no address or phone number on record.

He'd gone to California and become a ghost.

June squeezed Nora's hand. "I'm sorry about your window. And the bird in Hester's mailbox. I won't make excuses for my son, but I *need* to see him. I need to help him. I've been waiting a *long* time to make things right with Tyson."

She stopped talking when she saw Deputy Fuentes making his way to their spot in the shade. He dropped into a catcher's stance and offered June her cash box. "Should be all there. The perp didn't get a chance to open it."

"I need to come with you." Ignoring the box, June got to her feet. "That *perp* is my son."

If Fuentes was surprised by the news, he didn't show it. Instead, he straightened and put a steadying hand under June's elbow. June passed the ice pack to Nora.

"I'll meet you after I let Sheldon know what's going on," Nora told her. Water from the melting ice pack ran over the burn scars on her wrist and forearm.

"No." June's tone was firm. "I don't want anyone there. I need to do this alone."

Nora stood under the tree as June and Deputy Fuentes melted into the crowd.

She knew she should hurry back to the shop, but she ended up watching a little boy in the playground. He sat on the top of the slide, looking nervous. Eventually, he let go of the handrails and slid down, right into his mother's arms. She swung him around in a circle. The boy's face was lit with joy. So was his mother's.

June had memories like this from Tyson's childhood. But she'd missed seeing her son grow into a man. She'd missed experiencing his life. She hadn't had the chance to create new memories.

Though Nora didn't expect the meeting between June and her son to go smoothly, she desperately hoped that the long-awaited reunion would allow June to forgive herself. June had been paying for an innocent mistake for years and years. But it was time to let go of the past.

"Did they catch the guy?" Sheldon asked when Nora entered the shop.

"Yeah."

Sheldon fanned himself with a Nora Roberts cover flat. "There's never a dull moment around here."

Nora didn't feel like talking. "You should head home. Today's been crazy."

"I'm going horizontal for the next twenty-four hours. Tomorrow will be all about reading, stuffing my face, and a long, hot bath."

"That sounds like heaven. And you deserve it after today."

Nora wasn't going to wait until tomorrow to read. Tonight, she'd have Rose's diary in her possession, and she refused to sleep until she'd read it cover to cover.

When the sidewalk sale finally showed signs of winding down, Nora sent a text to Hester, asking her to stop by after closing the bakery.

Hester entered the bookstore and dropped into a chair. Her cheeks were pink from exertion and her blond curls were wilder than ever. Her shoes were dusted with flour and she had dried chocolate on her chin.

She rubbed her eyes with the heels of her hands. "Why am I here? I'll be sitting right here in a few hours and I'm dying for a shower."

Nora told Hester about Tyson.

Hester's mouth fell open. "After all this time, he tracked down his mama just to scare her? How could he write that on June's house? And why mess with us?"

"I don't know, but we need to support her however we can."

"Let's postpone our meeting until tomorrow night. We can be waiting here for June when she's ready to talk." Hester touched the chocolate on her chin and grimaced. "Besides, I still haven't finished this week's book."

The sleigh bells banged against the door.

"That's my cue," Hester said to Nora on her way out. "I'll call Estella. Let me know if you hear from June."

By closing time, Nora saw that she was going to need to update her display window. There wasn't enough inventory to replenish all the banned books she and Sheldon had sold. Also, the glass company was repairing the window on Monday, which would ruin the overall effect.

Nora looked at the signs Sheldon had placed behind each banned book.

RELEASED BY A READER.

If those books had been birds, they'd be flying by now.

With visions of books and birds in her

head, Nora drove to the Inn of Mist and Roses.

The inn's front door was ajar, and Nora could hear someone crying inside. The crying was interspersed with soothing tones. Nora recognized Patty's voice. Then Lou's. A man spoke next.

Patty and Lou were with Micah's parents.

Nora didn't want to attract attention, so she quietly slipped into the front hall and looked around. On a narrow table placed under a large mirror, there was the guest registry and a package wrapped in white tissue paper. A note with Nora's name sat on top of the package.

She read the short missive.

Please return this as soon as possible. I won't tell Lou that you have it until tomorrow. Tonight, we're having dinner with Micah's parents.

— Patty

The meaning of the note was clear. Take the book and go. Nora left the inn, noiselessly closing the front door behind her.

As much as she wanted to crack open Rose's diary, Nora needed to check on June and touch base with Jed first. Both calls went straight to voicemail, so Nora left messages for her friend and her boyfriend. She then ate a quick meal of soup and salad.

Normally, she'd eat and read at the same time, but Rose's diary wasn't an ordinary book, and Nora wanted to cradle it in one hand while carefully turning pages with the other.

After wiping off her little café table, she parted the layers of tissue paper. Rose's signature scent drifted into the kitchen.

"We finally meet," Nora said, gingerly opening the cover.

She was completely immersed in Rose Lattimer's world by the end of the first page. Rose's writing style was witty and conversational. She painted a detailed picture of her life as a young, married woman living in a beautiful house near the busiest intersection in town. The Civil War had begun, and her husband was gone, fighting alongside his fellow Southerners. Rose was worried about his safety, but she seemed more concerned about those already wounded in battle and the welfare of her neighbors.

It didn't take long before Rose stopped worrying and sprang into action. She took in the wounded from both sides. Turning her home into a makeshift hospital, she either nursed the men back to health or buried them in the churchyard. Though many shunned Rose for her behavior, others saw it as their Christian duty to help her.

One of the regular volunteers wasn't from Rose's social circle. He was a Cherokee named Chea Sequah. Rose wrote his name once. After that, she referred to him as C. It didn't take many pages for Nora to suspect that Rose had fallen in love with Chea. Rose wrote about C being big and strong. About his long, shiny, raven-colored hair. C was quiet. C was wise. He knew how to bind wounds, make poultices, and ease pain.

Because Rose penned her diary entries before bed, many pages were splotched with candlewax. Rose likely picked off the wax once it had hardened, leaving a pale, circular stain behind.

One night, as she sat at the ladies' writing desk in her bedroom overlooking the garden, Rose wrote an entry that was nearly impossible to read. Half of the page was covered by wax, as if Rose had been interrupted and had abandoned both her diary and the burning candle. Two lines midway down the page had escaped the wax. They read,

Most quiet need, by sun and candle-light,
I love thee purely, as men strive for right.

Nora looked away from Rose's lively script. Where had she seen that sun and candlelight reference before?

The tintype. A ripple of excitement ran through her. "By sun and candle-light" had been written on the back of Rose's portrait — that hypnotizing image of the self-possessed beauty in the white dress.

If Rose's journal was from the same year as her photograph, then it was written in 1862. That meant Rose would have used a quill or dip pen and an inkwell filled with black ink.

Nora had no experience removing wax from pages that weren't typeset. Normally, she'd used an iron and clean brown paper bags to remove chunks of wax, but the diary didn't belong to her. She couldn't risk damaging it just because she wanted to read the rest of the entry.

Getting up from the table, Nora decided to have a cup of tea. She put the kettle on and stared at the blue flames licking at the kettle's base.

In reading Rose Lattimer's diary, Nora had come to know her. Rose was a strong-willed, generous, and courageous young woman. She was also lonely. Her free time, such as it was, was devoted to reading. By and by, she'd fallen in love. The man was referred to only as C, and Rose wrote about him every night. By flickering candlelight, she dreamed of being with him.

C has to be Chea Sequah, Nora thought.

Rose had only mentioned his name toward the beginning of the diary, but she wrote about his midnight-black hair, his strong hands, and his dark, quiet eyes many times.

As the kettle gurgled, Nora wondered why the entry with the line "Most quiet need, by sun and candle-light" was covered in wax. Had a wounded soldier needed Rose during the night? Or had someone else knocked on her door? Had she risen from her chair, her heart fluttering like a hummingbird, to find Chea standing in the hall? Had she invited him in, despite the risks? Had they made love while Rose's candle dripped like a leaky faucet onto her diary page?

When the kettle whistled, Nora poured the steaming water into a mug loaded with a bag of chamomile tea. She took the mug into the living room, opened her laptop, and typed the lines from Rose's entry into the search box.

The first result told her what she wanted to know. The lines were from "How Do I

Love Thee?", a sonnet written by Elizabeth Barrett Browning in 1850. The poem was only vaguely familiar to Nora, so she sipped her tea and read it in its entirety.

It was a poem about a woman deeply in love with a man.

Not your husband, Nora silently spoke to Rose. *He wasn't there. You barely mention him, but C comes up again and again. C is the man you loved by sun and by candlelight.*

Nora knew she was jumping to conclusions, but her theory felt right. Rose Lattimer had fallen in love with Chea Sequah while her husband was away. Though the Colonel had died in battle, the Lattimer line had not. Had Rose been pregnant when he left?

Nora thought of the bird carved into the hidden niche.

"I need to know when Rose's husband died. And when her first child was born," Nora muttered to herself as she returned to the diary.

Believing she'd find the rest of Browning's poem under the wax, she decided to move forward. Turning the stiff, heavy page, she kept reading.

As the nights passed, Rose's prose changed. The dreamy, girlish quality of her descriptions of C matured. They became more intimate. More tender. Her obvious happiness lasted for several weeks. And then, the tone of her entries changed again.

She began to worry about the future in a way she hadn't before. She hinted at changes. And of the need for deception.

The last page mentioned her leaving Miracle Springs to visit her husband. Though apprehensive about their reunion, she wrote that it was necessary. She believed all would be well upon her return and that she would be able to put her worries aside.

Her diary ended prematurely because someone had ripped out the final entries.

The missing pages raised several questions. Had Rose seen her husband before he died? Had her plans, whatever they were, fallen into place? Or had they failed?

Nora ran her fingertips over the ragged ruffle of paper left from the tearing of the pages and considered the meaning behind Rose's fatigue and her sudden aversion to certain foods and smells. "Changes. Deception. Necessity. Were you pregnant?"

The book had no more to say.

Nora was about to close the back cover when she noticed that the hinge had come loose. It had probably been damaged when the pages were torn out.

"I can fix that," she told the diary.

Nora gathered her book repair supplies from a cabinet built into the wall between the kitchen and the living room. Normally, she'd repair a broken hinge with binder tape. For old or valuable books, however, she kept a small supply of Japanese paper and PVA mix on hand.

It took love and skill to repair a broken book, and Nora prepared her workspace with care. Like Lou and Patty, she'd become attached to Rose after reading her diary. Nora admired the intrepid young woman. Rose had disregarded politics and propriety to help people. Her charitable spirit meant more to her than her reputation. It couldn't have made her life easy, but she stuck to her guns and assisted soldiers on both sides of the war.

Now, it was Nora's turn to help.

Her first task was to remove the old adhesive from the spine. As she was about to begin this task, she noticed a thick ripple in the endpaper. Where the endpaper met the hinge was a gap, and something poked out from the gap. Nora leaned closer to the diary. Was it a thread? A piece of twine?

Picking up her tweezers, she withdrew the object. The moment it was freed, Nora let out a gasp of revulsion and dropped it.

Laughing at herself for being spooked by

a lock of hair, she grabbed a magnifying glass and studied it. The lock was very small and had been tied with a thin pink ribbon. The hair was short, wisp-fine, and black. It looked too delicate to belong to an adult.

"A baby," Nora breathed.

She got up from the table. She needed to move. She needed fresh air. She needed to think.

Throwing on a sweatshirt and sneakers, Nora went outside and began to walk. Her thoughts swarmed around her head like gnats.

Danny in the river. Danny's pottery at the inn. Cherokee Danny. The red bird at Cherokee Rock. The red bird on Danny's pots. The red bird in the wall at the inn. Rose's lover was a Cherokee.

Was the bird a love note? An invitation for Rose's lover to climb the ladder to her bedroom? Had C knocked on her closet door, stepped into her room, and kissed her? Had he and Rose been too caught up in discovering each other to notice the candle burning, to see the wax pooling on the pages? Whose lock of hair had been hidden in Rose's diary?

For days, Nora had believed that there was a connection between Danny Amo-adawehi and the Inn of Mist and Roses. Rose Lat-

357

timer had been trying to tell her as much. She'd sent her sweet, sickly rose perfume into the air, but Nora had failed to translate her message.

She still couldn't decipher it. She was still missing key elements.

She walked to Miracle Books and looked in the window. The ceiling lights illuminated the empty spaces where the banned books had once sat. The tape covering the hole in the glass shimmered like a mirage.

Turning away, Nora walked on.

She crossed the street and entered the park. Evidence of the day's events still remained. Barricades and signs. A scattering of trash. But it was quiet. This was unusual on a mild Saturday night in April, but Nora was grateful for the tranquility.

She sat on a bench and wondered how June was doing. She sent her friend a text even though she didn't expect a reply. Estella and Hester were likely relaxing after the long and tiring day, and Nora didn't want to bother them with her disordered theories. She would see her friends tomorrow. Everything could wait until then.

Her phone sat in her hand. The screen glowed, as if waiting for her fingers to make contact. She ignored it, gazing out at nothing until the screen went dark again. In the distance, she heard the lonesome whistle of a train.

The grass around the bench was wet with dew. A paper cone sat on the ground at the base of a trash can. There were still a few threads of cotton candy stuck to the cone. The spun sugar glittered in the lamplight. Nora heard a rustling overhead. She raised her eyes to see a cloud of bats flying toward the gazebo.

Nora glanced back down at her phone. She pulled up her Safari app and typed "Chea Sequah" into the tiny search box. The first hit was a pronunciation guide. Nora clicked on the link and heard a man's voice. He said, "Chee-ah-seh-kwah." She replayed the audio file and spoke the name out loud. It was a good name. A strong and powerful name.

Returning to the search results, she found a link to a Chea Sequah on Facebook. The second hit led to another social media site. The third hit was a site of baby names and meanings. Nora clicked on it.

She was redirected to a preview page on Google Books featuring a book on baby names. Nora was thrilled to see Chea Sequah listed in the glossary. Unfortunately, the page with that name wasn't included in the preview.

Returning to the search results, Nora clicked on another baby name site. This time, she was taken directly to a page listing the name's origins (Native American) and its gender (male). The last line explained the meaning.

Nora read it again and again, her eyes swimming with tears.

"Chea Sequah," she whispered into the quiet night. "Red Bird."

Chapter 17

Memory is the diary that we all carry with us.

— Oscar Wilde

The sun had barely risen over the green hills when June sent a group text asking her friends to meet at her house at noon. Because her morning would be divided between church and a visit to the county jail, lunch would be simple fare.

Nora replied that she'd be there and turned back to the Sunday paper. She'd already circled several yard sale ads and planned to be among the first shoppers at each address. After hitting the yard sales, she'd check out the flea market. She also needed to return Rose's diary.

Pulling on a semi-clean pair of jeans and a Dr Pepper T-shirt, she parted her hair down the middle and wove it into two French braids. This hairstyle worked well with her moped helmet.

The first few yard sales were a bust, but the last one was a gold mine. Nora found a seventy-fifth anniversary box set of Nancy Drew books in excellent condition and a handful of vintage Enid Blyton Famous Five novels. Nora had a special affinity for Blyton's books. As a girl, she'd wanted to be like those fictional children. She'd longed to roam the countryside searching for smuggler hideouts, cook meals over a campfire, and spend the majority of her time without adult supervision.

"I'm downsizing," the woman told Nora. "It's hard to let these go, but I have to do it."

"They'll be adopted by new readers. I hope that makes it easier to part with them."

The woman smiled. "I've been in your shop, so I know they're going to a good place. I have more boxes inside. They were too heavy for me to lift, but you're welcome to look through them."

Nora ended up making several trips from the woman's house to Miracle Books. In addition to the Nancy Drew and Enid Blyton novels, Nora bought a Beatrix Potter set in its original shrink wrap, a collection of American Girl books, the Little House series in pristine condition, a handful of

Sharon Draper's clubhouse mysteries, and several unread Erin Hunter Warrior books. The woman was so pleased by her sales that she gave Nora a dozen Golden Books for free.

The successful shopping trip would plump up the bookstore's diminished inventory, which was good. Even better, Nora had been able to dwell on her favorite subject: books. For two precious hours, she hadn't thought about Danny, Micah, red birds, or any of the people connected to the Inn of Mist and Roses.

After unloading her moped basket for the final time, Nora drove to the flea market.

She couldn't enter the big barn without thinking of Danny. Memories of their one and only meeting replayed in Nora's mind as she walked up the first aisle. Nothing caught her eye and she turned down the second aisle. She stopped short when she saw Marie at the booth she used to share with her husband.

There was no pottery on display, only Marie's baskets and a selection of loom-woven blankets. Marie sat in a folding chair, her face buried in a book. Nora was happy to see that she was reading one of the titles from her kindness tote.

"Hey, Marie."

Marie looked up, saw Nora, and became instantly animated.

"I was hoping you'd come today," she said, dropping her book on a table. "I found something. Can you come around back?"

Nora didn't have to be asked twice. She hurried around the end table, taking care not to bang into the beautiful baskets or the display of beaded jewelry. "Is all of this yours?"

Marie followed Nora's gaze. "No. I got in touch with two Cherokee artisans who've been looking for a place to sell their stuff. They're both women around my age with kids. We're going to try splitting shifts. We're hoping to earn a little money on the weekends."

Nora was proud of Marie. It must have taken a gargantuan effort to reach out to those women in the midst of her grief.

"Sounds like a great idea." Nora gave Marie an encouraging smile.

Marie touched her belly. "I need to earn a living. The money in the bank won't last forever. I have to try. I have to be what this baby needs me to be. I'm eating. I started reading the books you gave me. And I looked through Danny's memory boxes. That's what he called his two old suitcases stuffed with papers and pictures."

She moved around the booth, searching for something. When she looked under the table in the center of the booth, she found her purse sitting on top of a cardboard box. Next to her purse was a padded envelope.

"Lots of things in Danny's memory box were from before we were married. I never saw them. Like this old poetry book. It was in a leather bag. I think it's a saddlebag. Along with this." She opened the envelope and took out a lump of stone. It was gray with veins of white. When Marie flattened her palm, Nora realized that it wasn't just a stone, but a carved animal effigy. Of a bird. A bird made of stone.

Nora's fingers stretched out. She yearned to touch the stone. "What is it?"

"An old Cherokee pipe," Marie said, handing it to Nora. "Made of soapstone. I thought it might be tied to the red bird name, so I asked Danny's mom about it. This pipe was her grandmother's, and it's been passed down from generation to generation, just like the Red Bird nickname. Always to a girl. Danny didn't have a sister, so his mom gave him the saddlebag. I guess he put it in his memory box and forgot about it."

Nora turned the pipe over. The sculpture, though primitive, was undeniably charming.

From the proud jut of the bird's breast to the curve of its beak, it was full of personality.

"Sweet and strong," Marie said. "Like the red bird from the Cherokee story."

Nora had been thinking the same thing. She looked at the stone pipe and thought of the red bird's kindness, of how he'd come to the wolf's aid when no other animal would.

"It feels good to hold," she said, reluctantly giving the pipe back.

Marie proffered the poetry book next. The small, delicate volume in crimson leather and gilt had patterned boards and endpapers. Brown spots marred some of the pages, but most were clean. The book was beautiful and quite rare. All this time, Danny had been in possession of a very old, very valuable copy of *Sonnets from the Portuguese* by Elizabeth Barrett Browning.

"This is in incredible shape."

Marie shrugged. "I think it was wrapped in a baby's gown. One of those fancy white christening gowns. It's mostly yellow now, especially the lacy parts. I think it's as old as the saddlebag." She stared at Nora. "Can you tell me what these things mean?"

It felt surreal to Nora to be in the middle of the flea market, surrounded by the din of shoppers and the aromas of buttered popcorn and candied nuts, knowing that the most valuable treasure in the building was in her hands.

"I believe Rose Lattimer fell in love with one of Danny's relatives. A Cherokee man living near Miracle Springs during the Civil War." Nora tapped on the book's cover. "I also believe that a poem from this book was *their* poem. Couples have *their* song, but Rose and Chea Sequah had this poem. Chea Sequah means 'red bird.' "

Marie smiled a small, sad smile. "That's romantic. And impossible. A white woman couldn't fall in love with a Cherokee, and a Cherokee wouldn't dare look twice at a white woman. Today's Cherokee deal with discrimination all the time, but nothing like they faced back then."

"Theirs was a secret relationship for many reasons. Rose was also married. Her husband, who was almost twenty years her senior, left Miracle Springs to fight in the war. I can't say this for sure because I don't know the genealogy of the Lattimer family, but I believe Rose had a baby *after* her husband left."

Marie's eyes widened. "Red Bird's baby?"

"These are just theories. I'm going to spend the rest of the day researching the family and the house. I'll let you know what I find. In the meantime, I can tell you this. That poetry book is worth some money. I'll look up its value and give you an estimate but handle it with care."

"Okay." Marie put the book back into the envelope. As for the pipe, she curled her fingers around it and held it close to her chest.

Nora hated to leave her alone in the booth, but she had to finish her shopping if she wanted to be at June's by noon. She thanked Marie for looking through Danny's memory box and suggested that she share their conversation with Sheriff McCabe.

At Beatrice's booth, Nora found a stack of Shaker boxes, a cast-iron bulldog door-stop, a posy vase in green glass, an art deco dressing mirror, and a Victorian bride's basket.

"I saw you talkin' to Marie," Beatrice said as she wrapped Nora's purchases. "How's she doin'?"

"She's tough," Nora said. "But I wish she didn't have to be. She has a long road ahead of her."

"All the dealers took up a collection for her. Word has it she's pregnant. I hope she'll move to town before the baby's born. We'll help her out. That's what the folks in this

368

town do. We take care of people."

Beatrice's words resonated with Nora. By the time she showed up at June's with her laptop case and a bouquet of gerbera daisies, her determination to figure out what happened to Danny was stronger than ever.

But it wasn't stronger than her concern for June.

Nora knocked on the front door and heard June call out, "Come in!"

She was in the kitchen, arranging sandwiches on a platter. Nora gave her the flowers and a big hug.

"Grab that iced tea, would you?" June gestured at a pitcher on the counter. "I thought we'd eat on the back porch."

Hester and Estella arrived a few minutes later. They both hugged June and sat down, waiting for her to speak.

"Yesterday was a helluva day," she began. "I've been dreaming of seeing my son for almost twenty years. *Twenty years.* And when I finally got to see him — to talk to him — he had nothing to say."

Hester and Estella exchanged worried looks. Nora kept her gaze on June.

"The sheriff finally got him talking. I'm grateful to him for that." June put her hands together as if in prayer. "Tyson's in serious trouble. He came here looking for money.

369

Not a few hundred dollars. Not even a thousand. Big money. Because he's in big trouble. The kind you get when you screw over a drug lord."

June's friends stared at her in astonishment.

After the moment passed, Hester said, "You've tried to send him money in the past. If he needed it so badly, why didn't he just take it?"

June spread her hands. "Because he never read my letters, he didn't know that I've been putting money aside for him. He remembered the name of the town on my letters and used every penny he had to catch a Greyhound to Charlotte. He hitched the rest of the way here. He didn't have a plan. Rage and fear pushed him on. And the drugs. He had those too. He's been using for a long time. They've taken over his life."

"Is that why he did that to your house?" Estella asked.

"Partially," said June. "He's still mad at me. I think the drugs helped him hold on to his anger. He hasn't tried to let it go. My son has been in a fog for half of his life. I don't know what's left of the boy I raised under all that mess, but I need to find out." She glanced at her friends. "I can't do that without your help."

Hester started to speak, but June held up a warning finger. "This isn't easy, but I'm asking you and Nora to refuse to press charges against Tyson. I need to get him in a treatment facility as soon as possible. I have to . . ." Her throat closed around the rest of her words.

"We'll do whatever you ask," Nora said, reaching over to take June's hand. "Whatever it takes."

June squeezed Nora's hand before turning to Hester. "Your man won't be happy about this. He wants Tyson to pay for scaring you."

"I *was* scared, but I'm not anymore," said Hester. "Don't worry about Jasper. He'll come around."

"I know how you could get him to come around." Estella gave Hester a playful nudge.

The women laughed.

"Lord, I needed that," June said. "Life has been way too serious lately. Go on. Dig in."

She passed the sandwich platter to Nora and a bowl of fruit salad to Estella. She then poured glasses of iced tea, humming softly all the while. Her face was full of hope. She looked ten years younger. Nora smiled at her. June responded by giving Nora's arm an affectionate pat.

Hester speared a strawberry on her fork

and pointed the fruit at Estella. "You always want me to talk about my man, but what about you and Jack?"

"There's nothing to tell because we haven't done anything." Estella's eyes glittered. "Jack is courting me like the gentleman he is. We've kissed, but that's all. He wants to get to know me without the physical stuff getting in the way, and I feel the same. For once, I want to take it slow. I want every second to be stamped in my memory."

Nora raised her glass. "Here's to believing that good things come to those who wait. To June and Tyson, and to Estella and Jack."

Estella knocked her glass against June's.

As the meal progressed, Nora was content to listen to the music of her friends' voices. They floated into the air, light as balloons, now that they knew June was okay. As for June, her voice was as warm as a midday sun. Her son had finally returned to her. He needed her help. It didn't matter that they'd been estranged for years. It didn't matter that he'd painted her house with anger. It didn't matter than he was an addict. Tyson was her son — the boy she'd been missing with her whole heart. And her boy was here now. Her prayers had been answered.

Nora was happy for June. Happier than she could express. But the happiness she felt was tinged with sadness because she couldn't help thinking about Micah's parents. They'd lost their son forever. And Danny's child would never know him. These truths bothered Nora. They dimmed what should have been a bright, celebratory moment.

"Nora?"

"Sorry," she said, seeing that her friends were staring at her. "Did I miss something?"

"We were saying that we're worried about you." June jerked her thumb toward the house. "There's a reason you brought that laptop, and I'm guessing that it's not because you want to show us cat videos."

Estella grinned at June. "You could be a YouTube sensation. The Pied Kitty Piper of Miracle Springs. You could get tons of free products."

"Like what? Cans of Fancy Feast?" June threw a grape at Estella. "Do you want to talk about those damn cats, or do you want to let Nora answer my question?"

With a coy wink, Estella popped the grape into her mouth.

"I need research help," Nora said. "Which is why I have my laptop. Between that and your computer, June, we could run multiple searches at once. If we can't find all the answers online, I'll visit the archives in the town hall basement tomorrow."

Hester made a time-out gesture. "What's this about?"

"Danny. Possibly Micah. The Inn of Mist and Roses. Lou." Nora touched the soft petal of a pink gerbera daisy. "I think it all began as a story of forbidden love. What I don't know is how the story ended."

"Endings are important," said Estella. She was leaning forward, eager to hear more. "Haven't you read a book that was incredible until the end? When it falls flat, you're so disappointed. That last scene, those last lines — they have to be just right."

Hester glanced at Nora. "Maybe we're supposed to make sure this story has the right ending."

Nora looked at each of her friends in turn. She was lucky to have them in her life, and after she swallowed the lump in her throat, she told them as much.

The tender moment was cut short by the appearance of a large orange tomcat with a torn ear. His pink nose quivered as he caught the scent of food. Hester cooed at him while Estella tossed a piece of ham into the grass.

"Don't encourage the beast," June protested.

The tom purred and rubbed his body across June's shins. She grunted in annoyance but gave him a bowl of egg salad.

"Don't tell your friends," she whispered. He purred even louder.

After the tom gulped down his food, he found a square of sunlight and began what was sure to be a lengthy bathing process. The four friends left him to it and went inside to clean up their lunch things. When they were done, they followed June into the living room.

June and Hester volunteered to research the Inn of Mist and Roses. Nora asked them to dig around the Madison County property records database and to take notes on sale dates, owner names, tax records, and anything else they could find on the building's history.

Nora wanted to focus on the genealogy of the Lattimer family, starting with Rose's husband, the Colonel. Since Estella had a smartphone with an oversized screen, Nora asked her to read up on the history of the Eastern Band of the Cherokee Tribe, especially those members living near Miracle Springs in the 1860s.

"I guess we're tabling our book discussion

until next week," Hester said, pointing at the copy of *An American Marriage* by Tayari Jones on June's desk.

June glanced at the book. "It was definitely well written, but I'm not in the mood to talk about a black man behind bars."

The rest of the women murmured in agreement and got to work.

Nora was good at researching the past. During her tenure as a librarian, she'd helped lots of patrons locate family records. Most states had online genealogical databases that were divided into county databases. Madison County was no exception. Not only did Nora find records on the Lattimers, but she also came across an article about the time the Lattimer House had served as a makeshift hospital during the Civil War.

As she read everything she could find on the family, Nora thought about Lou. Lou was interested in genealogy. When she was a girl, Lou had come to Miracle Springs with a sick grandmother. Lou's dream had been to buy Lattimer House and turn it into an inn. Lou was a Lattimer. Lou had read Rose's diary, which meant she knew the meaning behind the red bird carved into the inn's wall. What other family secrets could Lou be keeping?

The afternoon wore on. The four women read, took notes, and occasionally shared a discovery. For example, Estella said, "The Eastern Band of Cherokees had to go into hiding to avoid being rounded up by the government. The feds were going to send all the Cherokee West. I'm talking about the Trail of Tears here. The Cherokee that hid from the feds didn't become legal citizens of North Carolina until the 1860s. Things couldn't have been easy for Rose's lover. *If* he was her lover."

"He was," Nora said. "Rose's husband was wounded in battle. She traveled to a field hospital in Virginia to see him, un-doubtedly hoping to fool people back in Miracle Springs into believing that she got pregnant during this visit. But there's no way. Her daughter was born six months after the Colonel's death."

June swiveled in her chair to face Nora. "She could have been a preemie."

"I doubt she would have survived. Rose named her baby Ava Claire Lattimer. Ava is Latin for 'bird.' I'd bet the bookstore that her father was Chea Sequah. Red Bird."

Hester held up a pencil. "I found part of Rose's will online. She left the house and all the property to her daughter, Ava Winston. I assume Ava got married."

Nora consulted her notes. "Yes. Rose's daughter, Ava, married James Winston."

"What's interesting about the records is that the deed is in Ava's name," Hester said. "Just hers. Ava Lattimer Winston."

Estella lowered her phone. "Nineteenth-century female empowerment? Who got the house next?"

Hester ran a finger down her notebook page. "Claire L. Cecil.

"Ava and James had four children," said Nora. "Three boys and a girl named Claire. Claire married John Cecil. It looks like the house was passed down to the daughters of the family. Hester, can you search for a document that says as much?"

"I can tell you that Lou and Patty didn't buy the house from the Cecils," June said. "I've been clicking on tax records, and it looks like the Cecils got behind on theirs. They didn't pay for three years and ended up borrowing against the house. Some company called Glenn Development LLC offered to buy out the loan. John Cecil signed the paperwork."

Nora stared at the names she'd written on her notepad. "Hold on. Was John's name on the original deed? Up to this point, the house has been passed down to Lattimer women and only women."

"Which is what Rose wanted," Hester added firmly. "The ladies were the only legal owners of the house. Their husband's names were never added to the deed."

Nora tried to absorb everything she'd heard so far. Had Rose written her will to protect Ava and her future children? Had she wanted to be sure that Ava enjoyed the same freedoms she'd known as the mistress of Lattimer House?

"We need to find out if John Cecil had a legal right to sell the house," Hester said with feeling. "It's not just a house. I mean, it's gorgeous and historical and all, but it's not worth that much on its own. But the *land.* The original parcel goes behind the house and just *keeps* going. We're talking about a stretch of land that leads from the business district to the Meadows. Once the Meadows sells out, the land will be worth its weight in gold."

Estella stared at her. "Yeah, a development that big can support a few strip malls. A grocery store. A new elementary school. That land is the future of our suburban sprawl."

"We're making Neil Armstrong–sized leaps," June said. "Lord knows we have reason to distrust real estate folks after last year's fraud case involving the Meadows and our crooked bank, but that doesn't mean this LLC is bent, or that John Cecil is a bad guy."

"We'll see." Estella picked up her phone and fired away at the tiny keypad. "Glenn Development, eh?"

The other women watched her for a moment. When it was clear that her research wasn't going to produce immediate results, Hester asked Nora, "Did the Cecils have kids?"

"No."

"You know, we can use that ancestry site to search for Rose's complete will," Hester said. "We'll have to pay a fee to access the database, and there's no guarantee that it'll tell us anything useful. Her will was written so long ago that it can't be relevant now. Can it?"

Estella stopped looking at her phone. "I have a client who came in for a cut and color two weeks ago. While she was processing, she told me about a trust that's been in her family for two centuries. Oh, what was it called?" She snapped her fingers. "A dynasty trust. My client's family has a vacation home they can't sell because of this trust. They have to pass the home to their kids, even though nobody wants it."

"I'll pay the fee for that ancestry site,"

Nora told Hester, and dug her credit card out of her purse. "Let's see what Rose planned for her descendants."

Rose's will was very thorough. It contained a specific inventory of items, a list of beneficiaries, and a separate trust stipulating that the Lattimer property was to be passed down to a female Lattimer in perpetuum. The current female owner could sell it only if she was of sound mind and body.

Hester printed the will and handed the stack of papers to Nora. "Since Claire Cecil didn't have kids, who would have inherited the house if it hadn't been sold?"

Nora rubbed her temples. "I need to make some kind of chart. Ava had three sons. Those sons moved away and had a bunch of kids. Their kids had more kids. There could be a dozen female heirs by now. Including Lou."

June waved her hands in frustration. "Hello? Are you forgetting about the other branch of this tree? The non-white branch? If Ava is half Cherokee, and Danny is one of her descendants, then you've got more potential female heirs."

Danny.

Nora was transported back to that moment on the bridge. She saw Danny's body in the river. That image dissolved to be replaced by the memory of Marie sliding a protective hand over her belly. Finally, Nora saw Lou, tenderly running her fingers over the inn's mantel.

Had Lou killed Danny to keep his children from claiming their birthright? Had she killed Micah because he knew what she'd done?

"We have lots of information. And theories," Nora said. "But we have no concrete evidence against Lou or anyone else." She indicated their collective notes. "Hester, can you and Estella take all this to the station and explain it to the sheriff? He can decide what to make of it. In the meantime, June and I can stop by the inn. I need to return Rose's diary and June made socks for Micah's parents, so we have a reason to swing by."

Estella shot her a dubious glance. "Are you going to bring up Danny's name while you're there? Because that doesn't sound smart. Lou could be dangerous."

"Patty too," Nora agreed. "But what can they do? Bludgeon us with candlesticks in front of Sheldon, Micah's parents, and the Gentrys? Don't worry, I'm not going to mention Danny. I'm going to set a trap. After it's set, I'll tell McCabe about it."

Estella folded her arms across her chest.

"What's the bait?"

Nora smiled. "Something you see every day."

"A dwindling bank account?"

Nora touched the end of her braid. "A lock of hair."

CHAPTER 18

We need to haunt the house of history and listen anew to the ancestors' wisdom.

— Maya Angelou

There were no workmen at the inn. The rocking chairs on the front porch were vacant. No one moved about the yard. The place had a somnolent feel that gave Nora pause.

She thought of Micah's parents. Of their grief. Hoping she wasn't about to disturb them, she rang the doorbell.

June put a hand on her shoulder and whispered, "You got this."

Nora smiled at her friend. June's touch bolstered her resolve. She wasn't afraid of being hurt. She was afraid of discovering that Lou and Patty were killers. It was a discovery she didn't want to make, but here she was, preparing to trick them into a confession.

Patty answered the door. Her blue and purple curls were wild. Her face was puffy from lack of rest.

"I hope this isn't a bad time," said Nora. "I wanted to return the diary and June has a gift for the Fosters." Nora quickly introduced June to Patty.

Patty opened the door wider. "I was about to make some tea. Would you like a cup?"

Nora and June accepted the offer with a unified murmur of thanks.

As they walked down the hallway toward the kitchen, Nora asked Patty about the suitcases at the bottom of the stairs.

"The Gentrys are checking out," said Patty. "They would have left earlier, but they stayed a little longer because of . . . Micah. They've been so nice to us. And to the Fosters. We'll be sorry to see them go. At least, we still have Sheldon."

"He might be here until you open for bookings in June. It'll take him some time to find a house."

Patty filled an electric kettle and told Nora how thrilled she and Lou had been when Sheldon said that he'd decided to make Miracle Springs his home.

"If you hadn't hired him, we would have made up a position for him. It would break our hearts to see him leave, especially after losing Micah."

June made a sympathetic noise. "This inn is more intimate than a big hotel. I can see how you'd get attached to your guests."

Turning on the kettle, Patty said, "I don't think we'll ever forget our first guests. The rain brought them to us. Stuck inside together, we bonded pretty fast. And even though Micah spent lots of time in his room, he would seek out Lou or me and pitch in with whatever project we were working on. He'd paint, clean, do yard work. Sheldon's our resident comedian and our shoulder to cry on, and the Gentrys have supported everyone with kind words and little treats. They gave us this tea the other day after I told them about the garden I was planning for Lou."

Nora took the tin from Patty. "Rose Petal tea? I've never had it."

"It's supposed to help you sleep," said June. "Didn't work for me, but nothing does. I have to get outside and move. That's the only thing that'll give me a few more hours of z's."

Patty's face brightened. "Are you the Cat Lady?"

"Thank you for not adding 'crazy' to that title." June spread her hands. "Yeah, that's me. It's not a role I auditioned for. The cats are the crazy ones, not me."

"I want to get a cat, but Lou's worried that our guests could have allergies or a general aversion to cats." Patty reclaimed the tea tin and scooped loose tea into a strainer. "Honestly, I can't imagine cooking breakfast for anyone who hates cats. I don't understand people who hate animals. Any animal. It's an automatic strike against them in my book."

June told Patty the story of how she'd inherited a herd of cats. Next, they spoke of sleep remedies. Nora didn't have much to contribute to either conversation, so she placed Rose's diary on the kitchen table and listened to the other women talk.

As the kettle came to a boil, Patty pointed at the old book.

"Lou's in her room. Do you want to take that to her? I could put your tea in a pot and give you a tray. It's definitely cookie time too. There's no sense in having tea without a cookie."

This woman cannot be a killer, Nora thought.

But she'd come to the inn to shake things up, and no matter how much she liked Patty and Lou, she had to follow through with her plan. For Marie's sake.

Though the tray Patty gave Nora had two

handles and was easy to carry, she had no idea how to keep it balanced and knock on Lou's door at the same time.

What would a Julian Fellowes butler do?

Improvising, she thumped the door with her elbow and said, "Lou? It's Mr. Carson."

Lou opened the door and laughed. "Well done. I'll keep you in mind if we ever offer room service."

Glancing down at the tray, Lou saw Rose's diary. Her face drained of all color.

Without looking at Nora, she pointed down the hall. "The last room on the right is a temporary storage room, but there are two chairs and a little table facing the window. It's a pretty spot."

Nora followed Lou to the room in question. Lou didn't close the door behind them. Instead, she hurried to clear papers from the small table. She then took the tea tray from Nora and carefully set it down.

"Oh, Patty made shortbread. My favorite." Lou poured the tea.

Nora took her cup and brought it to her nose. The steam carried a faint scent of roses. "I've never had rose tea before, but it seems perfect for this room. A hundred years ago, we would have been looking down on Rose's garden, right?"

Lou's eyes strayed to the diary. "Patty told

me that she sent that home with you. I guess you know Rose's secret now."

"And yours."

Nora didn't know who was more stunned by her comment, her or Lou. It had just slipped out.

"Having Cherokee blood isn't something I need to hide," Lou said in a conversational tone.

"No, it's something to celebrate. Is that why you bought Danny's pottery?"

Lou picked up a shortbread cookie. She broke off a corner with her fingers and popped the piece into her mouth. After a sip of tea, Lou leaned back in her chair and sighed.

"I lied to you about that," she said. "The night you asked if I'd met Danny and I told you I'd never heard of him? That wasn't true. I met him in the flea market, but I knew who he was long before then. My son gave me one of those DNA test kits for my birthday a few years ago, and when I saw the results, I was floored. And fascinated. I started searching genealogical records to learn more about my colorful roots. Finding that" — she pointed at the diary — "confirmed my hunch that Danny and I were cousins."

"Did you tell him?"

"I never got the chance." Lou shook her head with regret. "We only talked twice. The first time was at the flea market. The second time was here. He brought me the blackware and I wrote him a check. I wanted to tell Danny about our connection, but it wasn't the right time."

Nora glanced at the unopened moving boxes stacked against the wall. "Are you a pottery collector? Or did you just want Danny's pieces?"

"I've never bought a piece of pottery in my life," said Lou. "But I felt guilty. This house could have belonged to Danny's mother or grandmother. Instead, it was sold. I was lucky enough to buy it, but I knew I couldn't be happy here without making amends to the Cherokee side of my family tree. Rose never married Chea, but he was the real patriarch of my family."

"Did you know about him before you read her diary?"

"I've been wondering about Chea Sequah for a long time. Right before she passed away, my mother gave me a painting of a handsome Cherokee man. I'd never seen the painting before. It had been wrapped up and stored in some closet for years. Anyway, Rose was the artist. I decided to update the frame, which is how I saw the poetry couplet written on the back of the canvas."

Nora remembered Rose's portrait. " 'By sun and candlelight, I love thee purely.' "

Lou's smile was brilliant. "Yes. That was part of the couplet. The important part."

"What did Danny say when he learned that you two were related?"

"That's just it. I never got the chance to tell him." Lou's hand started shaking. A trickle of pale brown liquid sloshed over the rim of her teacup, across her saucer, and onto her jeans. Lou frowned at the spot and kept talking. "Danny came over with five pieces of blackware. I bought them all, using money budgeted for renovations. I asked if he wanted to stay for coffee, but he was in a hurry. He was planning to cook a surprise dinner for Marie. I didn't want to tell him about our connection when he was rushed and distracted, so I asked if he had more pieces of art pottery. He said that he had a few boxes, and I told him that I wanted to buy every piece. I asked him to deliver them to the inn the following Sunday."

Nora remembered what Beatrice had said. "Danny told another flea market vendor that a stranger had come into his life. That was you. He said that he didn't know if you were a gift or a curse. Since you offered to buy his most expensive pieces, why would he have mixed feelings about you?"

"I don't know. Maybe because I asked him to bring the pottery and his wife. I wanted them to join us for dinner the Sunday he died. I wanted to meet Danny's wife, and I wanted Danny and Marie to meet Patty. I wanted us to sit down together — to get to know each other. I have no idea why Danny drove to Cherokee Rock. I never asked to meet him there. And definitely not so early in the morning. I asked him to come here for supper."

If Lou was telling the truth, then someone must have sent Danny a message changing the time and place of the meeting. Had it been Patty? Had she been trying to keep Lou from spending funds earmarked for the inn?

"I can understand why this house means the world to you. You're a Lattimer. But what about Patty? Is she equally invested in this place?"

Lou seemed surprised by the direction the conversation had taken. She broke off another piece of shortbread and ate it. "Patty and I have been best friends for almost twenty years. My husband passed away and Patty's been divorced for ages. We came here because we didn't want to spend our golden years in a rocking chair. We both wanted to create a warm and welcoming home for people away from home. Patty and I both have grown children, but they're very busy and don't have much time for us. We still have lots to give to people, and we decided that we'd be quite happy spoiling strangers. So yes, Patty is an equal partner in this dream."

Nora wanted to believe Lou. She wanted her to be innocent of wrongdoing. She wanted Patty to be innocent. She wanted to see their dream realized. She wanted to tour the inn when its transformation was complete and be dazzled by its beauty. She wanted to see the rose garden in bloom and to know that Rose Lattimer's spirit of hospitality lived on through this pair of female caretakers.

Trying to organize her thoughts, Nora looked around the room. Her gaze fell on a box labeled ART SUPPLIES. "Do you paint?"

"Just walls. Patty's the artist."

Nora thought of the bird at Cherokee Rock. Of the Cardinal Red spray paint. "What medium?"

Again, Lou was taken aback by the abrupt change in subject. "Watercolor. Landscapes, for the most part. She's very good, but it'll be months before she'll have time to paint again."

Unless she already painted her most memorable work. A red bird on a rock, Nora thought.

"I'm sorry about lying to you," Lou said, reclaiming Nora's attention. "I didn't want you to think I had a hand in Danny's death. I didn't want you — or anyone else — to know that I was supposed to meet him on the day he died. I was scared that I'd be blamed. I know I should have come forth sooner. I've since told the sheriff everything I just told you."

"I guess you and Patty both had rock-solid alibis," Nora said. "After all, you had a houseful of guests."

Relaxing a little, Lou picked up the teapot and topped off her cup. "We sure did. The rain had everyone feeling blue, and Patty wanted to make a special breakfast that Sunday morning to cheer us all up. I heard Patty in the kitchen well before six. She made cinnamon rolls, bacon, and an egg casserole. She asked me to handle the fruit salad and the coffee. I was worried about Patty having enough energy to cook for Danny and Marie that night. *If* they came over. I'd given him my number and was hoping he'd call and accept my invitation, but he never did."

"Marie didn't seem to know about the dinner," said Nora. "She didn't even know Danny was selling the art pottery to you. All she knew was that he might have a buyer."

Lou shrugged. "I have no idea why Danny wanted to keep the deal a secret. Maybe he wanted to surprise her. I don't know. I didn't know him. I wish I had."

Nora put her hand on top of the diary. "You said that the house was trying to tell you something. Did you already know about the unusual terms of Rose's will?"

"I got a copy for my genealogy file. But that was a long time ago. I don't remember any unusual terms." Lou's eyes narrowed. "Why are you so interested in my family history?"

Because it led to murder, Nora wanted to say. She bit back the words, remembering that she'd come to bait Lou and Patty, not to try to force either woman into a confession.

"I guess I got caught up in it because of Rose," said Nora, doing her best to sound contrite. "Seeing her portrait and finding all those roses in her books. Looking at her sketches and reading the Browning poem she'd copied into her diary — I was captivated by her. You were right. Rose Lattimer was an incredible woman. I'm grateful that I had the chance to learn her story."

Lou didn't respond and Nora felt like she should fill the silence.

"It's not just Rose," she continued. "Like you, I only met Danny once. But I've visited Marie twice now. I feel protective of her. She's in agony because she doesn't know what happened to her husband."

"Of course she is. I can't imagine what she's going through." Lou's eyes were sorrowful. "I still want to help Danny's family however I can. Rose would have expected nothing less."

The words sat between the two women.

Nora glanced outside and thought of the room right next door. Patty's room. It had once belonged to Rose. Which meant a very long time ago, Rose had stared out her window and seen the same blue hills Nora now saw. She'd probably rocked her baby daughter to sleep by that window. She'd admired the rose garden during the day and the starry sky at night.

Had she wished on a star? Had she sent prayers to the heavens that she might marry the father of her child one day?

Judging by her diary, Rose had grabbed moments of happiness whenever she could.

She and Chea Sequah couldn't be together. They could never know true peace and contentment in a world filled with discrimination, but Rose made sure that their daughter was free to live as she saw fit. As heir to the Lattimer estate, Ava would have money, position, and independence.

Turning from the window, Nora said, "When the pages were torn out of Rose's diary, the hinge was damaged. I repaired it as best I could. And I found something during the repair. It might help you bridge the gap with Marie and serve as a connection to the child she's carrying."

Lou's face filled with wonder. "She's pregnant?"

It was hard not to be moved by Lou's evident delight. Nora nodded and said, "I found a lock of hair hidden inside the back cover of Rose's diary. It's black, and I'm pretty sure it belonged to a baby. I put it in a little baggie. But with all that's been happening at the store and to my friends, I forgot to bring it. I'll be having dinner with Jed, the guy I'm seeing, at the Pink Lady tonight. I could give it to you then if you and Patty would like to join us."

Lou hesitated. "It's hard for me to imagine us having dinner after all this." She gestured between herself and Nora. "We haven't exactly gotten off to the best start."

"Maybe not," Nora said. "But I believe in second chances. Let's shake hands, apologize, and start again."

Lou's expression of relief was so infectious that Nora wished they truly could be friends.

She held out her hand. "I'm sorry for being intrusive."

Taking Nora's hand, Lou gave it a hearty shake and said, "I'm sorry for being dishonest."

"Friends?" Nora asked when Lou let go.

With a smile, Lou said, "Friends. We'll see you at the Pink Lady. The milkshakes are on us."

June was waiting on the front porch. As she and Nora walked to her Bronco, Nora saw Bo loading suitcases into their rental car. The ID tag attached to a purple bag was sticking outside of the trunk. It would be crushed when the trunk was shut, so Nora jogged over and pushed it out of the way.

Bo, who'd been struggling with the handle of a carry-on-sized bag, thanked her. He then pointed at the inn. "Georgia's doing a final sweep of our room, but I know she'd want me to tell you that we're sorry we never made it to the bookstore while you were there. Next time?"

Nora returned his smile. "Next time."

Inside June's car, she sighed. "Just when I thought it was impossible, things have gotten even more complicated."

McCabe's expression was inscrutable as he listened to Nora. When she was done outlining her plan, he folded his arms across his chest and glowered at her. Feeling like a student who'd been sent to the principal's office, Nora steeled herself for a reprimand.

"You've forced my hand, Ms. Pennington. I have no choice but to see this through with you," the sheriff said. "However, I want you to understand something. You are a citizen. You are not an officer of the law. Even with years of training, it's impossible to be prepared for all that can happen when a suspect is cornered. This is why officers of the law try to avoid making arrests in crowded public places. If you'd thought things through, you'd realize that there would have been other ways to get this done."

Nora's cheeks grew hot. She'd expected McCabe to be irked by her plan, but not angry. She was surprised by how much his anger bothered her. He was her friend. Wasn't he? Couldn't he see that she was here because she knew she couldn't see this through on her own?

"I asked Hester and Estella to come to you with what we found today. I'm here for the same reason. To tell you what I know and to ask for help," she said. "I'm not trying to be something I'm not. My friends and I want to help Marie. We want to help her, and the Fosters, find a little peace."

"I didn't see much peace in tonight's forecast. You've set things in motion that I don't have the time or the manpower to undo. If you'll excuse me, I need to call a meeting."

June was waiting for Nora in the lobby.

"How'd it go?" she asked.

"McCabe is seriously pissed at me. I can see his point, and I'll make it up to him when this is all over. Are you going to see Tyson?"

Though visiting hours were almost over, June was going to use every last minute. She didn't have much time left with her son.

Tomorrow, Tyson was being transferred to a treatment facility just north of Asheville. The center had first-rate addiction recovery programs and incredible mountain views. The moment June had heard of an opening at the center, she'd called to secure a place for her son.

"Good luck tonight," she said, giving Nora a hug. "Listen to the sheriff. You were right, he is a good man. Trust him to finish this thing."

"I will."

"And be careful. No fires, no injuries, no accidents. I want to talk about books at our next book club meeting. Got it?"

Nora smiled. "Got it."

Jed was waiting for her in a booth in the middle of the diner. Jack had the night off but had come in to share a meal with Estella. They sat at the counter alongside two people Nora didn't recognize. Hester and Andrews were in the booth behind Jed. Andrews was in plain clothes.

He wasn't the only deputy present either. Fuentes was at a table for two, working his way through an order of loaded nachos while perusing the paper. Nora had seen the hostess in her brown and khaki uniform that afternoon. She was now wearing a Pink Lady bubblegum-pink polo shirt and white slacks.

"The stage is set," Jed said when Nora slid into the booth. "Do you think they'll come?"

"I'll be worried if they do and worried if they don't." She reached across the table, her palm facing up in a silent invitation.

Jed took her hand in his. "I hope they do. That way, you'll have to sit next to me."

Seeing a couple walk past the window, Nora said, "Your wish has been granted."

Lou and Patty entered the diner and looked around. Nora stood up, waved at them, and sat down next to Jed. She put on her best and brightest smile as Lou and Patty settled in across from her.

With her belly full of butterflies, Nora introduced everyone.

A few minutes later, after their orders were placed, Jed asked Lou and Patty how the renovations were coming along. The women talked about projects and deadlines and Jed regaled them with funny anecdotes of the patients he'd treated as a result of DIY projects.

"People assume most of the injuries are from band saws or nail guns," he said at one point. "It's never as sexy as that. Usually, it's a fall from a ladder or an electrical shock. If not those two, it's a foot stuck through a rotted board. You think getting a splinter is bad? Try a hundred splinters."

Lou and Patty laughed, and by the time the food arrived, Nora had almost forgotten her real reason for being at the diner. She managed to eat half of her fried catfish before she remembered and had to put her fork down.

"Aren't you hungry?" Patty asked.

Nora wiped her mouth with her napkin. "Actually, I was thinking about how I sat in this same seat during the week of rain. When I looked out the window, I saw this man in a white T-shirt standing at the entrance to the alley. I felt like he was staring right through me. It was creepy, especially since I'd seen him outside my shop the night before. It had been raining then too, and he'd been wearing that same white T-shirt."

"Was it the man Sheldon saw?" Patty asked.

Nora nodded. "Turns out, he's June's son. He hasn't seen her in twenty years, but he traveled all the way from California to scare her."

Lou stopped eating. "Why would he do that to his own mother?"

"Because he wanted her to pay for a mistake she made a long time ago. He forgot how she'd raised him with love and tenderness. He forgot about the sacrifices she'd made for him. He forgot everything but his anger. That emotion was more powerful than the past he shared with her. More powerful than all the good things she'd done for him."

"What happened?" Patty asked. "Where is he now?"

"His mother is getting him help." Nora didn't want to dwell on Tyson. She had only brought him up to make a point. "Hopefully, the two of them will reconnect. They'll forgive each other. Sometimes, though, family members do things that can't be forgiven. Which is why I mentioned this story in the first place."

Lou and Patty exchanged puzzled glances.

Nora explained how she and her friends had read Rose's will. She went on to say that the sale of the Lattimer House by the Cecils might not have been completely aboveboard.

"I don't mind that I had to buy it instead of inheriting it," Lou said. "What matters is that it's back with a Lattimer now, and Patty and I can invite people to stay under its roof."

"Someone else isn't happy with this arrangement. Someone else — one of Rose's descendants — killed two people for the chance to claim the house and the land that belonged to the estate. That someone hopes to sue for ownership."

Lou's bafflement deepened. "I don't understand."

"Have you met all of your cousins?" Nora asked.

"No. I have a bunch and they're scattered all over the country."

Nora produced a piece of paper and slid it across the table to Lou. "This one's been right down the hall."

Lou unfolded the paper and frowned.

"This afternoon, I saw a monogrammed luggage tag that raised my suspicions. Sheriff McCabe discovered the rest. The people standing between your cousin and the Lattimer House were Danny and you. Danny has been dealt with. You're next."

"This can't be right," Lou protested. But as she stared at the name on the paper, her face transformed. Her doubt was replaced by horror.

Nora took out the plastic bag containing the lock of black hair. "If you want to protect yourself and Patty, if you want to help the sheriff find out exactly what happened to Danny and Micah, then you'll have to trust a bunch of people you barely know."

"Are you one of those people?" Patty asked.

"Yes," said Nora.

Lou looked at Patty. They held each other's gaze for a long moment before Lou turned back to Nora. "Tell us what we need to do."

Nora pressed the lock of hair into Lou's hand and said, "We need to interrupt your murder."

CHAPTER 19

Tears are only water, and flowers, trees, and fruit cannot grow without water. But there must be sunlight also.
— Brian Jacques

Patty explained that she and Lou always had a nightcap before heading off to their separate bedrooms. It was their way of unwinding and reviewing the day's events. They'd sip their drinks and split a chocolate bar. They both loved dark chocolate with almonds and bought seven bars at the start of every week.

Because the library was still being renovated, they had their drinks on the front porch or in the dining room. Their cocktail of choice was a gin and tonic. The gin was kept in the sideboard along with a supply of wine and other liquor. Patty also kept wine in the kitchen to serve with dinner, but she and Lou had finished a bottle the day before and had yet to open a new one.

Spiking their bottle of gin with GHB, the same drug found in Micah's body, wouldn't be difficult. The gin was stored in an unlocked cabinet in a room at the front of the house. Anyone could enter the room, add the drug to the gin, and be gone in a matter of seconds. Lou and Patty tended to use the back door, as did the workmen, and the front door was kept unlocked until one of the women locked it around eleven at night.

Danny's killers had to make Lou and Patty disappear. The inn would never change hands as long as they lived, and too much had already been risked to back out now. Nora knew this. The sheriff knew this. And by the time the waitress had cleared away their dinner plates and asked if anyone wanted dessert, Lou and Patty knew it too.

Saying good-bye to Lou and Patty outside the diner was one of the hardest things Nora had ever done. She had to settle for a casual wave when what she really wanted to do was embrace them. It didn't matter that Officer Fuentes would be following at a distance as Lou and Patty walked back to the inn. It didn't matter that Sheriff Mc-Cabe had been hiding in Sheldon's room since this afternoon. It didn't matter that measures had been taken to keep the two women safe, because Nora kept remembering what the sheriff had said to her in his office.

He'd said, "It's impossible to be prepared for all that can happen when a suspect is cornered."

Were he and his team prepared? Would Lou and Patty make it through the night unharmed?

Lou and Patty, best friends and business partners, were bait for a killer. They were targets.

And it was Nora who'd assigned them these roles.

"I can practically hear the gears in your head turning," Jed said as he drove toward her house.

"I'm never going to be able to sleep tonight."

Jed reached over the center console and took Nora's hand. "You could go for a midnight stroll with June and the cats." After a beat, he added, "Or we could sit by my scanner and listen while we wait."

"Yes. Can we please do that?"

Jed made a U-turn and headed for his house. "Do you want to hang out in the Curious George living room? We could grab a leopard chair and play cards — something to pass the time while we listen."

Nora smiled at him. "That's sounds good. Thank you. For going through this craziness with me."

He gave her hand a squeeze. "I want to go through things with you. The hard stuff. The scary stuff. That's what I want."

Neither of them spoke again until after they were inside Jed's house.

Even though it was April, Jed lit a fire. He told Nora that the giraffe chair was chilly, but she knew that he'd seen her rubbing her arms on her way into the house. She drew a chair covered with a leopard drop cloth closer to the fire and stared at the flames.

"I don't think I've ever wanted a drink so badly," she said.

Jed sat in his leopard chair and studied her. "You haven't had one in weeks, and you don't need one now. I'll make some coffee and entertain you with my knowledge of police scanner codes. You'll be too fascinated to think about grape juice."

Nora flashed him a grateful smile as he walked toward the kitchen. Settling deeper into her chair, she wished Henry Higgins was around. There was something extremely comforting about the sight of a dog napping by the hearth.

But Henry Higgins was with Atticus. The

dogs were officially on duty. It was their first case, and Nora was as worried for their safety as she was for Lou's and Patty's.

Many fates hung on the next eight hours. By morning, things would be resolved. Or they would be worse. There was no in-between.

Nora gazed at the orange and gold flames and thought of all the people who'd gone from being strangers to being tied to one another. The women of the Secret, Book, and Scone Society; Patty; Lou; Sheldon; Jed; the sheriff and his deputies — they were like thin tributaries pouring into a wide river. The river's current was fast. It swept them all forward, driving them toward an uncertain future.

Jed returned carrying two mugs of coffee. "I know this won't be as good as Sheldon's, but I did buy some mugs. I liked your idea of having things made by local artists to perk up my depressing kitchen. I am now the proud owner of four mugs, four soup bowls, and four dinner plates. I might have to throw a party now."

Nora laughed and kissed him as he leaned over to give her the mug of coffee.

"That's better," said Jed. "Now for our game. I'll tell you a code and you tell me if the officer is reporting a sewer leak or is on stakeout and needs a bathroom break."

Nora laughed again, causing a wave of coffee to crest dangerously close to the rim of her cup.

The game didn't last long. There were too many serious codes on the list, and the ones symbolizing violent acts kept reminding Nora of the hazards McCabe and his deputies might face during this night.

"Are you worried about Henry Higgins?" Nora asked Jed after he'd tossed the list aside.

"No. He's in good hands with Angela. The woman is a total dog whisperer. She doesn't like people much, though. If she had a choice, she'd spend all of her time with four-legged officers."

Nora shrugged. "I know lots of people who prefer the company of dogs. Sometimes, after dealing with a bunch of prickly customers, I can see their point."

Jed talked about Henry's training and Nora shared highlights from the sidewalk sale. Mentioning the banned books reminded her that she needed to redo her window display tomorrow. She mentioned this to Jed before telling him about meeting Lily.

"I guess I can take those pink flowers off now."

Jed pulled a face. "You should leave them. They've kind of grown on me."

"Was that a pun?"

"Yep, and I can come up with lots more. The closer we get to midnight, the worse they'll get." Jed reached for Nora's mug. "But first, refills."

Time passed. Nora and Jed fell silent. They drank their coffee and listened to the police scanner. Eventually, the warmth of the room, the sound of the crackling fire, and the muted voices on the scanner lulled Nora to sleep. She didn't remember drifting off, she simply dropped off the edge into darkness.

Which is why she was disoriented when Jed shook her shoulder.

"Nora," he whispered. "Wake up. It's going down."

Nora's eyes snapped open.

"Lou and Patty?" she mumbled. Her mouth was dry, but her mind was alert.

"The sheriff has two suspects in custody. I nodded off, so that's all I caught."

Nora got to her feet. "Will you drive me to the inn?"

Jed already had his keys in hand.

The Inn of Mist and Roses was shining like a lighthouse beacon. Every window was illuminated with a soft, yellow glow. Swirls of red from light bars on the sheriff's department cars danced over the building's white walls.

"No EMTs on the scene. That's a good sign," said Jed.

Nora couldn't answer. Every muscle in her body was tensed. She was ready to jump out of Jed's truck the second it came to a stop. She had her seat belt off and was out the door before he could turn off the engine.

He called after her, but she didn't pause. She ran straight into the inn.

Men and women in uniform milled about the vestibule. The strobe of a camera flash created a disco effect in the dining room. Nora heard the sound of footfalls on the stairs as well as voices coming from the kitchen.

She pushed her way through a knot of deputies and hurried to the kitchen.

When she saw Lou and Patty sitting at the table with Sheriff McCabe, a low, guttural cry of relief escaped from deep inside her chest.

Lou was the first to notice her in the threshold. She stopped talking and rushed over to Nora, pulling her into a fierce hug.

"I was so worried," Nora whispered into Lou's white curls.

"We're fine. We're tough old birds," Lou whispered back.

Images darted through Nora's mind. The bird-shaped stone pipe. The bird carved into the secret wall of the library. The nickname passed down from generation to generation.

"Yes, you are," she said.

Sheldon, who'd been busy at the sink, walked across the room to greet Nora. "About time you showed up," he said. "You missed all the drama."

"What happened?"

"The dogs saved the day," he said.

Lou put a hand on Sheldon's arm. "She's going to want to hear it from the beginning. Come sit with us, Nora."

Though she was a little apprehensive about joining Patty and Sheriff McCabe, Nora agreed.

When she sat down, Patty smiled at her and said, "Welcome to the party."

McCabe managed a curt nod before getting to his feet to hold Lou's chair out for her.

He's not making me leave, Nora thought. *That's something.*

"Bo and Georgia?" she asked the table at large. "Where are they?"

"Deputy Andrews is processing them," McCabe said.

Patty shot him an admiring glance before looking at Nora. "The sheriff had them on his radar since he interviewed everyone about Micah. The Gentrys said they'd spent the day visiting the folk art museum, but when the sheriff called to check their alibi, he learned that the museum is currently closed. Their roof leaked during our big rain and they won't open for another week or so."

Nora turned to McCabe. "I never thought you dropped the ball for a second. I knew you were looking into everything and everyone, and I know that investigating takes time. I wasn't trying to do your job. I just happened to stumble on these seemingly important connections. And I was seriously worried that Bo and Georgia would get away. Or worse — that they'd hurt someone else. I'm sorry if I complicated things or got in your way."

McCabe's gaze softened a fraction. "Though catching the Gentrys in the act will certainly strengthen the case against them, putting citizens in harm's way is risky and foolish. Mr. and Mrs. Gentry had reached a point of desperation. After murdering Danny Amo-adawehi and Micah Foster, they believed they had no choice but to finish what they'd started. As you predicted, Ms. Pennington, the couple spiked the gin in the dining room. They weren't going to stop there, however. I told you that cornered suspects can be unpredictable. And extremely dangerous. Do you want to see what the Gentrys had planned?"

Lou covered her hand with her mouth as if to stifle a cry.

Patty jumped up and put her hands on Lou's shoulders. "Come on, let's get you a real drink. Coffee isn't going to cut it."

"If you're having wine, make sure you uncork a fresh bottle. You don't know what's tainted with what," Sheldon said, and followed the two women into the hall.

"Why did Lou react that way?" Nora asked McCabe when they were alone.

McCabe opened the door leading from the kitchen to a small mudroom and gestured at the space.

Nora couldn't see from her vantage point, so she walked over to where McCabe stood. She immediately understood what had upset Lou so much. There were a dozen plastic gas cans on the mudroom rug. Every can was full.

"Jesus," Nora whispered. "They were going to burn the inn?"

McCabe hooked his thumbs under his utility belt. "Looks that way."

Nora was floored. "But this is the *Lattimer* House. Georgia's a *Lattimer*."

"I don't think Mrs. Gentry cares about family history outside of a desire to become wealthy from it. She would have burned down the whole town in exchange for the land. It's a large parcel and will be worth a huge chunk of change in the not-too-distant future."

Nora stared at the cans. She thought of the brand-new kitchen behind her with its gleaming appliances and soapstone countertops. She pictured the finished library, book-lined and cozy. She saw a roaring fire in the hearth and plump reading chairs. She thought of the freshly painted hall. Of the wide, welcoming front porch. She thought of the flowers Micah had planted.

And then, she saw all of it being devoured by flames. She saw the charred carcass of the house that had been home to Rose, to her daughter, and to many daughters after that.

The house where Rose had hidden her diary — where Chea Sequah's bird had been walled over — might have been smoke and ash by dawn. All the history. All the memories. Gone.

"Thank God you were here," Nora murmured. "You stopped it."

418

"Luckily, yes," said McCabe.

Nora heard Sheldon's laughter down the hall. "They would have killed Sheldon too."

"They couldn't leave witnesses or evidence. They hoped the fire would erase all traces of their crime. Except the arson, of course. But they'd be in Tennessee by the time our investigation was in full swing. Or South Carolina. Or Virginia. It doesn't take long to cross into another state from here. They'd drive back to Ohio, and by the time we had the Toledo police speak with them, they'd have a tidy story ready to share. They'd already checked out, so they couldn't be responsible for the fire. Confronting Mrs. Gentry with her family tree wouldn't prove anything either. People could suspect her, but she and her husband could still go to court and sue for the land rights."

Nora felt a tidal wave of hatred for the Gentrys. It flowed through her with such force that she actually looked around for a place to release it.

"Hey," the sheriff said, reaching out a supportive hand.

She ignored it. With a snarl of fury, she said, "There's no guarantee they'd end up with the land. Yet they were willing to gamble all these lives for their day in court.

Danny's baby will never know her father because of the Gentrys. Micah's parents will never see the man he'd grow into because of the Gentrys." Her eyes bored into Mc-Cabe's. "Tell me you'll make them pay."

The sheriff put a hand on Nora's back and steered her to a chair.

"I get angry too. I do. But you can't let the rage win. The best thing we can do right now is to keep clear heads. We gather evidence. We interview the suspects. We search their car. We —"

"Find the nails to drive into their coffins."

Sheldon chose this moment to reenter the kitchen. "Sheriff, I know you're on duty, so no grape juice for you. Nora? You look like you could use a nip."

Nora considered how lovely a glass of wine would be right now. She could practically feel her fingers curl around the narrow stem of the glass. She saw the wide bowl filled with burgundy liquid and smelled the fruity, woodsy bouquet. She exhaled and said, "No, thanks."

Sheldon settled into the chair next to Nora's. "I'm too wired to go to sleep. So tell me. How did you know who the bad guys were?"

"I saw a luggage tag sticking out of the trunk of the Gentrys' rental car. The trunk

420

was open, and I didn't want the tag to be crushed when Bo shut the trunk, so I pushed it out of harm's way. The monogram on the tag was E. G. G., which made me assume that Georgia was going by her middle name. When I mentioned this to the sheriff, he told me that Georgia's first name was Elizabeth. After a little more research, he discovered that she was a Lattimer. And Lou's cousin. Elizabeth Georgia Lattimer Gentry."

Sheldon whistled. "This is some *Days of Our Lives*–sized drama."

Seeing that Sheldon was settling in for a chat, McCabe gestured toward the hall. "Deputies are working in the bedroom the Gentrys used. We're done with the dining room, but we have to process the mudroom and other areas. It would be best if you saved your chat for the morning."

Nora looked at the sheriff. His message was clear. There was work to be done. Important work.

"Now that I've seen Lou and Patty, I can probably sleep," she said. "You should too, Sheldon. Tomorrow, it's back to books and coffee for us."

At the bottom of the stairs, Nora paused to hug Sheldon. He smelled like wool and oranges.

Lou and Patty came out of the dining room to wish him a good night.

"Before you go, I thought you might like to see this," Lou said to Nora, and led her into the library.

Unlike the other rooms, the library was deserted.

With no furniture and the floor and mantel covered in protective sheeting, there was a stillness to the space that was immediately calming.

"This is where Rose was photographed," Lou said, pointing at the wall across from the windows. "I think she was looking at Chea Sequah or at the hidden panel that led to her room. Either way, I think he was the source of that secretive smile."

Nora thought of the beautiful young woman in the white dress. "When I first saw the tintype, I thought she was holding a rock in her hand. I now know that it was a stone pipe. A Cherokee pipe shaped like a bird. Marie has it. She's your family too. So is the child she's carrying."

Lou's face glowed as she whispered, "A baby."

Her delight made Nora smile.

"That child can be a fresh start for all of us. Rose and Chea Sequah's children." Lou clasped her hands. "I have so many ideas. I

422

need to talk to Patty about them." Her joy-ful optimism was infectious. "I am *never* going to sleep tonight, but I hope you do. Thank you for saving us. And our dream."

Lou gave Nora a quick hug and left the room.

Nora turned to face the wall once covered by bookshelves. The wood was scarred and scratched. Toward the middle, there was a dark recess in the wood. The opening to the narrow passage leading to a ladder.

Using her cell phone as a light, Nora turned sideways and entered the niche.

The light bloomed over the interior wall, and she saw the bird. She traced its simple but graceful lines with her fingertips. It was a love letter etched into wood, a tattooed invitation to share a life. A family tree had grown from their secret love. One of their descendants still lived in their house, and she was ready to fill it with new memories.

"It's over, Rose," Nora whispered. "Lou's safe. Danny's family is safe. The house is safe." She put her hand flat against the wall. "You can rest easy now."

Nora half expected to hear a creak of wood or the subtle moan of the foundation settling, but the room was completely silent.

After waiting a few more seconds, Nora walked down the hallway and outside. She was ready to find Jed and go home.

When she stepped onto the porch, she was met by the sound of gentle rainfall.

The rain smelled like roses.

Micah's parents stopped by Miracle Books on their way of out of town.

After taking them to the circle of chairs by the ticket agent's office, Nora asked Sheldon to make three coffees.

"I'm truly sorry for your loss," she said. "I wish I'd gotten to know your son while he was here. Would you tell me about him?"

The Fosters were more than happy to. They sat in Nora's book-filled haven, sipped their Cuban coffee, and talked about Micah. They spoke of how he'd been a nature lover since he could walk. That he'd always been a quiet, sweet boy who would have grown into a quiet, sweet man.

Tragically, Micah had noticed red paint on Georgia's index finger. He could have ignored it, but he was concerned that she would accidentally stain her shirt or get paint on her bedspread, so he brought it to her attention. His thoughtfulness sealed his fate, and days later, the Gentrys invited him to join them on a sunrise hike to a famous landmark. After being stuck indoors for a week, Micah jumped at the chance.

According to his parents, he didn't know that their destination was Cherokee Rock. He didn't know that Danny had also met Bo and Georgia there. At the sign of the red bird. He only knew to expect clear skies and a memorable view, which is what he wrote his mother and father in his final email.

Micah hadn't known that he was being driven to his death. Like Danny, he had no idea that the ancient rock was to be his gravestone, forever marking the place where he'd taken his last breath.

The sheriff learned that Danny had been struck on the head and tossed in the river.

As for Micah, he'd been given a fatal dose of GHB on the ride from Miracle Springs and Cherokee Rock. The drug had been mixed into a thermos of herbal tea. Bo and Georgia dragged him into the woods and left him there to die.

The Gentrys were back at the Inn of Mist and Roses before anyone knew they'd left.

They'd murdered two innocent young men.

All for the chance at wealth.

Not a sure thing. Just a chance.

After nearly an hour of talking, Micah's mother put down her cup and gestured at the bookshelves, which surrounded them like protective walls. Each wall was filled with colorful books. Books of all shapes and sizes. Books made of the unwavering power of the written word.

"Sheldon told us about your bibliotherapy, and we were hoping you could help us. We're not looking for books on grief. Not today. Today, we want to find books to honor our son's memory through his love of nature. We want to send copies of these books to every college library in our state. It would make him happy to know that kids like him could read the books that touched him in here." She put a hand over her heart. "After the great outdoors, he loved books most."

"We've already decided on *Walden* and Bill Bryson's *A Walk in the Woods,*" Micah's father added. "Those were two of his favorites, but we'd like a few more titles."

Nora was glad to have something to offer the grieving parents. "I can help with that. Just give me a few minutes."

After whispering to Sheldon to plate complementary book pockets for the Fosters, Nora began pulling titles from the Nature section. When she was done, she carried the stack to the checkout counter.

By this time, Micah's parents had finished their pastries and were ready to be on their way. They examined the books Nora had set out for them: *Coyote America: A Natural and Supernatural History* by Dan Flores, *The Lost Art of Reading Nature's Signs* by Tristan Gooley, Michael Pollan's *The Botany of Desire,* Barbara Kingsolver's *Prodigal Summer,* and *The Thing with Feathers* by Noah Strycker.

"Please accept these as a gift," Nora said when they approved of her choices. "I'd like to honor Micah's memory too, and the best way for me to do that is by sending you out the door with a bagful of books."

Mrs. Foster was too choked up to reply. She managed a nod. Her eyes glistened with gratitude and grief.

"We'll see you again," Mr. Foster told Nora as he held the door open for his wife. "This is the place where our son left this world, so we'll be back to visit him."

Sheldon joined Nora behind the checkout counter. Sliding an arm around her waist, he gave her a quick squeeze and said, "How about we tackle this pathetic window display, eh, boss?"

Nora turned to the window. "About that. I have an idea."

People went out of their way to stand in front of Miracle Books. They tended to congregate in the early morning or as day

427

was giving way to night. The light was perfect at those times. It fell upon the window in soft, golden waves. It made everything more enchanting than it already was.

What most people saw first were the trees. Their trunks sprouted from piles of green crinkle paper and rose toward the ceiling. Books roosted on cardboard branches. The branches were surrounded by yellow, gold, and green paper leaves and tissue paper cardinals. The treetops were strung with twinkling fairy lights.

As the bystanders' gazes traveled down from the leafy canopy of books and lights, they noticed the reeds lining the foil paper river. Handmade baskets sat among the reeds. Each basket held a book on arts and crafts. Battery-powered lanterns nestled in between the baskets, casting a gentle, flickering light onto the blue and silver foil river. The longer people stared, the more it looked like the river was alive. Rippling.

The river wound behind the baskets until it reached the other corner of the window. There, it transformed into a muddy bog made of flour, water, cocoa powder, and bronze glitter. Beautiful pieces of pottery rose out of the shimmering mud, and because they sat on clear plastic platforms, they seemed to float in midair. The piece that rose the highest was a nut-brown pottery bowl. A tissue paper cardinal perched on its rim, right on top of a tiny chip. Books on making and collecting pottery were lined up on a faux rock outcropping.

The window did more than showcase nature. It showed the connection between man and nature. It highlighted nature's beauty and its bounty. It was alive with creativity, color, and words.

It was Danny's window.

It was Micah's window.

It was Marie's window.

It belonged to all those known as Red Bird.

The onlookers had no idea that the window had been designed with these people in mind. But they felt the significance of it. They stood on the sidewalk and felt something stir in their hearts. They felt their ancestors calling to them. They felt the need to walk in the woods. The desire to make something with their hands. And they felt the all-encompassing magic of books.

They waited until the bookshop was open for business.

They waited in front of the window.

And when Nora unlocked the door and

they went inside, they found exactly what they'd been looking for.

CHAPTER 20

There is no friend as loyal as a book.
— Ernest Hemingway

Spring had come in like a raging lion. It tried to go out like a lamb but never got the chance because summer came along like a ravenous python and swallowed it whole.

Mild days and nights were instantly replaced by humid air and relentless sunshine.

The locals didn't complain. They thought back on the April rains and the havoc they'd wrought. They thought of their flooded shops and houses. And they remembered the fallen footbridge. And a man they'd known only as Cherokee Danny.

They no longer called him by that name. Everyone in Miracle Springs now knew who Danny was. And Micah Foster too.

They also knew the names Georgia and Bo Gentry. The people of Miracle Springs devoured every detail about the couple that had committed two murders and planned on committing three more. They knew the Gentrys had been denied bail. That they'd pled guilty to a laundry list of charges after it was discovered that Bo had told a Toledo physician that he suffered from narcolepsy. The physician recommended a polysomnogram and a multiple sleep latency test. Bo refused both and declared that he'd find his own solution. After all, he was only interested in getting a prescription for GHB.

Between the physician's statement and evidence found on the Gentrys' home computer showing the purchase and receipt of a GHB kit from the Netherlands, the couple's fate was sealed. Hoping for a reduced sentence, they became very cooperative.

They told the authorities how they'd gotten Danny's cell phone number from a note in the inn's kitchen. They used a burner phone to send Danny a text message. Pretending to be Lou, they requested Danny meet at Cherokee Rock at six in the morning. Apologizing for the hour, the fake Lou explained that she needed to be back at the inn by seven to serve breakfast to the guests. She added that she'd buy whatever pottery he brought at whatever price he requested. She would pay cash. It was an offer Danny couldn't refuse.

The fake Lou told Danny to wait at the red bird painted on the rock. He complied, and when Georgia approached him, explaining that Lou had sent her to complete the deal, Bo snuck up behind Danny and hit him on the head with a rock. The couple dragged Danny's body to the river and threw him in. The torrential rain and the collapsed footbridge helped to disguise their crime.

The Gentrys didn't need the GHB to kill Danny, but they needed it to get rid of Micah. They'd disposed of the thermos that had been filled with the fatal rose tea, but the woman who ran the tea shop remembered them well.

"They were such a *nice* couple," she told a local reporter. "You could have knocked me over with a feather when I heard what they did. They even told me about the young man they were getting the tea for. They said he loved being outdoors and went out of his way to be helpful. That couple used my lovely tea to kill him. Tea is supposed to make people feel good. It's not supposed to be a weapon. This world has enough weapons."

After reading about her in the paper, Patty had contacted the teashop proprietor and said, "We're trying to fix all the things the Gentrys tried to ruin, which is why I'm asking if you'd like to sell your tea in our gift shop. It's not open yet, but we're lining up local artisans now."

Marie had told Nora about the gift shop several weeks ago. Her smile had been electric as she shared the big news.

"I'm going to be the manager of Red Bird Gallery and Gifts. We'll sell my baskets, pottery, quilts, blankets, June's socks, candles, woodcrafts, glassware, jewelry, and homemade food. We'll also have candy, honey, soup, herbal tea, and different types of jerky."

Nora had been thrilled by the announcement, but she'd been even more delighted to see Marie's smile. She didn't smile often. The hole left by Danny's loss was too deep for that, but she was trying.

Sheriff McCabe had barely locked up the Gentrys when Lou and Patty reached out to Marie. They wanted her to share ownership of the inn, but Marie wasn't interested in their dream. She wanted to chase her own by establishing the area's first local artisan gallery. Lou and Patty loved the idea. The rose garden project was put on the back burner and the renovation of the carriage house was given top priority. The shop would be on the first floor and the second-floor apartment would be the future home of Marie and her baby. Lou and Patty would live in what was once the gardener's cottage.

The activity at the inn seemed contagious. Suddenly, merchants all over town were refreshing façades with fresh coats of paint or adding new signage. Drought-resistant summer plants burst from pots lining the sidewalk. Newly washed windows gleamed in the sunlight.

Nora had done some improvements to the bookshop as well. She'd had railroad wall lanterns installed around the front and rear entrances. The lights chased away the shadows while drawing attention to the window display. Now, Miracle Books was just as inviting at night as it was during the day.

Business had been very good for the last six weeks. Sheldon's salesmanship added extra money to the till. He called in sick at least once a week and was usually back the following day. Upon his return, he moved a little slower and spoke a little softer. He was surprised to discover that people liked his quieter side too.

On the third week of June, Sheldon spent three days in bed. He was miserable, so the

Secret, Book, and Scone Society paid him a visit.

June rubbed his forehead with peppermint oil and gave him an update on Tyson's progress.

"I'll see him next weekend," she said. "The doctors say he's doing really well."

"A gold-star student. I bet he gets that from his mama." Sheldon smiled tenderly at June.

Sheldon was fond of June. They'd been thick as thieves ever since the sidewalk sale.

June pulled something out of her tote bag. "This gold-star gal's been doing some thinking. About you. You like to give, but you don't like to take. We all think that's something you need to work on."

"It's true," said Estella. "Without you, my business might be closed by now. But the Pink Lady Day saved it. And me. The same women who spread rumors about me behind my back are my newest customers. They're getting highlights and massages, trims and pedicures. And your idea to offer mani/pedi parties with booze? I've already booked six of them."

Sheldon gestured at Nora. "It was all a ploy to get this one to be more adventurous."

Nora touched a strand of pink hair. "Who

says the blondes have all the fun?"

Hester approached Sheldon's bed and handed him a small bakery box.

"I'm not really hungry, sweetie," he told her with genuine regret.

"You might want it later, when you're feeling better. Just take a peek at it for now."

Sheldon opened the box to find a sugar cookie shaped like a house. The house had four windows. Three of them were blue. The fourth was a golden yellow.

"That's a bedroom," Hester said. "The light's on because the man who lives there is reading. Sometimes, he reads late into the night. But his roommate doesn't mind."

Sheldon's brows rose. "Roommate?"

June put a folded piece of paper on his bed. "You've been looking for a cottage, and it just so happens that I found the perfect place for you to hang your hat."

"If you ever see me wearing a hat, you'll know I've been abducted by aliens," said Sheldon. "Why should I cover my glorious silver crown?"

"You shouldn't. I have clients who pay hundreds of dollars for the silver fox look." Estella made a hurry-up gesture. "Come on. Look at the paper."

Sheldon unfolded the paper and then glanced at June. "Isn't this your house?"

She took his hand. "I was thinking that it could be our house. I don't want a husband. I want a companion. I use exactly half of my house. I figured you might like the other half."

The women waited for Sheldon to respond, but he just stared at the photo. "What about Tyson?" he whispered after a lengthy pause. "Won't he want to come home after rehab?"

June shook her head. "He'll need to transition back into the world. He's better off in a group living situation where the right folks can help him make good decisions. I can't do that. He and I have too much history. But I'll spend my days off with him. I'll be in his life as much as I can. I saved all that money for a reason. Now I know what that reason is. I'm supposed to save my son. I prayed for the chance to do that, and the good Lord answered my prayer."

"And you're nagging me about being a giver?" Sheldon spluttered. "You're going to give me half of your house after knowing me for what, two months?"

"Not giving," said June. "I'm going to charge you rent."

Sheldon looked relieved. "I hope it's a fair price. I don't think I'll ever win an argument with you."

June gave his hand a pat. "Just admit that I'm always right and we'll never argue."

Everyone laughed.

"What about the cats?" Nora asked.

"I love cats," Sheldon said. "I can't wait to start naming them. Rum Tum Tugger. Mungojerrie. That big tom should be Growltiger."

June wagged a finger at him. "I hope you don't let them inside. I've told those beasts a hundred times that they are never, ever, coming in. I don't care if it's raining or snowing. I am not a feline hotel."

"Maybe we can start with a few cat houses on the back porch," Sheldon mused aloud.

"Does that mean you're moving in?" Estella asked.

Sheldon looked at June. "We're not exactly Bert and Ernie or Felix and Oscar. We're more like a plump, chronically ill Ricky Ricardo and a black Lucy."

June threw back her head and laughed. "Oh, Ricky. We're going to have such fun."

On the last Saturday in June, Marie stopped by Miracle Books. She held a plastic bag and wore an unusual expression on her face. Nora had seen the same expression on young children. It was the glow of anticipation. Marie was dying to share a story. Or to show Nora something.

Noting the sheen of perspiration on Marie's forehead, Nora led her back to the circle of chairs and served her a glass of ice water.

Marie drank half of it down in three swallows. "Thank you. I didn't realize how thirsty I was until I saw the water." She put a hand on her belly. "She must be thirsty too. All I do these days is drink and go to the bathroom."

Nora refilled Marie's glass and sat down in June's chair. The soft one with the purple velvet that wrapped around Nora's body like a hug. "Do you know the baby's gender?"

Marie's smile was dazzling. "She's the next Red Bird."

Nora didn't mean to cry, but she was too overwhelmed by grief and happiness to hold back her tears. "You knew it from the start, didn't you?"

"I did."

"I can't wait to meet her," said Nora. She'd never been a baby person, but this baby was special. Through her genes, this baby would bring Danny back to life. She would also join two branches of a family tree that had never so much as leaned toward each other before. She was the future Rose had planned for all those years ago.

Looking for a distraction, Nora wiped her eyes with a napkin and pointed at the bag. "Do you want to show me something?"

"I sure do," said Marie. "Remember that poetry book I had at the flea market? The one you said was worth a pretty penny?"

Nora's cheeks burned in shame. "I'm so sorry. I forgot to look up its estimated value."

"Don't worry about it. Anyway, this might change how much the first volume is worth."

Marie pulled the tissue-wrapped object from the bag and peeled back the layers to reveal not one, but two books.

"Oh my." Nora's words came out in a rush of breath. "Where did you find the second volume?"

"In another suitcase. I thought Danny had one memory box. But he had two beat-up suitcases. The second one was covered in a blanket. On top of that was a pile of sweaters Danny never wore. I never nagged him about being messy because we have separate closets. A person has a right to his own mess as long as it can be hidden behind a closed door."

Nora listened to Marie's reply with only

441

half an ear. Finally, she jumped out of her chair and said, "Keep drinking that water. I'll be right back."

She grabbed her laptop from the checkout counter and carried it back to the purple chair. While Marie watched, she found an online auction that had sold identical editions of the Elizabeth Barrett Browning volumes. The results were eight months old and didn't reflect the percentage the seller had to pay the auction company. Nora smiled.

"I'm glad you're sitting down," she told Marie. "Because the books you carried in here are worth twelve thousand dollars."

Marie's mouth fell open.

"I can sell them for you, free of charge. I have an account at one of the best sites on the Internet for buying and selling rare books."

"I can't believe you'd do that for me." Marie looked down at her lap. "I thought I lost everything when Danny died. Having this life growing inside me kept me going, but you, June, Lou, and Patty have given me hope. It's easier to go on when you have that."

The women sat in companionable silence for a few minutes before Marie suddenly exclaimed, "I almost forgot! The twelve-thousand-dollar news distracted me. I found something else in that suitcase. It really belongs to Lou, but I had to show it to you first. Without you, well, we'd all be worse off."

She dipped her hand back into the plastic bag and pulled out a manila folder. "Take a look."

Nora opened the folder's metal clasp and withdrew a thin sheaf of papers. Nora instantly recognized the aged paper, the black ink, and the elegant penmanship.

"Rose," she whispered, and glanced from the papers to Marie's face. "Danny had the missing diary pages?"

"I think Chea Sequah had them first. How else would Danny have gotten them? They're mostly about Rose's pregnancy and the plans she had for her baby. I think Chea tore them out and hid them to protect the woman he loved. And his unborn child. If anyone found out that Colonel Lattimer wasn't the father, Rose's reputation would have been ruined. Their baby would have been an outcast."

Nora smoothed a crease on the top page as she read a couple of lines. She longed to devour every entry, to finish learning all she could about Rose. But an image of the diary surfaced in her mind. She remembered

443

the hinge she'd repaired. And the lock of hair she'd pulled from under the endpapers.

That lock of hair had since been analyzed. Genetic testing made it clear that Lou and the child were related. The person who didn't share an iota of genetic material with Ava Lattimer was John Cecil, the man who'd claimed power of attorney for his mentally incompetent wife and had sold her ancestral home without her permission. He'd convinced his wife's GP that she was suffering from dementia and needed to move to an assisted living facility. Claire Cecil was actually suffering from a B12 deficiency, and her dementia symptoms began to resolve as soon as she received the proper treatment. But by the time she proved mental competence, Lattimer House had already changed hands.

Nora slid the diary pages back into the envelope. "Lou once told me that Lattimer House was built to hold secrets. That might sound romantic to those of us that love the notion of hidden passageways or hiding places, but I'm beginning to think that a house without secrets is the happiest kind of home. Look at the secret Rose kept. John Cecil was next. And after him, the Gentrys. Secrets seem to run in the Lattimer blood. And their house was built to hold them."

"I talked to Lou and Patty about having a cleansing ceremony," Marie said. "Danny's mother has done hundreds of them. I'm going to ask her to cleanse the house, the outbuildings, and the grounds. It's time to purge all the negative energy. It's one thing to paint and install new plumbing and wiring, but what that place really needs is someone to chase away the shadows. And the secrets."

Nora looked at the envelope in her lap. Marie was right. It was time to let go of the secrets. Rose's should stay where they belonged: in the past. No one knew how her diary ended up inside the hearth wall, but Nora guessed that Chea Sequah or Ava had hidden it there. Someone had cherished Rose's words and didn't want to destroy them. That someone had believed that her secret thoughts and desires were as much a part of the house as the stone and timber. And maybe they'd hoped that one day a future Lattimer would learn the truth about her heritage and celebrate the knowledge.

Marie left the poetry books with Nora and picked up the envelope. "I'll give these to Lou so that she can have the diary repaired. Bringing the pages back together is kind of a reunion of Rose and Chea's story." She touched her belly. "It's hers too. An origin story."

"Sue Monk Kidd said that 'stories have to be told or they die, and when they die, we can't remember who we are or why we're here.' Danny's story will live on through your daughter."

The two women embraced.

Nora watched Marie walk away. Even now, she felt protective of her. Marie was going to be all right. There would be bad days ahead. Plenty of them. But there would be good ones too. More and more as time marched on. And that was a life worth living.

Not long after the Gentrys' sentencing, in which Bo and Georgia received life without parole, Sheriff McCabe asked Nora to join him for lunch.

"Pearl's been asking about you."

Nora didn't accept right away. Her friendship with McCabe had been strained since the afternoon she'd asked him to save Lou's and Patty's lives. Nora knew that things would continue to be awkward between her and the sheriff if they didn't hash things out.

Maybe today is that day, Nora thought, and told McCabe that yes, she'd like to have lunch with him.

As usual, McCabe offered to pick her up. When he met her in the parking lot, she was clearly distressed.

"My moped is gone," she said, turning in a circle with a stricken look on her face. "It was here this morning, but it's gone now. So is the helmet. Gone."

McCabe got on the phone with the desk clerk and asked for all officers to keep an eye out for a yellow moped with pink flower decals. "If they see a two-wheeled vehicle that looks like it belongs in a Dr. Seuss book, then they've found it."

Mumbling something about Sneeches, the sheriff turned to Nora. "Do you want to cancel our lunch plans? I'd understand if this puts a damper on your day."

"No. I can't do anything about it, so we might as well eat."

After making sure that she really wanted to go, McCabe opened the car door for Nora. As they drove out of Miracle Springs, he took off his hat and tossed it in the back seat.

"I'm not going to wait until we get to Pearl's to say that I regret how I responded to you the day you came to my office, looking for help. I felt manipulated, and that made me angry. In hindsight, I realize that you had nothing to gain by your actions. You were simply trying to keep two women from coming to harm. I apologize for my attitude. However, I would still prefer you leave the investigating to my department."

"Believe me, I'd prefer that too," said Nora. "Ever since I was burned, I've attracted trouble. If I didn't have June, Estella, and Hester, I wouldn't be able to handle everything that's happened over the past year. I moved to Miracle Springs for a peaceful existence. I've had moments of peace but they've all come with periods of wild upheaval."

McCabe grunted. "I know you don't look for drama. And when it comes, you deal with it better than most."

Nora shot him a sideways glance. "Does this mean that you don't want me to work for you anymore? Didn't you want me to do research or check facts?"

McCabe laughed. "I can't see you in our uniform."

Nora glanced down at her T-shirt, jeans, and red Chuck Taylors. "Yeah. That utility belt would add too many inches to my hips."

The sheriff parked in front of Pearl's and pointed at the front door. "Forget about inches and hips. There's a basket of hush puppies with our names of it. Please tell me

448

that you're going to split them with me this time."

Nora smiled at him. "I am. And I'm getting sweet potato chips, so prepare to loosen your belt."

"Yes, ma'am." He saluted Nora and then raced around the car to open the door for her.

They were both laughing as they stepped into Pearl's, their friendship fully restored.

Nora's moped wasn't found that day. Or the next. On the third day, Deputy Andrews stopped by the bookshop with news.

It was almost closing time. The afternoon coffee rush was over and most of the browsers had finished making their selections. Nora would get a few more customers looking to kill time before their dinner reservations. Because it was summer, she'd also get a family or two. They'd pop in to browse before heading to the frozen custard shop.

Andrews had held the door open for a family of five on his way in. He frowned as he watched them move deeper into the store.

"Are you scowling at my customers?" Nora teased.

"Honestly, I was hoping you could close a bit early. We think we found your moped,

449

but we can't be sure because it's been, ah, altered. If you could grab your keys and registration and come with me, I'll drive you to where it is."

Nora told Andrews to wait a moment and walked through the store. In addition to the family of five, three customers were still drifting around.

Returning to the front, Nora asked Andrews to give her a few minutes.

"Why don't you check out the Sci-Fi section while I close up?" she suggested.

"Okay. I finished *Fahrenheit 451,* so I need something new. I'll see what grabs me."

Nora cleaned up the coffee stations, though there wasn't much to do. Sheldon always left everything so tidy. She then removed the menu board from the ticket agent's window and turned off the lights in that area. By the time she was done, only the family of five remained.

"Can I help you with anything in particular?" Nora directed the question at the mother. "I don't mean to be pushy, but I'm hoping to close a little early tonight."

Because the woman looked slightly put out, Nora told her about the stolen moped.

"That's awful. I hope you get it back," the woman said. Glancing around to see where the rest of her family was, she lowered her voice. "I need a good book to read by the pool. My job's been really stressful this year and with three kids, I get pulled in ten different directions all the time. I barely see my husband. Life is so busy that I couldn't stop and smell a rose if I wanted to." She finished with a heavy sigh.

"I have just the thing for you." Nora grabbed the woman a copy of Liane Moriarty's *What Alice Forgot.*

The woman was instantly taken with Nora's choice. "I read *Big Little Lies* and loved it. I'm sure I'll love this one too. Thanks."

After paying for the book, she hustled her family out of the shop.

Andrews had selected *Artemis: A Novel* by Andy Weir. "I liked the movie version of *The Martian,* so I thought I'd give this a try."

With this final sale, Nora was ready to leave. She locked the back door and followed Andrews to his car. Once they were underway, she reluctantly asked, "What did you mean when you said that the moped had been altered?"

Andrews shifted in his seat. "It's hard to explain. You'll see for yourself in a few minutes."

It was clear that Andrews didn't want to say anything else. When he pulled into an

451

auto body shop two towns over, Nora was surprised to see Jed's Blazer parked in front of one of the garage bays.

Andrews led Nora into the garage. Something shaped like a moped was hidden under a black tarp.

Suddenly, Jed was beside her.

"Hey," he said, taking hold of her hand. "I thought you could use some emotional support."

Nora gave him a perplexed look. "If it's wrecked, it's wrecked. I'll be okay."

A man came out of a door marked OFFICE. He wiped his hands on a rag and smiled at Nora. "I'm Derrick. This is my place. You ready to see your ride?"

"I'm ready," Nora said, and tensed herself for the reveal.

Derrick whisked off the tarp and Nora stared at the moped. She stared and stared. It couldn't be hers. Her moped was yellow with pink flowers. This was something else entirely. Something wonderful. Spellbinding.

This moped was covered with books. Colorful, cheerful books. Books with tangerine, teal, lavender, saffron, lime, and cherry-red spines. There were even titles on some of the spines. Nora saw *The Mists of Avalon, I Am Malala, The Hunger Games, The Girl* with the Dragon Tattoo, Americanah, and The Handmaid's Tale to name a few.

This moped couldn't possibly be hers.

This moped was a bookshelf on wheels. It was a moving billboard of books. An invitation to run to the nearest library or bookshop and walk out carrying a pile of treasure.

Nora's thoughts were interrupted when she saw the graffiti-style writing just under the moped's seat. The words said, NEXT STOP: MIRACLE BOOKS.

"Sorry about making you believe that your moped was stolen," Jed said in a near whisper. He could see that Nora was still taking everything in. "It was the only way to give Derrick the time he needed. He works here and moonlights as an EMT. But he got it done." He winked at Derrick.

Jed waved his hand over the moped. "And Nora? These books? They're all about badass women. Because you're a badass woman."

Nora looked at Jed. "You did this? For me? It must have cost —"

"A bunch of people pitched in," he interrupted. "You're always doing things for other people, Nora, and those other people wanted to find a way to thank you. This is what we came up with."

Nora's gaze returned to the moped. Her heart was swelling with emotion. She could feel it rising inside her chest like a wave. If she didn't hold it in, she was going to burst into tears. But she didn't want to cry. After all, Jed had called her a badass. No one had ever called her that. She knew he'd meant it as a compliment. She knew he'd lumped her in with the amazing authors on the moped. She liked it. She liked it very much.

She turned to Jed and directed all of her feelings into an intense stare.

"Jedediah Craig, I have never said this to a man before, and I will probably never say it again, so listen up." She took a theatrical pause. "You are better than a book boyfriend."

Jed placed his hand over his heart. "Wow."

With a laugh, Nora threw her arms around his neck and kissed him. She didn't care that Andrews and Derrick were watching. She'd forgotten all about them.

When she and Jed eventually separated, Derrick stepped forward to present Nora with her helmet. It had also been customized and now featured an open book on a dark blue background. Some of the letters were blowing off the page as if coaxed into the air by a strong wind. As they left the white page, they were no longer black. They became a rainbow of dancing letters.

Nora couldn't wait to ride her moped. She couldn't wait for someone to roll down their car window and ask about the book titles on the moped's body. She couldn't wait for them to ask about Miracle Books.

When that happened, she would raise her helmet visor and say, "There's a book in my shop waiting just for you. Come find it when you're ready."

If they drove off and she never saw them again, she'd understand. But if they walked through her front door to be welcomed by sleigh bells, the scent of coffee, and a smile, she would find them a story.

She would find them a miracle.

READER'S GUIDE FOR
THE BOOK OF CANDLELIGHT

1. From the start, the weather plays a role in this novel. Have you ever experienced a flood or another major weather disaster that allowed you to identify with the townsfolk of Miracle Springs?

2. Nora buys a pottery bowl from a man the locals call "Cherokee Danny." Do you own a piece of pottery or another hand-made item that holds special value?

3. What was your initial impression of Sheldon Vega? Do you think he's a good fit for Miracle Books? What does he bring to the bookstore?

4. What's the significance of the red bird?

5. If you were to order something from the Miracle Books food and beverage menu,

what would it be?

6. Why was Lou a suspicious character for a good part of the book? Did you think she was guilty of something before Nora confronted her? Why or why not?

7. In what ways was Rose Lattimer, a woman who'd been in her prime during the Civil War, still very much a presence in the novel?

8. Banned books are featured in a Miracle Books window display. Have you ever seen a list of banned books or purposely read a book because it had once been banned? Have you ever felt a book deserved to be banned?

9. Who did you think the man in the white T-shirt was before his identity was revealed? Do you think June and Tyson will be able to reconnect?

10. Three romantic relationships are unfolding in this book. They include Jed and Nora, Hester and Jasper, and Estella and Jack. Which relationship are you rooting for? Which one do you think will be suc-

cessful? Which, if any, is unlikely to last?

11. Danny Amo-adawehi's pregnant wife, Marie, was dealt a crippling blow. What will she need to heal and move forward? What positives do you foresee for her?

12. Of all the book titles mentioned in this book, which title(s) are you most likely to read in the near future? Were any of those mentioned already a favorite?

13. Nora and Sheldon create a memorial window display at the end of the novel. How do the elements of that display tie into the plot?

14. What feeling did the end of the novel leave you with? Will you continue with the Secret, Book, and Scone Society series?

15. There are quotes preceding each chapter of *The Book of Candlelight*. Which was your favorite?

ABOUT THE AUTHOR

Ellery Adams has written dozens of mystery novels and can't imagine spending a day away from the keyboard. Ms. Adams, a native New Yorker, has had a lifelong love affair with stories, food, rescue animals, and large bodies of water. When not working on her next novel, she reads, bakes, gardens, spoils her three cats, and rearranges her bookshelves. She lives with her husband and two children (aka the Trolls) in Chapel Hill, NC. For more information and a list of bibliotherapy titles, please visit www.ellery adamsmysteries.com.

The employees of Thorndike Press hope you have enjoyed this Large Print book. All our Thorndike, Wheeler, and Kennebec Large Print titles are designed for easy reading, and all our books are made to last. Other Thorndike Press Large Print books are available at your library, through selected bookstores, or directly from us.

For information about titles, please call:
  (800) 223-1244

or visit our website at:
  gale.com/thorndike

To share your comments, please write:
  Publisher
  Thorndike Press
  10 Water St., Suite 310
  Waterville, ME 04901

CPSIA information can be obtained
at www.ICGtesting.com
Printed in the USA
BVHW030032281120
594401BV00001B/6